FACES IN THE FLAMES

FACES IN THE FLAMES

Fourth In a Series of Small Wars

PETER TATE

DOUBLEDAY & COMPANY, INC.
GARDEN CITY, NEW YORK
1976

All of the characters in this book
are fictitious, and any resemblance
to actual persons, living or dead,
is purely coincidental.

Library of Congress Cataloging in Publication Data

Tate, Peter.
Faces in the flames.

I. Title
PZ4.T22Fac3 [PR6070.A66] 823'.9'14
ISBN 0-385-01860-6
Library of Congress Catalog Card Number 75–21246

First Edition

FACES IN THE FLAMES

ANTECEDENTS

UNAM SANCTAM (One Faith), being an encyclical of Pope
Eugenio I.

"It has been considered timely to state that the Blessed Gospels
warn of the 'divisions' that will mark the days immediately prior to
the reappearance of the Beloved Son of Our Blessed Virgin Mary.
These are identified now by the Mother Church as manifestations of
the Evil Forces abroad in this sorry and suffering world.

"The Church herself has not been free of these demonstrations, although it should be stated in her defence that such failings were but
the imperfect understandings of imperfect men.

"Past sympathies have been misguided; the information available
to the Holy See was inadequate or partisan and the responses to her
genuine inquiries not always in harmony with the pacific aspirations
of the Church's intent.

"The day demands that she dissociate herself from the manners of
thinking which favour rulership by division, which seek to benefit by
confusion and fragmentation. Indeed, there is a single solution to
such wholesale anarchy and that is to present one face, to speak with
one voice, to acknowledge one truth.

"There is a danger in having not too much love, but love which is
so unquestioning that it embraces enemies and leaves the way open
for evil consequences. The Church's willingness to temper all its
deeds with affection is not so much a benediction as a weakness
which said forces of evil are swift to exploit.

"And if the hazard is that ruination may come from the very fac-
tors we welcome and applaud, then surely we may be entitled to dis-
criminate in a godly way.

"In the search for truth, where the heart so often rules the head, it
is a mistake on occasions to lean too far towards the apparently
oppressed minority. Their suffering is not proof in itself of their

rightness. This is how tears may cloud the eyes so that a proper understanding may be lost.

"Less than a decade ago, Pope Paul entertained in audience members of the liberation groups from the Portuguese territories of Guinea, Angola, and Mozambique and thus gave blessing to their partisanship.

"The result was a schism of no small kind between the Church and a nation which has been a strength and comfort to her since mediaevel times.

"We cannot fault a judgement which sought only to assess and apportion the blame. But perhaps we may have the humility to admit that subsequent events have shown our traditional ally's insight to be more penetrative than our own.

"For Portugal herself now writhes in the grip of these evil forces. The progressive thought which led her to fulfil the promise of self-determination to her colonies had a backlash at home so that she now suffers in her cities at the hands of political hoodlums.

"It is timely, then, to state our anxiety for her welfare and our desire to renew that cherished and sadly missed acquaintance; further, to record that we now extend the hand of Peter across the schism and across the sea in the hope that thus may be generated our spirit of one faith.

"In Portugal, the political animals are of a minority and the barricades and water-cannon of Lisbon mean little to the country people who comprise 80 per cent of the population and who still go about their business and their worship in a way that makes us feel ashamed for having been silent for so long.

"The Church proclaims her solidarity with the real power of Portugal, the power of prayer. The Church further proclaims her favour with the present leaderships of the emergent states of Zimbabwe where, too, dissidents still bid to sabotage the pure intention.

"Where an Establishment tries so hard to lay guidelines in all spheres of human experience, indiscretion dogs the unwary step.

"All the traditional power of the Church is to be brought to bear henceforth on these divisive forces, identifying them as the antichrist, outlawing them, bringing them to judgement and to daylight. The Church's influence is formidable and the precedents are clear.

"The Church will no more seek to elicit popularity with soft words and ambiguities. That one voice will be a strong one, one to be feared by those who practise evil. It will be unmistakeable.

"In this sense, we pray blessings and bounty upon our mission
. . ."

MORE THAN ONE FAITH*

"This declaration has become necessary in contradiction of attempts made to sabotage our sincerity and credibility in Black Africa.

"We were motivated initially by the plight of the Christian Institute of Southern Africa, now operating in isolation and under continuing ban from the post-Johannes Vorster government.

"Mr. Vorster, as the records show, concurred entirely with the reasoning of the Schlebusch Commission that the institute was 'conditioning public opinion to accept a possible, even an inevitable, violent change in the existing order' in order to produce 'a black-dominated socialist state.'

"Taken on its own, that restriction could have been survived—could even have been enjoyed, carrying as it did the threat of prosecution under the Suppression of Communism Act. If the fighting Church can now be accused of communism, then indeed our ideological opponents have gone as far as they can go without coming back.

"But the suggestion—rather, the INSISTENCE—that the CIA directly and the World Council of Churches indirectly—since that was the support group cited by Mr. Vorster—should achieve their results by revolutionary means cannot go unanswered. The institute and the council via this commission are pledged to nonviolent opposition to apartheid policies and to producing change by reasoning and persuasion.

"And now we discover that even apartheid, as we understood it, has taken on a new meaning. In a country adjacent to the borders of South Africa, we find that blacks are being divided from blacks and that the Church of Rome sits in the judgement seat.

"What is the rule of thumb? The Vatican has outlawed freedom

* Extract from a doctrine issued by the Anti-Apartheid Commission of the World Council of Churches in conjunction with the Christian Institute in Alienation (CIA):

fighters en masse, without testing their motives, without examining their precedents. They are branded as the 'antichrist'—and since our sympathies are wedded to them, we must presumably share their label.

"The encyclical of Pope Eugenio I, *Unam Sanctam* (One Faith), gives all people two chances—embrace the Church of Rome or embrace the 'antichrist.' It is an arrogance that cannot stand unchallenged.

"We are talking about Zimbabwe, where history, in truth, contains precious little credit for the Protestant church. By our apathy, our inadequate attempts to master local dialects or to instruct the natives in our own language, we left the missionary field wide open to zealous Catholic brothers.

"Our recent attempts to aid those we considered to be speaking with the true voice of the nations were attempts to regain lost ground —not because we were in contest with the Church of Rome but because we (and we thought the Vatican was of like mind) cherished the ideal that the natives should have the running of their own affairs.

"And so we find ourselves diametrically opposed to the Roman Catholic church—a position forced upon us by what we may now call the other side—a position where rightness and wrongness are identifiable by that small detail of sequence.

"We will not live with the epithet of 'antichrist' when we know that what we do is for the furtherance of truth and for the freedom of the individual. The Church of Rome no longer offers that motive. Since she has ruled us out of order, we hereby reverse and reiterate that allegation—and declare that wherever we find ourselves face to face over this issue, we shall render whatever steps may be necessary in order to secure the victory of good will and Christian principles.

"It is a pity that the moral leadership of the Western world shall come again to schism but the circumstances are not of our making. Therefore we make no apology for the way in which we react to them. It is a sacrilege for the sanctimonious Vatican to state that God is on her side. Further, it is a grave error of fact. He is on the side of freedom. And so are we. . . ."

THE HAGUE, Wednesday, June 27, 19—

DEATH IN A DEVIL HAT

A tourist attraction, put it no higher. The Afrikaners came up off the beaches of Lourenço Marques, moved by the dry southwesterly and the promise of an auto-da-fé for their delectation.

July mid-winter with the temperature at a gentle sixty-five degrees Fahrenheit and the long cold spells of the native Rand a long way away from their Mozambique thoughts.

Hardly a fever heat to moisten the brow, but there would be some ebony skins greased up today. The cabaret was prone to sweat.

The organisers had laid out a square of short-grass steppe overlooking Delagoa Bay and marked the concessions of the cashewnut sellers, the Coke merchants, the fruiterers, and the holy men. Now the tradesmen, the tourists, the priests waited, with excitement swaying them like a succession of savanna breezes.

There were twenty cages and thirty stakes, which meant 60 per cent real death, 40 per cent relaxation in effigy—a little higher than the crowd usually liked of symbolism but a major event, nevertheless.

The month of notice had been passed in various ways by the penitents and in great activity by the sponsors, who plastered city and village walls with edicts bearing all the high colour of bullfight posters.

In the last twenty-four hours, heretics from as far north as Beira had been trucked down the coast. Those who had died of endemic sleeping sickness before they could be called upon to make their fatal act of faith were the lucky ones.

But they would be here, too, in spirit and pasteboard, cut out lifesize and decked in coat of demons and matching tall hat.

Tremendous. The Coke was going down without touching the sides.

And on the outer edge of the square, a flutter of silk.

The banner led the procession. A scarlet surround framing a thorny cross with the tree of life on its left hand and the sword of truth on its right. Encircling the motif, the words *"Exurge Domine et Judica Causam Tuam*. Psalm 73."

"I became envious of the boasters when I could see the peace of wicked people . . . Haughtiness has served them as a necklace and violence envelopes them as a garment . . .

"They have raised themselves to the very heavens and their tongues themselves walk upon the earth . . . Surely you place them on slippery ground and make them fall to ruin. Oh, how they have become an object of awe in a moment, how they have been brought to their end with sudden terrors . . .

"For, see, the very ones keeping away from you will perish . . ."

These were the credentials, the answers to those who might question the moral dilemma, and after them came the cross, shrouded in black crepe, preceding the formal array of purple from the Pontifical Society for the Propagation of the Faith.

This was the bind, this necessary ceremonial. The crowd watched that from the corner of its eye with the main gaze flung to the rear of the parade.

"FLESH!" shouted one Boer in straw hat and shorts. "FLESH!" took up another on the opposite side of the square. They had been placed by Propaganda Fide to put the spectators in the correct frame of mind. The bloodlust, after all, was no more than righteous and the execution a kind of sacrament.

"FLESH!" It soon became a chorus, a corporate voice taken by the sea wind and flung inland towards the Transvaal border. "Flesh!" For the miscreants were not just sinners against the Church, they were aliens to humanity.

They were guerrillas.

Flesh, emerging now in conical caps and sanbenito smocks, bedevilled and licked with linen flames.

The live ones came first. Some were proud or appeared so, with principle stiffening their backs and deafening their ears to the voluble monks who marched beside them, beseeching them even at this stage to make a contrition. It would not alter their outcome. And the peace of mind offered was less than convincing.

Others were beginning to bend as they saw the instruments of their downfall. A small number had been soft from the initial questioning, when they discovered that torture pure and simple was the least of their pains. They had not understood the procedure and had not been told the charge. Then they had discovered that confessing to the sins they knew still wasn't what the inquisitors sought. Despair came easily when they found they could not compromise, even if they so desired.

At least there were no rolling eyes. If they did not understand, it was not because the creatures of their superstitions were standing in their way. The obscurity was deliberate and they put it down to politics. So much for education.

So much for their heroes, too. Joao Frelimo who walked with head high and dunce's hat achieving an almost jaunty angle that confounded his vivid sanbenito, had been calling back to them as they walked.

The idea of burning had not surprised him because he was versed in the precedent. In fact, it had inspired him with expression when he had spent the night wondering what words to use for his last.

Shouting back to them above the priests' chants and the crowd calls, quoting José Craveirinha loud and clear:

> "I am coal
> and must burn
> and consume everything in the fire of my combustion.
>
> Yes, boss
> I will be your coal!"

If they could just take a firm grip on that thought. If they could believe—imagine, if they had to—that these fires today could spread and take foul tourists and grinning *assimilados* and moaning churchmen and reduce them all to common ash . . .

No sweat on Joao Frelimo's brow, no line of telltale beads along his upper lip. "Keep cool," he called back. "Remember what they want and remember not to give it to them. That's"—he nearly fumbled and said "all"—"that's what we do now."

A firm resolve to take them through the inevitable. They loved him all the more for it.

And they felt very little fear; only sadness as they were drawn up to witness the relaxation of effigies. Pasteboard representations of their comrades who had cheated the Inquisition in the stinking cells of Beira and Inhambane, borne forth here by the servants of Propaganda Fide, and bent and twisted and stuffed into the tiny cages.

Still, the cry was for "flesh." Cardboard was one-dimensional. Cardboard did not scream or bleed.

And at a sign from the purple gentry, a line of troops moved into place behind the liberators and prodded them on bayonets towards the stakes.

"Cool," said Frelimo. He felt the blade pierce his back, felt the warmth of blood upon his vest. But it was no deterrent because he was bound for death anyway and the soldier would take the blame if he expired before he reached the bonfire. "Cool." A wound on the other side, but not so severe because the soldier was far more nervous than he was.

"Who can carry off the multitude," he said, "and lock it in a cage?"

"For Joao is us all," came the response from Eduardo, the Balante, who remembered the *Noemia de Sousa* refrain. "For Joao is us all."

The freedom fighters, deprived of mission, had a chant to answer the ecclesiastical simperings and the wolf howls from the fringe of the square. "For Joao is us all."

They kept it up while they were lashed to their stakes, while the military came to their toes with burning brands, while the brushwood and steppe grass caught, while flames rose and dispatched their lives in black smoke and dishonourable stench across the savanna.

A few of the tourists left their stomach contents and ice-cold Coke in a nice mixture on the steppe. The tougher individuals went back to the beach wondering why they felt vaguely cheated. They had stared death in the face, with the advantage that it was not their own. Few hit on the reason—it took a special brand of honesty to admit that the blacks had died like white men.

The traders counted their cash, the clerics counted the victims and withdrew for a day of benediction.

The Mozambique vultures counted their blessings. At autos up and down the coast, they were developing quite a fancy for cooked meat.

Another tourist attraction, another act of faith. It came back to Rico Scarlatti now as he lingered in the Vatican loggias of Raphael, looking for offence. In truth, he needed but little reminding and these present grotesques of Giovanni da Udine, Giulio Romano, and Raphael's other assistants put him squarely back in that sun-baked garden of Tuscany.

Rico Scarlatti, Siena lawyer, had taken up an impossible case against his will and had found himself briefed with a burning commission.

His client had been Shem. A younger man, a little clumsy in his ways with people. And that was a crime in these hanging gardens where the international peace and security organisation of the day had held him responsible for the world's ills.

Well, that agency was in decline, undermined by its own dexterity. The Tuscany gardens had helped. Scarlatti, in his small and late way, had contributed. But he had not given as much as Shem—and if Shem had crumbled the United Nations, what was left for Scarlatti?

The memory stayed so vivid because the question remained unanswered. It was there for recall at the sight of a gargoyle, at the slap of a sandal on a dusty road.

Shem had dealt with four situations involving unstable people. Psychologically, his intervention had been a disaster. As indications of good heart and good intention, the situations could hardly have shown him in a better light. If that had been the object of the game.

But it had not. By the time Shem had run the gamut of the complex, all but one of the inhabitants had reason to hate him and that one was dead. He was Che, imprisoned in his library and tortured by the very knowledge that surrounded him—

How far back does it have to go? asked Scarlatti in the sunlit seventh of Raphael's thirteen vaults. Every time I replay it, it gets harder to grasp. But there was really just one day, when the comedy finished.

He found a marble bench with a lion's legs and lost himself again to Garden Five, with Arthur Prinz, the interrogator, waiting for him like a keeper.

And Shem. It was good to see Shem again.

On the rolling lawn of the last garden, Scarlatti was making his statement. It was more than a plea, it was a declaration.

"You," he said to Prinz and the administrator who sat with him as a tribunal. "You are the guilty ones. Che was the weak link in your chain. The mistake you made was to surround him with truth.

"Che recognised you for what you were, whitewashers, illusion thinkers—and because he realised your error, you killed him . . ."

"That is ridiculous." Prinz lost his smile.

"So deny it. Better yet, explain to your—creatures—how you

came to employ such violence in these games of peace and how you now accuse a stranger of defiling your virtue by doing the self-same thing . . ."

"You are DISCHARGED." Prinz's tone was brittle and breaking up. "You are in contempt. You will be jailed."

"Then deny it," challenged Scarlatti. "Can't you lie? What kind of morality is that? Don't you know that the greatest deception is the perversion of the truth? At least be HONEST enough to lie."

He started forward. The interrogator stepped back. His chair went over and his papers went flying and his nerves went to hell. "Guard . . . GUARD!"

Scarlatti saw a movement out of the corner of his eye. A machine gun was being levelled.

"No . . . nononono." Shem whipped past the lawman's left side, running like a madman for the table or a soldier for glory or a winner for the tape or a . . .

Scarlatti threw himself in a flat dive for Shem's legs caught a heel on the temple, and lost contact—

When he came round, the scene was frozen in tableau and there was a hard echo receding, garden by garden, through the vast complex.

Shem was nowhere. Correction: Shem was BEHIND him, carried that way by a hail of bullets that had taken him in mid-flight and cast him like a broken doll upon the grass.

The blood spreading, brown, across the back of his denim shirt; the smoke coiling upward from the heated barrel of the gun which had pierced him and nailed him were the only movements in the whole of the world.

Alone, alive in the middle of a picture, Scarlatti walked to Shem. There was no doubt he was dead, torn almost apart by the Manslayer. But Shem had known it would be that way and had left instructions, unuttered, subliminal, that there was to be no grief. Just a purpose.

Finita la commedia. So it had come to this.

Scarlatti knelt at Shem's feet and removed his sandals. He kept one foot longer than was necessary in his hand—not that it would be noticed in this frozen time—and tried to inherit some of the draining warmth.

A rustle at his side. A girl dropped loosely like a puppet whose strings have been released.

She was trying to look at Shem but without much success. She looked at his outstretched hands, the grass six inches from his head. She kept her eyes averted from his terrible wounds.

"He ordered me not to love him," she said. "How do I do that?"

Scarlatti was moved by the wistful beauty of the girl. Suddenly he could understand a lot better why Shem had scampered to embrace death. "You don't have to worry," he said. "He saved you the trouble. He saved you all a lot of trouble."

"If he thought it was that easy . . ." Her tone broke. She rocked back and forward, crooning her sorrow, and because he could not bear the song, he went.

With the sandals dangling in his right hand, he followed the echo of the fusillade, preceded the echo of the whimper, through Garden Four, Garden Two, Garden One. The gate of whorled iron opened to his touch and he was on the road.

In the wall beside the gate, a plaque bearing the words: "And they will have to beat their swords into ploughshares and their spears into pruning hooks. Nation will not lift up sword against nation, neither will they learn war any more."

He read it and spat out the irony of it. Shem, namesake of the faithful son of Noah. Isaiah, doggedly communicating the peace promise of his God. Each just as dead now—and Scarlatti married to them both because he had seen the desolation and lived. He started to take off his Siena lawman's chisel-toed shoes.

Later, see him running. He had discarded his tie and opened his shirt to the waist. But he carried his jacket. At the next village, he could make a good trade—a well-cut business suit for a set of denims was quite a bargain and he could most likely pick up some provisions in the same voluble deal.

Shem had started inland from the Sea of the Middle Earth. Scarlatti would continue that course across the knee of Italy and thence wherever instinct or event transported him.

Shem had been ignorant until late in his short life of the necessity and desirability of ending it where death would do the most good. Scarlatti started out in full knowledge of this provision, but it did not worry him.

Shem had been the prototype, the hybrid. Scarlatti could build on that foundation. Someday, someone would build on Scarlatti.

Shem, stumbling through a kind of genesis, had managed to captivate one man. One man on the move was better than a thousand standing still. Maybe that was the heritage.

There was life. "Agip" billboards were springing up along the roadside. Pienza—2½ km. read a sign. In time, the Fiat density grew, the drivers hooting at the dishevelled Scarlatti as they passed, whipping up dust.

The frozen time, then, was gone. Scarlatti was taking on the real world. On an impulse, he turned his steps towards Rome.

End of flashback. See Scarlatti now, in denims for sure, but a wasted year older.

Scarlatti had spent that year washing in fountains, living off his lawman's fat in the bank, looking for trouble.

Last summer, he had thought Rome was a good idea and the Curia a fine windmill at which to tilt, but his legal training had sabotaged him. He had to get out of being dispassionate over cases. He had idled among the Vatican riches, hoping that injustice would seize him and propel him. But to what end? Beyond assassinating the pope, what was there? And the College of Cardinals could make another pope in as little time as it took to tell it.

So he wandered and he pondered. Days in cathedrals, nights in the Café Grecco on the Via Condotti, making glass rings on a table which might have propped up Gogol or Goethe, Byron or Liszt or Hans Christian Andersen, but did nothing to support him.

Twelve months of hoping the fire would not go out and it never burning lower than right now on this cold bench before the loggia doors.

Watching them shut, now watching them open. And emerging, a man he would never forget, a man who stiffened and paled in disbelief when he returned the gaze.

"Scarlatti?" said the man with a spectre of the familiar smile.

"Arthur Prinz," said Scarlatti, warmer than he had felt all year.

In the midst of life is death. Simeon had watched it make a slow meal of Tomorrow Julie for fifteen months and still the final breath caught him unawares.

Sweet lord, that—that . . . THING . . . growing inside her. It getting bigger, her getting smaller. When would it take over altogether? When would he be bathing and dressing a raw carcinoma?

That stage had not yet been reached. Julie's victory had been that she had died as herself. Smiling in her sleep at some moon meadow of the mind, smiling with Simeon clear in her eyes and his fingers tight in the small, yellow skeleton of her hand.

And Simeon, his eyes by no means clear, hands seeking some entry to her pale skin to wrench out the rot and plunge it under his own ribs. Delving in nonsense, willing himself dead in preference. Trying to give Julie life at the expense of his own. No selfishness in those diminishing months. No whims to go wandering. No self-pity. No feeling cheated because he was being deprived of a well-spring and a domestic and a lover and all the other things that Julie had come to be. Here, Julie—take my life. And then the bitterness in solitude that she could not.

Time running out and every second precious for use with words so far unsaid and yet—too many silences. Because the thoughts outgrew the vocabulary. Because the necessity crippled articulation. Never a word when you want one.

"I feel that, too," Julie had said, when he could play denial games with her no longer. "I love you. That sums it up if I should go right now. I love you."

Then again, when she saw the weight of futility sat heavy upon him, she would say: "It's not fair, that thought of yours. Why wish survival on me? Do you think it would be any easier for me without you? When I am dying, the least you can do is live."

"But if we could both—"

"Simeon . . . I can't help it. I'm innocent of my death. But if you took steps to join me, that would be a sin. I believe in a resurrection, you know that. How many times have I said to you that life without something better to follow makes no sense at all? How many times have I said that the manner of a man's death is more important than the manner of his birth? And why? You have to understand about death, Simeon. It isn't natural, it was never meant to be. As long as we know that, we can accept it as being only temporary."

There had been many other utterances, too, of a religious nature. With Simeon, such a belief was a gut feeling but uncommitted. He had never questioned that there must be something.

Many years ago, as he sat astride a swing in Playa Nine on the Pacific coast, he had tried to explain the mysteries by lumping them together and suggesting that a doctrine should be drawn from them.

But the doctrine was no good without a focus. To say everybody was right was to cop out of the question.

Somebody had to be wrong. No one would admit it.

As each castigated the other, then every line of thought seemed to negate itself.

Julie's faith was simple. Back to basics, Simeon had said wryly. As if basics were a weakness and modernity had to be a sacrament.

Back to basics, Julie had said. Back to the time of authenticity on the lake shores of Nazareth before two thousand years of controversy and schism and compromise and commerce had muddied the waters beyond perception.

Julie had sense and intelligence. If she believed, that was evidence in itself. And yet, if somebody had come to him and said: "I am intelligent. I must be right"—he would have banished the dogmatist from his hearing.

Julie believes. Therefore, I believe.

It didn't add up to much.

It was sentiment masquerading as academe and yet he could not shake it with disputation. Julie is love. God is love.

No spells, no superstars, no Jesus freaks. No religion getting on terms with the people.

The people have to get on terms. Another of Julie's deathbed pronouncements. The people have to make the effort and acknowledge their debt.

Debt for what? For green trees and fresh air, high seas and soft moments. All the ephemerals the evolutionists had never quite managed to explain.

And dying? No, don't thank God for dying. Thank His enemy for that. Appreciate the metaphysical balance. A force for good, a force for evil. What the one creates, the other destroys. And when the equation is love, what better way to upset it than to visit it with death.

"Simeon." This very July morning, when he had risen with the squirrels, pushed Julie's bed to the window and wrapped her against the morning breeze among the Hampshire pines, she had caught his wrist with her wafer fingers. "Simeon, don't be fooled."

Bread and milk, a little sugar. It went down painfully slowly and would come up with indecent haste but at least she would have the taste of it. Once she had said: "I'm the lucky one. You only taste a strawberry once [when she could rise to a strawberry]. I taste it twice."

"Simeon." Still her hand clasped his wrist with a small strength that devastated him. "Please find out. For both of us."

"Find out, lovely?"

"There has to be a right way."

"And where do I look?"

"The plains of Megiddo."

Perhaps the morphine was making her day cloudy already. The doctor had threatened LSD to gladden her weakening heart and give her sweet visions for comfort. Simeon had kicked him down the stairs. His impulse would have been to save her pain. But to squander her last few hours of consciousness was not his right. She wanted to talk and was prepared to stand the agony.

Though her torment racked his own body, Simeon kept Julie only to morphine and even then he did not know when she would lose track of thoughts. He feared the vegetable phase almost more than he feared the end. From that point, Julie would be on her own because he could not penetrate the coma. That they should be separated in such a way was more than he could bear.

"The plains of Megiddo. I'm not wandering, love"—and how could she be to say that?—"you'll know them when you see them because there will be no mistake. Clear cut, the two sides, the right and the wrong. Please find them."

Then she had slept and he had watched a formation of swifts sweep out from the gables above the window and recalled Richard Jefferies, the nature essayist who had marvelled as he died of consumption that spring could still come even though he would not be there to make a note of it.

While Julie slept he could weep and he did it now, empathising strongly between the Jefferies dilemma and their own.

Julie's hands were cold. He rubbed them gently, and finding no response, he began to chafe. Looking at her face, he found her eyes on him. Yet she could not see, just as she could not respond to warmth.

She had not said good-bye. But then, in her understanding, there was no parting. He closed her eyes gently and lay for an hour with his lips on her marble forehead.

This is how Arthur Prinz came into the possession of Pope Eugenio and vice versa.

The Garden Five experience had been a shaker, true, but Scarlatti was mistaken in his assessment that it alone had finished the United Nations. It was too private a disgrace.

It was a major matter only in the sense of proximity. The breakdown of the agency had been far more gradual, far more widespread. There had been public disgraces.

They came before and during the garden episode. They were evident, too, while Scarlatti was already closing the book on the organisation.

But the eclipse had never become total. Arthur Prinz, reeling among his papers and tasting failure in Garden Five, had ended the day with one determination—to ensure his own survival.

While so many top UN officials had suffered their ignominy in the open, his degradation had the virtue of being largely unseen. Since peerlessness was hard to find among the staff, Prinz discovered that, far from harming his prospects, he had actually enhanced his reputation.

Even so, the respect was worth very little when the fabric was crumbling, anyway. Thus he could not have timed his suggestion better. His plan, he told the Secretary-General's aide, Harold Messenger, was available to everyone.

And what was that?

He was going to embrace the Church.

Harold Messenger nearly gave the game away. The Prinz build-up had been to prepare him for a ticklish mission. Messenger, in his wisdom, had been looking for a likely marriage of interests and when word had come to him that Eugenio might be willing to hold meaningful talks, he had been seeking a fairly expendable member to test the ground at St. Peter's. Prinz had literally talked himself into it.

So why, Prinz had added, didn't they ALL embrace the Church?

From there, it was but a very short step to Rome.

At Rome, Pope Eugenio was ready with the hospitality and grateful, though not prepared to show it. Idealistically, the Vatican and the UN had always been fairly close together but their relationship had been more polite than intimate. The fact had made it difficult for Eugenio to phrase the favour he was seeking. Now, having the approach come from the other side gave him bargaining power.

Eugenio set aside the ceremony for Prinz's visit—which Prinz didn't mind; there were too many critics already trying to label these talks as last-ditch attempts to save face and credibility—and greeted him and fed him in the private apartments.

The working lunch reached the Napoleon brandy stage and the real talking started.

"As you know," broached Prinz, "my principals have always been glad of your formidable support. It is no use denying that circumstances seem to have conspired against us in the last couple of years. Here we are trying to do a conscientious good work and—"

He left the sentence for Eugenio to finish, so that he might learn from the response.

"Good works are not popular," said Eugenio. "I could say that we in the Church have a longer tradition of such misfortunes but, believe me, it does not make them any easier to bear."

"Then you have felt the frustration, too."

"Naturally. One cannot deal with the whole world, as we two agencies do, without running up against this same brick wall. In fact, it is not so mute as a brick wall—would that it were. It is insidious and destructive. It delights in the failure of men's best-laid schemes. It gains strength from the apathy and discontent that plague both our houses."

"You describe it to the letter."

"We even have a name for it—the antichrist."

Prinz had not been expecting quite such an enthusiasm to find common ground but he reasoned it was no bad thing. If Eugenio wanted to believe they had a common enemy, so much the better for his suggestion.

"Then you link it with communism."

"By no means. Well . . . by a very SMALL means. Communism may be a part of the same disease, but our main cause for concern is the uncommitted, unaligned sector of humanity—the impulsivist, if you like, who has no creed of his own beyond trying to undermine the establishments that exist. Such a person can find support from communism but usually ignores it—because even that requires a commitment he is not prepared to make."

Eugenio filled his own glass, pushed the decanter to Prinz. When the UN man was similarly supplied, he said: "It is very gratifying to find we have so many points of contact. I would even go so far as to say that each of our agencies might benefit from a more tangible link with the other."

Eugenio was wary. "What kind of a link?"

"Not a merger," said Prinz quickly. "Our individual standing is far too important for that. My principals were thinking more of a mutual use of resources. Now that your concept of the enemy proves to be so close to our own, I am prompted to add—a regular exchange of information."

"I don't know," said Eugenio. "I have a problem which involves your people."

"Our people? Some dispute?"

"No. No, it's more your sphere of activity than your membership —at the moment, that is."

"Potentially our people."

"That would be more accurate."

"I'd like to help but I'm afraid I still don't understand." So the pontiff demands a price, thought Prinz. All right—let's see if it is payable.

"It will not be held as a debt?"

"Good grief, Your Holiness. We are hoping to set up a worthwhile intercourse here. If you know of a matter that should be brought to our attention, that is normal procedure. We won't send you a bill."

"Right. Then it's Zimbabwe."

"Zimbabwe?"

"The former Portuguese colonies. As a federation, they are applying to join the United Nations."

"That's so. Formal inquiries are being made."

"Well . . . I would find it impressive proof of our entente if some pitfall should be perceived which might render them unworthy."

Prinz was surprised. Zimbabwe was a long way away from Rome and a subject he had not studied. "Could I ask why? It would enable me to provide my peers with a more convincing case."

Eugenio replenished the glasses, refreshed himself, and phrased his play. "We were speaking of the antichrist. The antichrist is RIFE in Zimbabwe."

"You mean—black magic? Juju worship?"

"Good heavens, no. That went out with missionary education. I'm talking about the witch doctor's modern counterpart—the guerrilla."

"The guerrilla? I wouldn't have said he—"

"Perhaps I was obscure. What I mean is that he now provides the kind of threat to thinking that we once encountered with the witch doctor. The present Zimbabwe government had its beginnings in such a movement. Now, having found a place in the world by certain small compromises, it still suffers the inroads of extremists—not only on itself but as a place of refuge for their activities elsewhere. The Zimbabwe authorities do not like that any more than we do. They have allowed us to set up a machine to deal with the terrorist heresy, but that is insufficient. Isolation is the only sure measure."

Prinz now had progressed from surprise to bewilderment. "But if the Zimbabwe rulers have afforded you these—facilities—how can you, in all conscience, act against what they want?"

"How indeed, Mr. Prinz? That is why I make the request that the decision to reject their application should come from the UN herself —and be in no way traceable to me."

"But that is—dishonest, Your Holiness." Prinz never mistook a chance for betterment. Here was something he could use.

"I did not make the rules, Mr. Prinz, and really, I have no need of instruction in morality. It is not dishonest in the context in which we live, and while we live, my first task is to provide and maintain hope. In order to keep that particular fountain unpolluted, I ask this boon. When I say it is a benefit to both of us, I speak advisedly. Once you allow the antichrist among your members, collapse will not be very far away."

"Surely only the legitimate government of Zimbabwe is ever going to find its way into our organisation. Aren't you being overly cautious?"

"Aren't you, Mr. Prinz, being somewhat naïve? The governments in these emergent nations can change overnight. Are you going to say the UN will go through all the elaborate rigmarole of expulsion if the new rulership also offers promises aimed at the good of its subjects? I have seen the growth of the antichrist. It is insidious. Show it a door and it will find a way to the other side. That is my conviction.

It is also, if you like, my—price, though I ask it for good scriptural reasons."

Whatever Prinz thought about it—emotional claptrap, political expediency, the feverish wanderings of an old man—it was all he could take back to his superiors and then, presumably, his job was done. What next?

First things first. Arthur Prinz requested the use of a telephone and put the deal to Messenger. He returned to the pontiff well pleased with the result. Then he made his investment for the future.

"My principals are in total agreement," he reported. "We understand and appreciate your concern over our African brothers and you can be assured that that understanding will be utilised when we come to deal with the Zimbabwe application. Now . . . I find myself at a loose end with our business completed. My feeling is that this liaison for which we aim might be well served if I had a position right here."

Across the Rome rooftops, campaniles were counting out the siesta hour.

"It's a little warm to organise that now," said Eugenio, "but if you present yourself and your belongings here in the morning, I can guarantee you a suite that will satisfy every aspect of your taste and artistry. Now I hope you will excuse me. I have a head full of thoughts and they weigh heavily."

Prinz stood up and proffered his hand. Eugenio took it without protest and shook it. There was the matter of the pontifical ring and the blessing but it was shelved by mutual choice. They had both been too close to earth for such esthetic considerations.

Instead, Prinz took the pontiff's elbow and guided him none too steadily towards his retiring room and saw him through the door.

Eugenio, reclining, gave exercise to the thoughts.

Prinz, meanwhile, came face to face with Scarlatti and panicked.

He fled the building, crossed St. Peter's Square with the haste of a fool, and lost himself in the Via dei Corridori.

Pope Eugenio I had outlined the spiritual side of his problem as though there were no other. Indeed, that was how he considered it— an isolated ramification. But there were others.

The cornerstone of his structure was the Prefecture of Economic

Affairs, which had now totally absorbed the Administration of the Patrimony of the Apostolic See and several trailing branches of the Vatican willow tree.

While Propaganda Fide still circumscribed all thoughts of faith and witness, the manipulation of money lay squarely with the streamlined department which had its offices adjacent to the Raphael loggias and Eugenio's private quarters. Those offices housed an impressive line-and-vision link with the business capitals and took their administrative cardinals fresh from Harvard Business College or the Turin think-tank.

Even so, the results were less than satisfactory in the terms of the Dow Jones index and the clatter of teleprinters these days was frequently drowned by the clamour of chickens coming home to roost.

Eugenio had declared the Zimbabwe machine a holy war and, in fairness to him, was sincere in that belief. But the fact remained that the Vatican had a lot of money at stake in its international dealings. True, there was infinitely more value in the treasures of the Church —but there could be no capital realisation of these while they were as important at the box office as the Mass itself.

So the need arose to safeguard those fractional but fluid assets involved in business—such holdings as oil and minerals and engineering.

In recent history, all these interests had been exercised in one arena—Caborra Bassa.

By an entirely arbitrary means, that same prestige project had become the focus of attention for every guerrilla, freedom fighter, mercenary, and carpetbagger north of the Cape. Eugenio's intelligence sources had told him it represented the whole travesty of black-white relations in microcosm and that was the attraction for the forces of disorder. His personal feeling was that this made the thing sound rather too respectable.

Despite his official tone of conciliation, he had little love for the remaining insurgents or for the new governments who had allowed him to conduct his campaign in their midst. What they—the insurgents and their moderate authorities which had sprung up among them—had done in their time to the missionaries dispatched via Propaganda Fide was distressing and detestable and he failed to see how anybody could explain it away by resorting to racist clichés. The people should suffer for their sins.

His conscience didn't bother him, then. His heart condition was right. The fact that every blown-up container train took its share of Peter's Pence was not the first consideration or the primary reason for action.

The terrorists were declared enemies of the Church. It was not just a matter of bandying a term like "antichrist"—they made clear identification possible, and this being so, his response was more than understandable . . . it displayed religious integrity.

Arthur Prinz, he suspected, was a wheeler and dealer. He had no more faith than any of the foe, but he still managed to make Eugenio nervous. Thus, he must be a professional frightener.

And it was fortunate that the Church had been able to secure his services at such little cost.

Thus the Prince of Rome arrived at an appreciation of his own fine wisdom and drifted into slumber.

He had achieved his purpose, gained a valuable interrogator for his machine, when need be, and made the man happy in the process. He could afford to be well pleased.

What he did not know was that, in rapid succession, something had happened to prick that particular balloon for Arthur Prinz.

Rico Scarlatti found a scrap of paper in his denim jacket, wrote the address of the Café Grecco on it, and handed it to one of the Swiss Guards.

"For Mr. Prinz," he said. "It will save him a great deal of trouble."

Then he took his elation back to the café to await events.

Prinz must have expected him to give chase and for that reason alone, he had not. He knew Prinz. The man would not let him alone now. There had been a score to settle and he had shown himself within striking distance. Quite by accident, as it happened. But he was glad. For the first time in many months, he was beginning to feel that Rome had been the right choice to make on that dusty road.

Almost the first consequence of the meeting was a new repertoire of visions. His thoughts transported him back to Siena. Then the life-style had been well-cut dark suits, small prosecutions for small misdemeanours, and a bottle of wine at the end of the day with the local police chief, Cosimo Giotta.

The brief that had taken him into the garden complex of the United Nations Temperate Environmental Control Agency had come via two of Prinz's aides, given a sinister gloss and a strong-armed persuasion.

He wondered whether the man still employed the same methods. Over his lasagna, he watched the café door, half-expecting it to swing wide to admit heavily-muscled messengers.

Instead, Prinz came in person, grabbing a glass from the bar, helping himself from Scarlatti's demi-litre of Valpolicella while the man was still struggling to accept the fact.

"I didn't give you a proper welcome earlier on," he said. "Forgive me. I was late for an appointment. It's good to see you."

Scarlatti took a little of the wine for himself and blessed his steady hand. "You can't mean that," he said.

"Of course I can. It means I have a chance to level with you. You quit that garden in Tuscany at such high speed, I had no time to say all sorts of things."

"Like what?"

"Well, I made a mistake. That was the most important thing."

"In not killing me, too?"

"Please spare me a little patience. I made a bad mistake with Shem. I believed in my actions even as he believed in what he was doing. Over the past year, it has been his belief which has prevailed. I wish I had the chance to tell him so."

"Your goons took care to remove that possibility."

"I didn't want it to happen. If the case had run its full course, he would have been alive today. Execution was never the intention."

Scarlatti could feel the old anger rising despite Prinz's representations. And with it came the assurance of familiar ground beneath his feet. Prinz could pretend what he liked but nothing had really changed. This was another ploy. The intervening months were as nothing and he was ready to continue the contest. "I can't help but find that hard to accept. Even if you didn't intend to curtail the boy's life, you sure as hell convinced him that was your plan."

"He was young—"

"Don't blame it on his youth. I saw it as clearly as he did."

"Look . . . I have to put up with your rancour. It's a small price to pay and I'm not quibbling. But if we are ever to advance from that damned garden, we have to discuss what happened there with

the wisdom of retrospect. Shem had a death wish. He was convinced
that the circumstances justified the ultimate sacrifice."

"Perhaps he was right."

"You tried to stop him."

And all of this was true, in the same way that all the UN evidence
had been true. Not in spirit, maybe, but in fact. And arguing about
the accuracy of spirit was either invalid or impossible.

"You said you had come around to his way of thinking," said
Scarlatti.

"I said it was his belief that had endured."

"Prevailed."

"Prevailed. Not that there is a great deal of difference. What I
meant was that each time I went over the episode—and that was often—Shem emerged as the hero and myself as the villain. I feel responsible."

"You WERE responsible."

"Well, I ACCEPT it. What the hell do I do about it?"

"You come to me."

"What?"

"You come to me and you say, 'I'm sorry for what I did. I wish I
could make amends!' I don't know whether you think I have some direct link to the tomb. Shem is just as dead to me as he is to you."

Scarlatti pushed back his plate. Before Prinz's arrival, he had been
eating with the appetite of eagerness. Now he had no stomach for the
remainder. He called for another carafe of wine.

Prinz watched him quizzically. "Is that to indicate that we have
nothing to share? Not experience or confidence or Valpolicella?"

"It's to indicate that I am thirsty and that I am going to be a lot
thirstier before this conversation is out. Now you can start this new
carafe or finish the old one or do whatever you like. We are SHAR-
ING this dialogue—all right?"

"Fine," said Prinz. "At last I feel welcome."

And he drained the first carafe.

Natural break. First overtures had been made and accepted, in
whatever prickly form. Neither man was disturbed by the silence that
lay between them while dusk came down on the Via Condotti and
the barman brought candles. Each, in his way, was preparing for the
next scene.

Scarlatti no more believed Prinz's change of heart than he would have accepted a novena from the Devil. He was curious now to find out why the man was trying so hard to get on the right side of him.

Prinz stayed cool. So far, the exchange had gone much as he had expected. Scarlatti was still fiery and introverted by turn. If he used the right bait, he was sure of a catch.

"I came to offer you a job," he said.

"Doing what?"

"Well, I'm just starting off—but I suspect I'll still be putting the question to people. Furthermore, the people I am dealing with are beyond the age of impulse. They are hardened lawbreakers."

"Has the pope gone into law and order?"

"Ecclesiastical law. I'll be talking to heretics."

Scarlatti was surprised indeed. In the first place, he hadn't bargained for such an enthusiastic welcome from Prinz and in the second, he had not thought heresy was still a charge.

"The crime sounds interesting. In this permissive age, how do you prove it?"

"By making the age less permissive."

"By prosecuting heretics?"

"How is YOUR faith these days?"

"I left the Roman church for reasons I outlined to you a long time ago. In short, that was Christendom and I wanted Christianity."

"How do you feel now?"

"No different—except that, since Garden Five, I have had a better idea of what a Christian looks like. And it wasn't from meeting you."

Scarlatti reached for his glass and the draught set the candle flame wavering. Something of the sort was already going on in his stomach. Prinz finding a way to carry on where Shem had left off? That was the greatest insult of all. "The Church condemns heretics," he said, to steady himself.

"They are seen as the antichrist."

"Tell me—what kind of people are seen as heretics? People like myself who have voluntarily shaken off the shackles?"

"Not at all. It would not be our policy to blindfold people who are seeking for the light. We shed the light on those who seek to blindfold."

"Neat but meaningless."

"We prosecute those who seek to make discord—terrorists, insurgents, freedom fighters, clouders of the issue."

28 FACES IN THE FLAMES

"And what did you have in mind for me?"

"You are a man with a wide experience of the process of law—even our kind of law."

"Your kind? You mean justice without innocence?"

"I'm not talking about the Garden Five travesty. You would soon see that I had learned from my mistakes. Your position would be as an impartial observer of my interrogations. You would keep records for public inspection when necessary of methods and durations. I fancy that a man so keen to find me at fault would be an ideal choice in the circumstances."

From the UN Charter to Torquemada's Articles of Inquisition, thought Scarlatti. It is, as Prinz himself says, a fine way to nail him if I am ever to achieve it.

It was an offer he couldn't refuse—and Prinz knew that.

Scarlatti was hooked for a certainty with the statement that Prinz's ambition was the same as his own. That was one carafe they would never share.

As Arthur Prinz made his deal with Scarlatti, so his principals discussed the progress of the day. It was mid-afternoon in Turtle Bay, Manhattan, and they sat with their backs to the work and their eyes on the river.

Andrew Buthelezi, Secretary-General to the United Nations Organisation, was an African, although so long departed from his native soil that the assegais of injustice therein had grown blunt.

Harold Messenger was his aide, a professional diplomat who had begun his trouble-shooting with Kurt Waldheim and had supported several S.G.s through prickly times since.

"I can't pretend I like it," said Buthelezi.

"You were enthusiastic," Messenger chided him gently. They both knew the score.

"To you, I can't pretend. To the casual observer, it looks like a good stabilising influence at work at last. To me—well, my skin tincture tells me it's treachery."

"You're too hard on yourself. We did what we had to do."

"What it cost us was a bit of a shock."

"Surely, Andrew, you weren't expecting Eugenio to forgo the chance of a profit. He may think he's fooling some people with his talk of antichrist. But Prinz knew—and it's no mystery to me. The Vatican is financially involved."

"Then why do we have to accept it? We're allowing him a free hand in Zimbabwe to treat people as he likes. God, I feel as though I've handed him the thumbscrew myself."

"No, no. We have no say in Zimbabwe, anyway."

"But we could have had."

"We couldn't."

"What do you mean? We could have accepted their application."

"No. It's out of the question."

"Now, yes, but . . ."

"Even before. Their application was still out of order."

"I'm sorry, Harold. I continue bewildered."

"Tracks twenty-two and twenty-five."

"Harold, I swear you are being deliberately perverse."

Messenger laughed and laid a hand on his friend's arm. "Railway lines into the marshalling yards at Lourenço Marques. Those are the lines used to ship oil into and minerals out of Rhodesia. We have sanctions of Rhodesia—they've been around for a long time, it's true, but they have never been rescinded. If the Federation of Zimbabwe wanted to join the United Nations, they would have to outlaw that traffic. This they would not do because it provides the backbone of their meagre income. We couldn't promise them alternative traffic because we have nothing going into Rhodesia and we are supposed to ban everything that comes out—"

"Let me get this straight. Zimbabwe is a sanction-breaker. While she remains so, she is disqualified from membership."

"In a nutshell."

"Then we have given Eugenio nothing."

"Precisely."

"But how long before he finds out?"

"As long as you like. If you'll pardon the expression, Andrew—until you blow the whistle."

A cat waves his tail and Andrew Buthelezi tapped his foot when irritated. His right shoe had been paying tribute to St. Vitus since Messenger had come off the phone to Prinz. "Is anybody else likely to tell him?"

"If you mean Prinz, the man may not have a heart but nobody can deny the head on his shoulders. Besides, he had been able to apply a little blackmail of his own."

"On whom?"

"On me."

"On YOU! What—?"

"It's all right. Everything is under control. It suits me to let him have his way."

"And what did HE ask for?"

"A chance to work for Eugenio—to liaise between us."

"I don't see he had to blackmail you for that. It sounds like a logical progression."

"Well, I would have thought so. But Prinz saw fit to apply some pressure when he suggested it. He politely brought the matter of the sanctions to my attention, also mentioning that Eugenio was out of earshot. And when Arthur Prinz does things like that, it means one thing to me . . . he has a little venture of his own in mind."

"Such as?"

"Who knows? It takes him out of my hair for a while—though not off my hook. I'll tell you frankly, Andrew—I don't like this entente any more than you do. If I can see a way out, I'll take it. And who better to keep me informed than a man who changes loyalties like I change shirts? The moment Eugenio crosses him, we'll hear about it. When we hear, it may be something we can use."

Andrew Buthelezi's right foot was motionless. He lay back in his chair openmouthed. "That's . . . ingenious," he said. "No wonder you stay in the navigator's seat."

Messenger settled back in his own chair and consorted with the tranquillity of the day.

He was almost dozing when the Secretary-General said: "Do you know, I'm more than amazed, I'm amused. So tell me something—does a man of your superb vision really have no idea what Arthur Prinz may be planning?"

Messenger opened his eyes out of courtesy but turned no gaze to his peer. Instead, he spoke as though the words were written in the blue sky above the river.

"Several ideas. One—he enjoys interrogation. Eugenio may be offering him something that will exercise his talents to the full. Two —he may have seen some kind of interest in this—holy war. Two-and-a-half—there's a theory he has about the UN function with which I do not necessarily concur. He thinks it is the open-endedness of our commission which has been our main weakness. He says that if we had given ourselves the power of exclusion, we wouldn't be dogged by intellectual anarchy—fringe groups, civil rights, that kind of mechanism. These, he thinks, are more of a hindrance than a help to us and unfortunately, circumstances often give strength to his argument. Three—he similarly doesn't like loners. He seems to have some morbid fascination with them since the Garden Five debacle . . . though where he is going to find a loner in this papal pot pourri, I don't know—and that's the truth, superb visionary as I am."

Buthelezi chuckled and stood up. "I'm relieved to find you are fallible. I was beginning to think you were a bit of a pope yourself."

"Perish the thought." Messenger was going to give himself a little longer in the chair. "But if Prinz or anybody comes up with anything that proves this link doesn't have the stuff of saintliness, I don't mind playing the devil's advocate."

And all this time, as events shaped to their course, Simeon mourned. The business of dealing with death had taken more from him than the death itself.

Julie had spoken freely of a resurrection and Simeon, thinking in nonsense terms, had thought that that particular miracle at least would require a body—though why bones or dust or organs rendered to earth and protein should make the manifestation any easier, he did not know.

And there, the law of the county lay against him. The graveyards were full and overpopulated with the people who had sought this Hampshire in their dotage expressly for a hole in the ground and a stone at its head.

Simeon's gesture was still too flesh-raw for him to see that he had done the same thing. In essence, he cursed these unknowns who had beaten Julie to the hallowed ground. Because now there was only cremation—and how could Anybody manage resurrection after that?

A corpse is a corpse, however beloved, and a corpse has to go. The funeral directors handled him with patience as though there was a matter of how as well as a question of when.

But in the end, it came to the same thing. Julie—what was left of her outside Simeon's mind—was committed to the flames. And when some reference was made to the ashes, Simeon bolted from the scene. Who can tell whose ashes are which, Simeon? Don't let it reach the level of farce. Julie speaking, in his mind.

Julie's face in the flames. Her very presence now as he perched on the clifftop with new wood under his hands and the scent of linseed melodious in the symphony of dying leaves.

Julie liked a trip on the water and thus they came to Hurst Castle, by ferry from Keyhaven. It was an awkward landing with no jetty and Simeon had to lift her over the bow.

His heart nearly broke, not with the effort but with the lack of it. Julie was losing weight fast and with bulk went energy.

While his nightmare vision was one of growth within her, the reality was the opposite—a shrinking, a passing away.

"That's a girl," he said, as he set her down gently on grass with the grim Tudor fortress hunched over them.

And it seemed as though Julie cowered, as though her very fighting nature was in retreat. "I don't like it," she said. "I wouldn't mind just—sitting here on the grass until the boat comes back."

Simeon faced the familiar dilemma. Did he let her give in to this loss of confidence? Or did he still credit her with the strength to dispute? They had been able to disagree, with love. And surely it was wrong to change that now, even though Simon's first feeling was to allow harmony in all things—wholesale, telltale accord.

"Julie, love," he said. "We have to give the place a chance."

"I don't." She wasn't playing the game. Perhaps she was tired. It left Simeon badly deflated.

He took her hand and led her into the shade. "I'm afraid it's a forty-five-minute wait. I was selfish to bring you."

"I wanted to come. Perhaps I even wanted to see the place. I just don't now. I'm sorry to be so fickle, Simeon." The strain was in her voice. "But that's no reason why you—"

Her hand was still moist from its trailing in the estuarine waters. He kissed it and tasted salt. "I'm not fussy."

"I really would like to know about it. It's a pity to have come all this way. We may not have another chance."

Julie, Julie, you're not even trying this afternoon . . . And then perhaps the fight was gone. Perhaps this was the downhill truth of it, the efforts becoming fewer and farther between.

"It's been here four hundred years. It's not going to disappear before we come back."

"What I want, Simeon, is for you to see it and tell me about it. Breathe some life into it for me. I don't like it because it is cold and foreboding. You can get rid of that for me. I'm all right here—really. You have a look and tell me what you see. Now GO!"

And Simeon went—through a hatch in the iron door, gathering postcards and Department of the Environment circulars as he went.

Thin grass and Ministry gravel and everywhere the smooth, tiny pebbles which undermined your footsteps and slowed your pace. He passed over rusting railway lines from the small-gauge which had conveyed shells to the gun bays ranged along the island side of the fortress.

In four centuries, the main change had been one of calibre, with the artillery of the twentieth century ruling out the cannon of yore and now only the ridges in the floor, which had taken the mobile parts and the great iron doors that had wound up on winches while barrels and gunners scanned the strait for fleets Spanish, French, German.

The keep was twelve-sided and gained by a set of outside steps that Julie could never have managed. Simeon stood on ancient flagstones and could think only of today or tomorrow.

At last something of the place's spirit got to him and he sought access or at least some view of how the sea ran on the island side with a crazy idea of escape, if ever he should need it. Escape from what? In the course of his short lunacy, he scaled steps so narrow and so close to the wall that he suffered vertigo when he tried to descend.

A weakness took him in the backs of the knees and he panicked, seeing himself marooned here and Julie an impossible distance away, with the ferry coming and going, coming and going until the day ended with them still apart.

It was the panic he needed. He cast himself down the steps with abandon and found safe footing by instinct. He skipped over the rails, trod pebbles, bent through the hatch, and burst into the sunlight.

Away across the grass, Julie was standing unaided with her back to the castle, watching the mainland. She smiled as he came level. "Did you enjoy it?"

Straightaway, another dilemma. Perhaps her effort had been to order him to leave her, knowing that the loving thing was to allow nourishment for his curiosity. Then again, how would she feel if he said he had enjoyed it, and her not with him.

"I never enjoy anything without you," he said. And there was something wrong with that, too.

"That's silly," she said. "I can't be with you all the time and forever. You shouldn't be afraid to appreciate something without me. I *told* you I didn't like it."

"You *also* told me," he said gently, "that you might well like it if I—warmed it up a bit for you. There's no pleasing you, lady."

She squeezed his hand. "Well, I've been satisfying a little curiosity of my own. The custodian has been tellling me what all these other buildings are. There's the Ministry house and the lighthouse keeper's cottage and those three"—she pointed across the pebble shore— "they're the original fishermen's cottages that the Ministry is doing up. There used to be quite a little community here. The man says the Department may even let them out as summer lodges. Can you imagine anybody wanting to spend a holiday here?"

"One priest spent twenty-nine years," said Simeon. "But he didn't have much choice."

"And my eternity is about twenty-nine minutes." Julie looked at her watch. The strap was loose, even though Simeon had installed a clandestine extra hole. He thought Julie didn't know and she let him think it. "Still quarter of an hour before the boat comes. Why don't you . . . ?"

"Enough is enough." And Simeon would not be drawn further.

He could have queued at the landing stage while she waited on the grass but they had been apart for too long. That top-of-the-steps feeling was still with him and he wanted Julie where he could touch her.

So they waited at the water's edge, Simeon shifting to hold both their weights on the treacherous pebbles, and the ferry was early.

The castle isle and its shingle neighbours lay awash of the mainland like pieces of jigsaw. While the ferry threaded its way among them, Simeon could not take take his eyes off the diminishing fortress and the shore people who leant as if against high wind to make progress across the pebbles. No number of trippers could lift the desolation from this place.

Eventually, Julie nudged him. "You still haven't said—"

"A mess," he supplied. "A bit of this war, a bit of that—and the remains of the last going rusty already. I don't mind seeing rust on history but not such recent history."

They went ashore at Keyhaven, resumed the car, found a teashop to banish estuary chills. Only then did Julie say: "But it stays with you."

Today, months later, making out the castle at a distance from his new, pine-fresh Thinking Seat, Simeon echoed the words and discerned their meaning.

Nelson Ojukwe closed the Bible and looked down upon his tiny flock. They took up no real space even in this mean property with its mud walls and perishing corrugated iron roof.

"So we learn," he said, "that things must get much worse before they get better. That we must not be surprised to find ourselves in fear of our lives. That, in fact, we should be happy to come to that situation because the hardship heralds paradise as surely as sunrise signals day."

Their attention was complete, their faith absolute. The warning might have set a lesser congregation to wondering, even worrying, questioning the rightness of its purpose. But not these ones. They were about their work in drought or monsoon, finding evidence in every condition of Christ's words upon the Mount—the indications that would prelude the fall of the literal Jerusalem forty years after he had uttered them, the happenings that meant destruction to a modern Jerusalem of false religion and rabid materialism. Evidence like earthquakes, plagues, wars, cooling love.

Nelson gave them love, they returned it in service. Thye told all they met how others might share in it—not selfishly guarding it or rationing it to favourites. Everybody or nobody, that was the score.

They were happy.

"Hold on tight to the Kingdom," he said. "Let go and you fall."

Then he bent his head in prayer.

The rest followed—all but Sami Ojukwe, brother to the speaker. Sami had chosen to play the role of Iscariot. He had fewer years than Nelson and that seemed to be a brand he must bear all his days.

In tribal terms, he was a man long since, but tradition didn't seem to matter in Nelson's new religion. Nelson counted the hours and the words, the quality of study and by those criteria, Sami was determinedly under par. The others might be won over by the promises of a life tending their own vines and sitting under their own fig trees but to Sami, that wasn't realistic. In fact, it was a dangerous fantasy.

Sami had seen his parents and their parents work for everything they had, only to lose it and have to start all over. That was the true hardship. And if anything better followed, it was only to be lost again.

Nelson could read how Sami felt in his reluctance over every task. Sami thought Nelson did nothing about it. But Nelson prayed. And even if the younger Ojukwe had known that, he would have laughed it off as another exhibition of the same illusion that led his elder brother to dwell on dreams. Nelson concluded in words that were not his own—though he blessed the source: "Even so, Father, not my will but Your will be done."

Anyway, Sami had taken steps. The harvest had suffered from lack of hands. And where were the hands? Knocking on door timbers, beckoning people to talk while the canes stooped and then crumpled, sabotaged by the weight of their own goodness.

Sami questioned any religion that sanctioned wastage and hunger. He saw the Roman missionaries with their straw hats pushed back to cover their necks and their hooks busy among the cane and knew that this truth of his brother's was a snare set by the Devil to imprison men's minds.

He looked now upon the mental captives, mouthing the prayer in the wake of his brother. Outside, dust was settling upon the beaten mud of the square, mud kicked up by the trucks which had arrived while Nelson spoke.

Nelson had seen them, too. There was little doubt in his mind about their purpose or their sudden presence. For that reason, he had let his sermon take a particular turn.

Without warning his flock in so many words, he had reminded them of what was to come and what was to follow. It was like dragging children to the tooth-man with the promise of a treat afterwards, he knew. He just hoped that their faith—and his faith—could stand up to the simile. The treat, in all sincerity, was so much greater. And so, in all conscience, would be the pain that preceded it.

He did not have to think long, either, to ascertain who had manufactured the arrival. In among his words to the congregation, there was a thread of meaning just for his brother.

"Lord, we know Satan will stop at nothing and nobody to achieve his purpose. Our brains can so easily become clouded with unworthy considerations. Sometimes if we do not immediately see your abundance, we begin to doubt it. Give us the strength to ward off such doubts and to know that in your time and not in ours, we will have understanding of all things.

"Be with our loved ones for they need not only your protection but your guidance. When understanding your purpose means so much, how active the Devil must be in muddying that comprehension. And for those who suffer such confusion, show them the same compassion Your Son showed upon the torture stake. Father, forgive them for they know not what they do."

But Sami missed it. He was watching the righteous army which was descending from the trucks. They wore the khaki and denim of a hundred brigades. Their uniforms were their faces, deep-lined with the sun. Eyes lidded like lizards, stubble where there were not full-grown beards. The foliage made a mystery of their mouths but not of the fact that many of them chewed and spat.

Nor of the fact that they were white. To a man.

Propaganda Fide knew that at least mercenaries could be trusted to come back for their money.

God, what have I done? begged Sami.

It was the skin that turned him round. While he could believe his actions were for the welfare of his people, he could feel them justified. But here, now, the justification had been removed.

These scum, these mongrels, these butchers, these outcasts of all societies except their own, these—whites—were coming to finish what he had started. Why?

They had guns. That had not been in the deal.

The straw hat missionaries had shown him the way and never mentioned these mercenaries. How could this rabble possibly represent a right attitude, an organisation in good standing?

"Nelson," he said, high-pitched because his throat was tightening. "Nelson, believe me, this isn't—"

And his brother brought the prayer to a casual close and waited for Sami. "Make no mistake, brother," he said. "This IS. No matter what you thought you were doing, it was taken out of your hands. This is inevitable. But please, Sami, see now the face of evil as it is presented to you."

The soldiers of fortune crossed the threshold, entered the shed, jostled Nelson and flock against the wall. With deliberation, they searched even the most intimate places, in public and without reserve; knowing that there was nothing to find but violating nevertheless for the sake of it.

A child began to whimper. His mother broke free of her shocked and frozen stance to pull him to her.

"Keep the monkey quiet," said a man with two pips on the shoulder of his stained shirt. "All of you, outside."

Sami hesitated and was jolted with a rifle butt. It was almost a comfort to know these soldiers weren't going to single him out and leave him alone.

He took a place near Nelson but could not stand the elder brother's gaze. He made idiot patterns with his toe in the dust.

"I'm sorry," he said.

"No talking," Two-Pips again.

"It had to come," answered Nelson. "For you and for us."

He was belted in the kidney region with a rifle butt and laid low.

"White trash," shouted Sami, pleading to share the pain.

But Two-Pips just laughed. "I'll allow you that," he said. "I'm told we owe you a favour."

That took the strength out of Sami's legs as surely as a blow. On his knees, he ploughed his face into the dirt and wept.

The rest of the congregation were making their own sense of the scene. They knew why Nelson had gone down. They could work out what had been meant by the comment that so crippled Sami. And they were seeing the words of the prayer and the text of the sermon in a new light.

Right now, the fact that they had been shouldered into some kind of order was doing them some good. At least, it removed the inclination to mill or run away.

Nelson had told them that if they should be singled out for persecution, it was a measure of their threat to Satan and a guide to their importance with God. They were comforted. After all, they had done nothing to warrant legal arrest. They did not have to worry about guilt or innocence. They could identify this for a certainty as a demonic whim. Nelson, riding out the agony in his back, straightening up to join them, saw it in their faces and was joyful.

He moved towards Sami but was forced back into the line.

Now the mercenaries were turning the flock and ordering it towards the trucks. They were levered onto the platforms, pressed together like cattle. There was motion from the motors.

And motion from Sami, for whom the engine sounds meant the rapid passage of chances.

He approached Two-Pips. "I have to go with them."

"Why? Listen, my bosses said thanks a lot. If you hear of any more . . ."

Sami hit the lieutenant, not with strength, because he did not have any, but just to get his touch on the man, knowing how such whites shrank from contact. He got a handful of shirt and spat into the grizzled features. "Now kill me," he said desperately.

Two-Pips swung a foot and took Sami's legs from under him. He swung the foot again and sank his toe in Sami's abdomen. "No," he said.

Wiping his face, he walked to the cab of the leading truck. He took ridiculous care to adjust his vile shirt. He swung himself aboard, gunned the ancient Leyland engine, and ran the truck so close to Sami that he had to drag his racked body out of the way.

"No," said Two-Pips. "You live with it."

Trouble found Simeon more surely than a pulp writer's storyboard strings. He and anxiety were a clinching argument for predestination. And when he thought things were at their lowest ebb, they got worse. That, at least, was a certainty in his life.

Life without Julie was more pain-strewn and problematical than he could have believed and even then there were these people waiting to catch and crucify his attention.

Two at the door now. Shades like black boxes over the eyes and Afro hair styles. Their appearance said activist; their introduction said civil rights.

Civil rights had left Simeon alone. The lunatic motley assembled for the Green Town episode two summers ago had been free from civil rights, possibly because they would have befuddled the issues.

The student following he had gained five years ago when he talked the tide back into the Gulf of California from his swinging Thinking Seat had been without such professional compromisers.

And here they were.

Bad news has a good circulation. The passing of Tomorrow Julie, while it led no one to believe that Simeon had become the more vulnerable, had nevertheless served to pin-point the man.

John Icarus and Adam Zed came sure-footed to the English seaside and found Simeon still impaled to the spot where Julie had breathed her last.

So John said: "Civil rights."

And Adam said: "May we come in?"

And Simeon said nothing, just stood back to make way.

"We heard about your bad news," said John. "When you lose a woman, it's bad enough. But when you lose someone like Tomorrow Julie—well, we expected to find you with a gun to your head."

"It's there," Simeon assured them. "But Julie won't let me pull the trigger."

The two Negroes traded glances.

"We all feel sick about it," offered Adam Zed. "Everybody who knew Julie loved her—you know what I mean?"

"I know." Simeon had not yet lifted his gaze from the floor.

Since he would not ask, they had to tell.

"We had something to say to you," said Adam. "Something we thought you might find interesting, something to take your mind off—"

"We know nothing is going to shift your mind from Julie," put in John Icarus quickly. "This was something you could think about as a sort of relief from—"

He dried up. Now Simeon was regarding them both in turn. "I guess I couldn't accuse you of being too pat. You don't have to keep picking your words. I know where I am. I know where Julie is. This —caution—isn't necessary. I give her all the thought she needs."

Icarus got the vibration first. "Then you want us to talk freely."

"For crying out loud, if only you WOULD." It was not criticism but a sincere plea.

"We're here about the holy war in Zimbabwe."

"Holy war? I thought the freedom struggle was over. I thought they had their own nation."

"The war still goes on for the Vatican."

"What?"

"An encyclical from Pope Eugenio called *Unam Sanctam*—One Faith. If you're not FOR the Roman church, you are against it and that makes you fuel for the Inquisition fires."

"Inquisition fires?"

"That, too, Simeon. Believe me, the world has been going on apace while you buried your dead."

Was that too callous? wondered Zed. But Simeon seemed undisturbed and Icarus had known it would be so. Act natural. Tell it as it is. Two truisms of a decade ago, still working today.

"And let me get this right." The prospect certainly had Simeon's attention. "These are the people of Zimbabwe who have been classed as the ungodly?"

"Not all. In fact, the legit government seems to be turning a blind eye to it. The—sufferers—are the extremist leftovers who thought old Mozambique sold out for too low a price and the guerrillas still active in Rhodesia and South Africa and hiding out in Zimbabwe. They are the antichrist."

"The ANTIchrist?"

"Eugenio's label."

"And as such, they are sampling the pleasures of the auto-da-fé?"

"You know the terms better than I do. If you don't believe us, we have a way in which you can see for yourself."

"Who is 'we'?"

"We is all brothers under the skin," said Icarus, deadpan, and caught a flicker of amusement, a hint of muscular spasm.

"So civil rights has spread to Zimbabwe."

"Civil rights is everywhere. We have moved out of the ghettos and into the open country."

"Because I always thought," said Simeon, "that civil rights was a waste of time, as impractical as it was optimistic."

"Maybe you could explain that." There was no missing the slight edge in Icarus' voice.

"I wouldn't deny there was a need for it, in theory," said Simeon. "I just could never see how it would work in practice. On the one hand, you had the white people expecting the blacks to forget everything that had happened in the past five hundred years and offer the hand of friendship, believing that life together could really start from scratch. On the other hand, you had the blacks who would be prepared to make the gesture being castigated by the blacks who wanted the debt paid, if not in full at least in token. It looked insoluble—and it looked as though the most blatant violation of rights was being practised within the enclaves themselves."

John Icarus relaxed. "For a moment there, I thought you were going to give us trouble. What you have done is to summarise the whole sorry state of the movement up to the time you stopped taking notice—what was it? Eighteen months ago? It's because we all came to that realisation that we have a form of survival today. The local issues were so damned self-destructive that we had to turn to the global picture. See, there's nothing wrong with the IDEA of civil rights, and the movement has a function and a purpose as long as it can focus attention on organisations and avoid the personal hangups."

"And the organisation in focus here is the Roman church? Well, how does the struggle break down? People versus clergy? Where's right and wrong?"

"It isn't clear-cut," admitted Icarus.

"Then what about your fear of hang-ups? Sooner or later, everything has to come down to a personal level. What do you think a person like me can offer to a situation involving such giant antagonists?"

"That's a lot of questions," said Adam Zed. "Let's see if we can make do with one answer. None of us can give any more than our best. Things go awry when people try to succeed by giving less. And your best is formidable. We need clear eyes and clear thinkers. You have a reputation."

"Undeserved," said Simeon.

"Then set about deserving it. As for right and wrong, you have to decide. You can do that by examining motives—and the best way to study motives is firsthand. Just take a short while to look at the enemy and I think you will decide they don't have virtue on their side."

"But do you?"

"Simeon . . . I don't talk about virtue because for me its meaning keeps changing." Icarus stood up. "I'll stick my neck out and say I genuinely believe they are more wrong than we are."

"They have the Bible and the sacraments."

"They don't read the Bible and the sacraments don't bear close examination."

"But the guerrilla's creed is bloodshed. Christianity is love. Are those two bedfellows any less strange?"

"I can't answer these things for you. I can only say there was no need for the Vatican to come into this at all. Rome's concern for the antichrist seems directly parallel with her business commitments and now I've put words in your mind. So come and see for yourself or forget it. I can give you a plane ticket and papers to get you there.

"I can say you would maybe find what you were looking for. But no promises—then no disappointments laid at my door."

Walking away from the seafront flat, Adam Zed asked: "Did we blow it, John?"

"I wish I knew," said Icarus.

Within his room, Simeon was talking to Tomorrow Julie's unfading memory face. "Hear me, lovely . . . I think perhaps I see the plains of Megiddo."

Arthur Prinz had sorted through his daily portfolio from Turtle Bay, Manhattan. The items arrived carefully jumbled among the stock and share dealings piped from Wall Street by teletype to the Vatican with only the operator's initials for guidance.

A lot of it had been bad punning from the lively Turtle Bay operators, only too willing to lend their humour to the strange new context. A few reminders that UN headquarters enjoyed hearing from him occasionally.

And a random item from England, where two of his minions, Frank Randall and Ronald Withers, were keeping busy with a civil rights tail job on his behalf. As he ran his eye down their list of stops yesterday, his eye was caught and held by a name.

It was a name out of the past. Not his personal past, like Scarlatti, but the general past.

About a year and a half ago. A record of an incident in Green Town, Illinois, when the U.S. government had been made to look foolish over two hundred white rabbits and two hundred Hiroshima survivors. A bizarre and entirely deliberate lesson to the establishment and quite a coup for the verbal anarchists of the day, who had made great play of the way the government had lined up a scintillating selection of minority groups for a hostile welcome.

The man at the centre of it had been Simeon. And here was the name again—in England this time, in rural Hampshire. Visited by two coloured operatives known to have links with Zimbabwe. It looked like a matter that might fall under both of Prinz's commissions.

He pin-pointed the location exactly on a map, memorised place names, was attracted to a site of natural isolation in the Solent.

He took the sheet with him for his audience with Eugenio and underlined the relevant meeting.

"That is something," he told the pope, "which requires my immediate attention."

"In England?" Eugenio lacked enthusiasm. "You have only just moved in here."

"And here I am based. But I must have words with this man. He won't come to me, so I must go to him."

"Am I to be given an explanation?"

"He has been consorting recently with people whose interest in Zimbabwe is at odds with your own—is that enough? Also, he is a known agitator, not only a political animal but a spiritual disruptor —a berserker, no less. And the antichrist, for sure."

"I didn't know."

"I'm telling you. This is one service you can learn to enjoy. Our information is fresh and undelayed. Your organisation already has the advantage of size. To that, you can now add speed."

"And you know this—Simeon?"

"Not personally, but by reputation. In fact, I once knew a man rather like him very well. A man called Shem."

"Both good Old Testament titles."

"That's as may be. Their effects on the environments they have occupied have been far more physical than metaphysical."

"Does he represent a danger to us?"

"I would say most certainly. I would say he is involved for no other reason than that."

"Will you bring him here?"

"I don't know." Prinz thought of Simeon, thought of Shem, thought of Scarlatti. He would have to take the lawman to have the interrogation in keeping with Torquemada's terms but once in England, there was no reason why Scarlatti should ever meet Simeon.

Prinz on his own could be sufficiently disconcerting.

"And how long am I to be without an inquisitor?"

"You won't miss me. You have plenty of your own staff capable of running the autos to your satisfaction. Believe me, my time will be much better spent if I can take this man out of circulation."

"In that case, perhaps my arrangements can help you. I do have arrangements in England, even . . . where did you say? Hampshire? . . . even in Hampshire."

Eugenio opened a compartment of his desk and drew forth a heavy directory. He thumbed pages and studied at a pace which infuriated Prinz. But he had to keep his temper if the leave was to be given.

"Ah, yes . . ." Eugenio peered over his pebble lenses. "Very suitable. It seems that in the days of the notorious James II, one of our clergy was restrained there for twenty-nine years. Lately, the British have been very apologetic. Perhaps it is time to call in the debt. I will notify the authorities and have the place prepared."

"What place?"

Eugenio turned the directory so that Prinz could read. He knew the name already from his recent scrutiny of the map.

"Well, I'm damned," he said.

"I trust not," said the pope.

The people versus Sami Ojukwe. They might not have subscribed to the views of Nelson and followers but they cared even less for the forces that had come to take them away.

Sami had thought he was doing the village a favour in organising a deterrent. That alone had been his motivation. But now, because the dissuader had proved to be a desolator, feeling had taken a full swing, so that the people who complained most when there were vacancies in the cane fields now gave their volume to the injustice wrought by the white man.

They had seen Sami suffer for his indiscretion but there was no sympathy for him.

Sami had no friend in any direction.

In three days, his physical injuries eased to a genital tenderness but the spiritual hurt was unrelieved. He was, however, able to consider the situation with something approaching composure. While nobody would volunteer him assistance, he knew there were some who could not deny him help.

He found one of the missionaries, Father Dominic, at the well.

In the three days, he had also found he could no longer bluster. It was not so much that he felt cowed: more, that if he wanted to make any progress at all, he had to adopt a correct approach that did not link determination with aggression.

"Father," he said. "I need to talk to you."

"Certainly, my son." The priest had him lined up already for the confessional.

"No." Sami wanted no misunderstanding. "I don't mean that kind of talk. I know my shortcomings and I know how to make up for them. I need practical help."

"Well, I—"

"Look, Father"—easy now, Sami—"I went through you to Propaganda Fide and we all saw the consequences. If I had anticipated them, perhaps my idea of what was right would have been different. On the other hand, perhaps one of you could have given me a more —honest—idea of what to expect."

"They will come to no harm."

"I find that hard to believe."

"They have been placed in care, that is all."

"For how long?"

"I have no definite information. Until such time as they cease to consider themselves a threat to our stability, I suppose."

"And who decides when that is?"

"They do. They indicate their repentance in their actions."

"And if they do not consider they have done anything wrong?"

"They will. It is only a matter of common sense. Look, Sami— perhaps I shouldn't tell you this, but that . . . pickup . . . looked a lot worse than it was. These soldiers have to play the part, you know, otherwise they would fail to convince."

Sami considered his bruises. "They convinced me. They left me in no doubt if they treat an informer so, they have even less respect for a wrongdoer."

"You did provoke them, Sami. I know you were upset and they

knew, too. But don't you see that, in the circumstances, they could only react in that one way?"

Father Dominic had drawn his water. Converts hovered to take the weight of it but his brotherhood decreed that he bear his own burdens as well as any others he could shoulder.

"So I don't have to worry," said Sami. "Nelson and the others are quite comfortable and certainly safe."

"Definitely."

"Where?"

"I—I couldn't say."

"Is that the truth?"

"Sami! I am surprised that you should doubt—"

"Don't be surprised at anything, Father. That is the lesson I have learned."

"You'll have a hard job retaining your faith, Sami, without a capacity for wonder."

"Not the way Nelson tells it. In his understanding, the things happening in the world today are entirely predictable—as from about two thousand years ago."

"That is his understanding, not ours."

"And where is that understanding now?"

"I've told you I don't know, Sami, and that's the truth. There are several places he could be."

"All right, then—which one would you say is the most likely?"

"Sooner or later, Lourenço Marques."

"Then that's where I start."

The younger Ojukwe turned from the well and started towards his hut. "Sami." Father Dominic had his arm. "Sami, Nelson is wrong."

Sami eased his arm free gently. "Maybe. But he is not as wrong as I have been."

CASTLES AND
BARBECUES

Sun high, wind low, and Simeon treading the yellow grass above the brazen sea. He took the walk because it had been their shared procedure and a step in Julie's step was a word in his ear.

Even today, with no other soul upon the cliff top and the unseasonal autumn heat reminding him of Pacific shores of long ago. The heat only. No other factor yielded a single association. This place was so—DIFFERENT.

Whether that was a good thing or a bad, he could not say. But on that other cliff top, on a rusted and complaining swing, he had spoken of this place with affection, separated from it by many years and with vision glossed.

Now, having returned to see Julie to her death in bland and loving circumstances, he had found it beautiful in every way but the original. And when he broke it down, the original appeal had been merely magnetism. Come back and you'll like it—as simple as that.

Well, the boast had been true to its promise, the forest behind an added bonus that they could take at the leisurely pace that Julie's advancing condition decreed. He had much cause to thank this place—each roadside poppy and azalea, each springy blade of grass upon this cliff top.

Thus, he trod now, knowing that footfalls were as essential to this herbiage as rain; knowing that somehow, in some way, the human pressure shifted sand specks, dissuaded weeds, evacuated parasites, and otherwise prevented the turf from perishing under a dry and abrasive silt.

The walker gave the cliff top service, the cliff top gave it back. Here was pleasant place occupied by pleasant people.

Simeon had noticed in past tours that the wooden benches which allowed them frequent rest when Julie's vile passenger was almost too heavy to carry were marked in the forehead, so to speak, with the identities of their donors and the details of their motivations: "In memory of my loving wife, Katherine, who treasured this spot."

The practice moved him, but not visibly. Julie must not see how and why it struck a chord in him.

And Julie, in her turn, had said nothing of the markings. What should she say? "Do this for me, Simeon." And sabotage all efforts he was making to keep her happy. "What a charming idea." A hint. A reminder that very soon, it would have a use for him? No, Julie said nothing.

In any event, she felt that it had registered with him. He would do what comforted him without any premature prompting.

On unsuspicious errands, he made discreet inquiries. He saw carpenters and engravers. Even while Julie lived, he notified the district council of his intent and sought their permission by word of mouth. He wanted no written authority that might fall into the wrong pale hands.

The councilman was sympathetic. "You may think your request is unusual," he said. "In its timing, you know? But by no means. The —survivors—often have these thoughts before they even reach those situations. They prepare to go on loving the partners they are to lose. And they want no painful delays. They resent the graves that have to stay unmarked until the earth settles and the grass grows—but even that, I think, they would have found preferable to the latest method —the anonymity of the ash. I honestly feel our cliff walks may soon become cluttered with benches. But in the meantime, of COURSE you can have a seat on the cliff top wherever a site is available and as soon as you are—well—ready."

And Simeon knew what that meant. As soon as Julie's eyes closed upon the scene.

"There's just one thing—"

Simeon waited, wondering. Payment?

"Some of the donors are very POSSESSIVE—do you understand me? In short, they can't bear to have anybody else using their benches. We—it's an awkward situation and very painful—we have to point out that what they are actually doing is providing a facility for people who might have a lot in common with them. We try to make them understand that although we can safeguard their gifts against vandalism and abuse, we can't control who sits on the benches. And we try to make that clear at the outset. There have been—difficult scenes. Sometimes, the bereaved just hasn't realised the eventuality and he goes along to sit with his loved one for a couple of hours and it hits him. We can promise welfare but not—intimacy."

"Thank you." It was something that had not occurred to Simeon. He was no less determined to provide the memorial but he was grateful, too, that he had been warned.

He thought about it and the man gave him silence.

"What if—?" The question caught in his throat. A sudden poignancy stung his eyes. "What if there isn't room for you when you want to sit there?"

The man smiled. "People are very accommodating. A lot of them know that cliff-top context well. They get to recognise the donors. Some of the veterans will even move when they see you coming. It is all as friendly as that. But even when you don't have such an acknowledgement, you only have to ask."

All this going through Simeon's mind as he walked on the yellowing grass and he not really knowing why until he saw, up ahead, the bench he had placed at the spot where he and Julie had used to pause and listen to the sea far below, sucking at the pebble beach, and count the seconds between flashes from the lighthouse on the island.

The bench—and a man sitting on it.

The sight chilled him like a vision fulfilled, but he shook off any stupidity about the supernatural. This was bound to happen. He was equipped to deal with it. He advanced with rapid steps.

The man paid no particular attention to his approach but his own appraisal was acute. He scanned the man's dress for buttons or buckles that might scratch the wood. He looked for sandwich bag or bottle that would stain or litter. He assessed posture, position of feet. He concluded the man was doing no harm.

"Excuse me."

The man looked up. Pink, well-scrubbed features. Hair receding from a centre point. Cold blue eyes. No immediate response.

"I wonder if you would mind moving. This seat is—in memory of my wife."

The man read the plate on the back rest. " 'Until tomorrow, Julie.' Charming. Simple but effective. Then you must be Simeon."

There was space alongside him and he made no motion to rise. "I've been waiting for you."

Simeon sat, breathing deep against nausea and anger. The councilman had said nothing of sharing.

"Waiting for me?" He still wasn't really taking it in.

"I knew you would have to come here eventually."

"I don't HAVE to come here. I want to—and I come often."

"I didn't mean it like that. I meant if I wanted to be sure of meeting you, this was the place to be. I was sorry to hear about"—the man tapped the seat—"your wife. A young girl. A terrible tragedy. But in a way, a relief from her suffering. The Lord giveth, the Lord taketh away . . ."

A strange choice of words because the man didn't look like a cleric. For that reason, perhaps, on the suspicion of an insincerity, Simeon reacted strongly. "That's not what Julie believed."

"No?"

"She believed the Father of Life was not also the Father of Death."

"It's a matter of conjecture, I suppose."

"With her, it was a commitment."

"And with you?"

"Julie always talked sense."

Simeon was bothered that the conversation had come so far in so short a time. He had missed this kind of exchange during the last year and a half since he and Julie had withdrawn from the world but he had not forgotten the methods of villainy employed at Playa Nine and Green Town, Illinois. He was being led, that much he knew for a certainty. And so far, there had been only one other call made upon him—from Icarus and Zed. The guerrilla faction against the Church. Here now was a man using phrases like the "The Lord giveth . . ."

The man broke in upon his analyses. "Then you miss her as an adviser, too."

"She's left me a good stock to draw upon. I suppose you're from the Vatican."

"Prinz," supplied the man. "Arthur Prinz. From the Vatican secondly and from the United Nations first of all. You could say that I am also an adviser."

"To whom?"

"To those who would benefit from my interest."

"And I take it I now number among those fortunates."

"As the men of the cloth observe, 'I am here to save you from yourself.' It would be a pity if bad counsel should add to your present pain. Your record has you as impulsive, Simeon. Now I am not saying that is in any way a bad thing. But I do feel you might stand warning when people have taken advantage of your emotional wounds."

Simeon watched the long waves making their fall around the curve of the bay, whitest where they met the shingle causeway to Hurst Castle, bleak even in this golden afternoon. He felt weary beyond respite and he cursed the man sitting beside him and the others who had come and dragged him by the mind back into the real world.

"You can't persuade me that any one of you is better than any other," he said.

Prinz shuffled his feet on the dry earth before the seat. "I can understand why you feel that way. All I can say is that if you were ever ready to get down to cases, you might be surprised how you would choose."

"Is that a straightforward denial of the claims that have been made?"

"I don't know. What claims?"

"These civil rights people told me the Church had declared a holy war on the freedom fighters as a cover for safeguarding its own business interests."

"I've heard it before." Prinz rode the allegation easily. It might be right, for all he knew, but Eugenio had insisted his concern was purely spiritual and that was all Prinz was empowered to concede.

"And how do you answer it?"

"Our intention is clear. The disruptors have been identified as the personification of the antichrist. As such, they must be removed to a place where they cannot go misleading nations—and that is in the interests of BOTH my employers. 'Antichrist' is an adopted term—for me, anyway. But it amounts to the same thing."

"And you remove them by another adopted term—the Inquisition. How does the UN feel about that?"

"They're content to leave matters in my hands. 'Inquisition' is an emotive word. Brings visions of cruelty and torture and all that is most replusive in oppression. Extreme methods were used, occasionally by misguided people, but only in the face of greater violence. The effect if the heresy of the day had allowed to continue unbridled —a universal breakdown of the Spirit—was unthinkable."

"Today, the Church sees the same spectre?"

"Believe me, it's not a figment of anybody's imagination. Massacres of missionaries amd church workers predate our own definite steps by some considerable time, Simeon. We TRIED using discussion. We CONTINUE to debate the pros and cons of causes— witness ourselves here and now. But for many, I'm afraid, the appeal to reason is a waste of time."

"So you kill them."

"That's a little trite. We follow the guidelines laid down in the Revelation of St. John the Divine concerning the fate of persistent unrepentant wrongdoers. When destruction is inevitable, the where and when become purely academic."

"And who decides?"

"Decides what?"

"At what point the case becomes hopeless."

"The Father of the Church."

"Eugenio?"

"If you like. More specifically, whoever occupies the throne of St. Peter. Look, Simeon, I don't know what your response was to Icarus and Zed—"

"Believe me, no less sceptical."

"—but you have to make up your mind one way or the other."

"Or not at all."

"That's too easy for you. You talked about Julie's commitment. Now she's gone, you have to make your own"—Prinz indicated the name plate—"in memory of her."

Simeon stood up to ease the cramped muscles in his legs. The move brought Prinz to his feet also.

"What it boils down to is this," said the interrogator. "If you accept our word you can be a valuable ally to us. On the other hand, if you give that value to the forces of evil which must be wiped out, you must be prepared to share their fate. The choice is between life and death. Think of it."

Then the man was gone, striding across the cooling turf to the road.

Life or death. A quick way to join Julie, maybe. Then again, perhaps the wrong way because it brought with it no answers. Where did virtue lie? Could the Church be so misguided that the truth lay with unbelievers? Was the only advantage of Icarus and Zed that they had got to him with their version first?

Simeon let himself down in the precise centre of the seat. It was good to be alone, at least. And hot upon the heels of that sly comforter came the realisation. Alone, he wasn't—not any more. And somehow, without Julie, he had to choose the right company.

The new-found spirituality of Sami Ojukwe had taken its first knock. When you have never been south of the River Save, Lourenço Marques is about as inaccessible as the moon used to be.

Sami did not know geography but a map would have shown him there was precious little choice of traffic. The Beira-Salisbury main line lay nearly one hundred miles to the north of him. Two hundred miles to the south, another line dropped out of Rhodesia, followed the Limpopo through Gaza, and ended up at Lourenço Marques.

He could trek to the coast and try his luck on the Beira-Inhambane road. At Inhambane, he might take passage for Lourenço Marques. If he had a week to spare.

But then . . .

He was reckoning without the mineral railway, too new for the maps, the southbound arm of the line that started at Caborra Bassa.

The Caborra Bassa project itself had been ended short of completion because terrorist activity had strung out the work for too long. Dutch, Belgian, and Portuguese engineers had demanded high prices for their time and hazard. With money running out, the multinational consortium had needed to rethink their plans and decide how best to capitalise on what remained intact. They had the beginnings of a railway line. If they laid it to the Indian Ocean coast and then southward away from Tete Province, which had been a Frelimo stronghold and still held security for the guerrillas, it was possible they could break even or at least limit their losses.

The mineral producers could be interested. Already, the wages demanded by their jungle hell-drivers had climbed to movie-star levels. Lorries travelling alone or even in convoys could be jumped or hijacked a lot more easily than a good strong train.

That was how the line came into being. Sami knew it was there only because some of the men had been away to work on it and come back with enough money to snub the cane harvest.

Last year, the villains had been the railroad workers; this year, Nelson and his followers. At least, the former had been able to enjoy their misdemeanour. They had even brought themselves back into good standing by being available this harvest.

And Nelson's group had disappeared altogether.

Sami had not been infected by Nelson's enthusiasm for persecution. He did not see it as a sure step towards a paradise future. It was as it was. An acquaintance with pain for an unknown duration.

To be sure, he believed the promises when Nelson was with him. But on his own, he was not sure what he believed, how deeply he felt it, how dearly he held it.

He only knew he had played a rotten trick on his brother and his friends. Pain or no, he had to find them and get on terms with them. That was the only workable atonement.

In the dawn, he scanned the family food pile and took his share. That day, he travelled fast, but at the end of it, the tall-grass terrain had changed little.

He found a stream, mixed his flour, made his flat cake of bread. He spread a layer of sugar in the pan, burned it to a toffee, and then added cashew nuts. Once that was cool, he broke the toffee into small, irregular pieces and transferred them to his plastic carryall, one of the new kraal necessities. All but one piece, which he sucked while he thought of the morrow.

At mid-morning of the following day, he broke out suddenly onto the precoastal scrubland. By noon, he had found the railway line and seen his first train.

Purely by chance, he had struck the line north of a water cistern. Since the locomotive was diesel and not steam, he wondered what use it had for the water.

Yet steam there was aplenty—and as he approached, he could see why. The halt was at the top of a steep climb. Now, two coloureds in overall pants were walking down either side of the train hosing the wheels.

The open trucks were carrying columbo. He knew that from the relics the trackmen had brought back. Columbo talantine. For making steel in Britain and America. The railway builders had been happy to sound so authoritative.

When the train restarted, he would be down this bank and up into one of the trucks. He didn't know how far he would get or what kind of a ride, but at least he would be heading in the right direction.

But now, suddenly, there were more than two men and the hoses were spurting unchecked onto the rails. The conversation was animated. The newcomers had rifles but they were making no move to bring the guns into a firing position. It was more of a discussion than a threat.

Some half-a-dozen men in stained khaki shorts and shirts were on the track gesticulating to the locomotive engineers.

And alongside the track, the scrub was moving without a breeze.

Then a rifle cracked. It took the talkers by surprise and one of them went down, moaning. The others unslung their guns and dived into the scrub.

The railmen started for their cab at a run and there were more shots. From his high spot, Sami could see the whole of the train. The firing was coming from the caboose, slung into the centre of the open cars.

Now whatever force stirred the scrub was moving parallel to the track to a point opposite the caboose. The shooting from the van was spasmodic without seeming to make any impact and the men in the grass were saving their ammunition.

Fifty yards to the rear of the train, three coloureds scurried like hares across the line and down into the undergrowth on Sami's side of the game.

They came back towards the caboose and when they were level with it, one man discharged his rifle. It was a signal for a barrage of crossfire, orchestrated with the whine of ricochet. The bullets were not penetrating. That lasted a full thirty seconds and there was no atom of response from the van.

Then the firing stopped, for strategy or for want of ammunition. Heads bobbed above the grass.

Sami saw the caboose door slide wide. He watched a terrifying spaceman figure emerge, bulky, grey, with glass for a face. This vision, too, bore a hose. But when he triggered it, flame burst forth.

Another adjustment and it was reaching the grass and still no answer from the guns.

The tinder flared, with flames moving faster than even a desperate man could crawl. Leaden-footed in some nightmare, Sami heard screams, saw men rising with limbs and torsos ablaze.

The manslayer in the asbestos suit withdrew his scythe of fire and retreated into the cab.

Puking on the hair-and-bone smell of it all, Sami heard the door on the other side of the car roll ajar, saw the flame reach out and overtake fleeing fighters, igniting their path and running them into the inferno.

Bodies burning long after life had been snuffed. And now in manner slow and sinister, the train began to move, quitting the scene without haste out of relish and not reverence.

Sami went, too, at a faster pace. No matter how long it took him to reach his brother, he could not travel by this railway.

He fled inland, retracing his route, while the vultures settled for another barbecue.

Simeon on his sunset seat and a shadow larger than a homing gull hovering above him. A helicopter descending upon the gravel car park beside his affinitive turf.

He scanned the cliff top for the curious eyes. There were none. This was the sherry hour, the hour of changing for dinner when the belated holiday makers became hotel guests and retired folk retired from the scene.

In two hours, one last walk along the cliff with the dog and home to bed.

Simeon was the exception. He ate when he felt like it—which was seldom—and changed for freshness, not appearance.

If anybody had wanted to be sure of singling him out, they had chosen well. That was how he knew this was not just some air-sea rescue operation.

The helicopter grounded. The engine shut off. The rotors lost impetus. Somebody within was making the same careful inspection that he had just made.

Perhaps he should have run, made for the trees in the lanes behind the cliff walk, skirted hacienda-style bungalows, and lost his callers in one of the abundant bunnies that led down to the shingle shore.

There was no panic. He could plan an escape route as fully as that. But he could not take it. If his fortunes of the past five years had taught him nothing else, they had given him a healthy respect for inevitability. When somebody was after him, the easiest way was to be caught.

Besides, other elixirs were moving through his veins. A development here could bring him closer to that confrontation which Julie had named. And again, a hasty exit would leave the helicopter here and this seat unguarded. His pursuers could decide to take out some spite with a hatchet.

All this reasoning and only now did someone step forth from the craft.

The callers could come from Arthur Prinz, from civil rights, or some third party. If it was any clue, there were two men and they were Caucasian.

"Mr. Simeon." In unison. They extended their hands.

"I'm Ronald Withers," said the one who was neat, fair, slightly florid.

"I'm Frank Randall," said the dark one—and from his grasp, Simeon was able to delineate that he was at least trying to be the stronger of the two.

"You have the look of security men," said Simeon. "I have run across you in a dozen different guises."

"That's what we were led to expect." Withers managed to make the comment sound like admiration.

"Then you have the advantage over me."

"How do you mean?"

"I was not—led to expect you. I suppose Prinz sent you. Which one of you flies the helicopter?"

"I drive," said Randall. "Anything and everything."

"And why are you here?"

"Mr. Prinz wants to talk to you."

"Is he with you?"

"Mr. Prinz is not a good traveller," said Randall.

He had his foot up on the arm of the bench and was testing the joint for strength. It creaked in protest. Simeon tried to take no notice but his eyes kept wandering back to the exercise. They knew they had made their point.

Withers said, "Mr. Prinz said that last time you entertained him on your premises. Today, he would like to return the hospitality."

"His refinement takes my breath away. How far do I have to go to sample this—hospitality?"

"Not far."

"Then why the helicopter? Couldn't you have come by car?"

"Not easily," assured Withers.

"Across water?" Simeon was already beginning to chill to a certain realisation. Irony had figured heavily in all these conflcits—if it WAS irony. The alternative was a string of coincidences so unlikely as to hint at supernatural engineering. "Why so secretive?"

"No secret." Randall withdrew his brogue from the bench. "Just that in the time it takes to tell you, we can be there."

"Why does he want to see me?"

"He didn't tell US, Mr. Simeon. We're just paid servants. He merely ordered us to invite your presence."

"And not to take no for an answer."

"Why 'No,' Mr. Simeon? We understood you were old friends."

"Believe me, not that old."

"Well, Mr. Prinz seems to think so. He told us to treat you with considerable respect and he seems to know an awful lot about you."

How much? Simeon wondered. And how up to date? Does he know what I value now? And just in case there might still be some doubt, he moved away from Julie's seat most casually, towards the helicopter. Wherever he went, it was less hazardous than an insistence to stay here.

The cliff top receded and he did not look back, although the effort cost him dearly. He weighed it up as the craft bore him low across tidal lakes and mooring places, a route he knew well but not from this angle.

The posts marking shallows had given the setting a Venetian slant when he and Julie made their water trip. From above, the posts just emphasised the definite direction.

A short flight but a long journey, and robbed of that vital backward glance, he felt distinctly unprepared for Hurst Castle.

Civil rights was just the minimum explanation for John Icarus and Adam Zed. It was no lie but it was a mere small percentage of the truth. If they had said their employers included the World Council of Churches—who, over the years, had overtly and covertly provided material support not of a prayerful kind to the freedom forces against colonial oppression—it would have looked too much like a confrontation between Protestant and Catholic . . . a clerical carve-up perhaps not attractive to Simeon.

But that was how it broke down. Since Rome had had the arrogance to declare that she was the sole exerciser of Divine Will, Protestant consciences had been inflamed. It had been such lofty claims, after all, that had fired the Reformation, and here was the Vatican trying to pull the same stunt again. Now, who would be the Martin Luther? The analogy was apt as the WCC sat in their premises at The Hague and paid polite attention to the comments and thoughts of their host congregation, the Dutch Reform church, whose beginnings went right back to the Lutheran treatises of 1526. The reality was rather less so. They had always had plenty of Luthers. The problem had been in controlling those who wanted reform just for the sake of it.

To that end, they had given a good deal of credence to the United Nations—and now the "political expression of God's kingdom here on earth" (as American churchmen had described the UN's forebear, the League of Nations) had begun a dalliance with Rome.

Time, then, for the World Council of Churches to make their own way. When the lines were drawn, they were seen to include the civil rights movements. If Icarus and Zed had been more extreme in their partisanship, they might have been beyond reach. As Black Muslims, they would have embraced a different divinity. But as moderates, they worked to make all men equal, a motivation very much in sympathy with the Vatican's opponents.

It had not concerned the Protestant church particularly that many of the freedom fighters they championed took their thoughts from Chairman Mao and their advisers from Hanoi and North Korea.

The real opponent was the other force that claimed God as its own. Time enough afterwards to come to terms with those who didn't claim God at all.

That was the ideological basis for Zed and Icarus. Naturally, they had to believe in it where they understood it—and they had been looking for hints of a religious leaning when they sized up Simeon.

Now John Icarus wrote and Adam Zed stamped authority on the Simeon portrait he had procured by telephoto lens during one of Simeon's cliff-top patrols.

"On balance, I think we were right," said Icarus. "He knows about Christianity. I would say he favours it."

"But does he favour our way?"

"I'm not going to test him with dogma. He has his own way and it seems accurate enough. For him, the criterion is love and he gets that in total from Julie. It's impeccable. He can be trusted to come to his own conclusions."

Zed chewed a cigarillo. "He made a plea for us to be open with him. Do you think we could have been more so?"

"I think we could quite safely have dropped the whole scene in his lap but it's a lot to carry first off. There was nothing wrong in what we told him."

"Except that we named the villain without naming the hero."

"Not true. We talked about good as opposed to evil. That's our motivation, man. The World Council of Churches is only part of it. If he was feeling he wanted to make up his own mind, it would have been a real put-off."

"Maybe you're right."

"Look, Adam, men of conspicuous virtue are hard to find. You don't squander them by telling them more than they can take at one time."

"He denies it. He says the reputation is misplaced."

"Whether the man measures up to his image is an intangible. The fact is that he attracts people. And the other team is here. You saw the Prinz of Darkness on the cliff the same as I did. Now what is his interest unless it is to win Simeon to their side?"

"He could have been just telling Simeon to keep clear of us."

"Do you believe that? Prinz is the UN's man at the Vatican—do you think Eugenio would pass up a chance like that?"

"I don't think Prinz would. Whatever Simeon is, he isn't a Catholic and Eugenio would not back anybody he couldn't count on."

"He's putting his money on Prinz."

"Maybe he has a hold, John. When I found Prinz nosing around, I got a strong feeling it was for his own satisfaction and not to gratify any pope."

"Which only goes to show what kind of concern Simeon is getting, Adam. That's why we have to hang in. Now let's get to him Code Three with these papers. It's sunset and I know where he'll be."

So sure was Icarus that he fed good money into the meter at the gravel car park before he looked at the turf and the Julie seat and found both empty.

Sami Ojukwe ran until the giant grasses closed about him and still did not stop. Somehow he felt that if he turned around, the trail would be stretching back behind him, straight and true, as far as the eye could see, to charred scarecrows and a casual train.

He reached a thick clump of trees—Rhodesian teak and baobab, eugenia and acacia, threaded together with feathery lichen. Their density slowed him. Gradually, common sense halted him altogether.

Another few steps and he would have run right on to the guns of the blacks who now rose from cover to view him. Their mongrel dress tied them in with the guerrillas who had fallen by the railway. Sami's first feeling was an unreasoning terror, which had the victims clothed again in good flesh, overtaking him unseen and barring his path.

"Hold there!" The speaker wore a fatigue cap, a tattered shirt with unmatching chevrons on either sleeve, and washed-out khaki shorts. The language was mainstream Bantu and Sami understood it without difficulty. The phraseology was obviously a colloquialism.

"I hold," he said. Wide-eyed and shaking, he put up his hands.

The other took a step forward. "You can lower your hands. Are you being chased?"

Yes, by ghosts, thought Sami. He said: "I—I have just come from the railway."

That seemed to make the necessary sense. The gunmen started to talk among themselves. Sami's interrogator held some kind of command and he silenced them quickly.

"What happened there?"

"It was terrible." Sami would have difficulty putting the scene into words.

"For the train?"

"No, for the—for your people."

"What do you mean?"

"They were—wiped out."

"All of them? All dead?"

"I saw from a distance. I cannot tell you the number. Just that nobody escaped."

"Perhaps some are just wounded. We will go and see."

"No survivors." Sami had to lean on the grey trunk of a baobab, retching drily. Even talking about it brought back that nauseous essence of bone and hair.

The guerrillas waited without patience. Sami articulated the devastation as best he could between gulps of air. "One man . . . with a pipe that sprayed out fire—"

"Flame thrower," said the man with the chevrons.

"In a van in the middle of the train . . . he had a"—and what was it? A uniform? An overall?—"a suit that covered him all over. Glass where the face should be. He just set fire to the brush on either side of the train . . . where your friends were hiding . . . They were burned alive . . . I heard their screams . . . Nobody escaped . . ."

Somebody at the back of the group set up a wail of mourning and was cuffed into silence. The rest had let their rifles go to the ground.

"I'm Eduardo," said the leader. "You will get to know the others as we go."

"Go where?"

"We have to move quickly now."

"Yes, but I—"

"You what? You've seen what these pigs do. Are you saying you don't want to be with us?"

"No, I—I have a journey of my own to make. My own war with the pigs, if you like. They took my brother and many of our people and I have to find them."

"Do you know where to look?"

"Lourenço Marques. One of their holy men said."

"And they're the worst of the lot. I'd show them a couple of the old Monomotapa's tricks . . . Well, I'll tell you frankly—I don't believe a man on his own can get anywhere against this bunch and I'd sooner have you join us. Zimbabwe knows, we could do with some more recruits now . . ."

Sami was choked again. "Is that all it means? Vacancies to fill? Are your people so disposable? No, thanks. I'll stick to my own war."

Eduardo shrugged his shoulders. "When you've seen death as often and in as many forms as I have, you'll know better than to dwell on it. If you lose one encounter, then move straight on to the next—and the sooner, the better."

Before he could philosophise further his attention was arrested by a sound, faint but growing. It was an engine sound, a dry, monotonous drawl. As it came nearer, so it split into different pitches—the persistent drone of mechanical operation and then a whistle, as of sticks passed quickly through the air.

"Helicopter."

With two deft blows, Eduardo had felled Sami. He was shouting to the others. "No good staying here. They've followed this sonofabitch. Split up. Belly through the grass. And for Mono's sake, make sure you don't shake a single blade of it."

The guerrillas moved off without hesitation. Sami, sick of the ground, managed to get to his knees, swayed to his feet, so that the reprisal bullet fired by Eduardo as he dived into the tall grass went between Sami's legs instead of into his head.

Then the helicopter was passing above him, obscured by the flat top of the acacia, and heading onward over the grass.

For the second time that day, Sami looked upon blazing death. He saw the chopper go, saw drums falling from it, saw them split to put forth napalm, the great equaliser.

But this time at least, there was less to see. One flame looks much like another.

When the follow-up party on foot reached him, he had fainted.

Commander Two-Pips looked down on him and smiled.

"So you wanted to go to Lourenço Marques," he said.

The castle was as Simeon and Julie had left it; indeed, as the Second World War had left it.

If he had been expecting Prinz to convert the place into a latter-day Llerena—and his mind, for all his control, had run on such a theme—then the question was soon answered. There was no friendly gateman to supply information as they ducked through the open flap of the massive steel door. The rusting rails lay as thrown down for the Cinque Port defences and the lighthouse near the cottages outside the castle had been abandoned in favour of the red and white signal light atop the battlements.

Ships came and went to a different tidal tune and never suspected that the sinister castle on the Solent might house a sinister function.

With ample and monstrous walls providing three good sides to the old gun emplacements, the labourers of the present occupant—presumably the ubiquitous Randall and Withers—had provided a fourth from the native barbed wire. They had wound it about a wooden frame. When they had confined Simeon within the emplacement, they just replaced the frame.

"If you wanted to," said Withers, "you could push your way out. You might even get clear of the castle, but it would do you no good because the helicopter is the only vehicle here—we've cleared all boats, big and small—and the pebbles are so tricky on the causeway that we could—pick you up before you had gone a hundred yards."

Simeon regarded them across the vicious barricade. "You said Prinz wanted to talk to me. Is this pantomime necessary? I want food and I want warmth and it is up to Prinz to provide. Tell him I'm here."

"He KNOWS you're here," said Randall.

"REMIND him I'm here and I'm not impressed with his definition of hospitality."

Did Prinz also know of his prior link with Hurst Castle? The location had been picked out with alarming accuracy. Such a man might have information on all things. Such a man might also be so versatile in terror that he could lead his subjects to believe he had total knowledge when all he had was a gift for aggressive psychology.

Simeon had expected to be overwhelmed—by memories, by the oppression of the place. But now he was happy to find himself healthily annoyed with the liberties Prinz was taking. If he could only hold on to his anger, he might have the strength to get through whatever Prinz had to offer.

And here came Prinz. He stopped beyond the barbs where the shadow was less profound. The sky, clear an hour before, had filled with small clouds that seemed to be catching the last rays of sunshine on their westward surfaces and robbing the earth. That quickly, the heat went out of the day.

"It's good to see you again," he began. "I'm grateful for your co-operation."

"You made pretty certain of it," said Simeon. "You don't have to thank me. What do you want?"

"I was hoping our exchange might be a little less blunt."

"What the devil do you expect? You reach down from the sky, bring me to this mausoleum, and still you want finesse. You must be joking."

"It wasn't meant to be so brutal. There's a lack of accommodation here—"

"Where's YOUR bed—in the next emplacement? Come on, Prinz. If you want something out of me, you pay for it."

Randall and Withers watched Prinz, waiting for a sign. A sign to do what, Simeon did not know—either put on some pressure or move the barricade. The heavy stuff would come sooner or later, for all Prinz's talk of refinements.

"Well, well," said Prinz. "You seem a little more sure of yourself today. That may be a good thing and it may not. From it, I infer that you have come to a decision. I hope it is the right one."

"The only decision I have made is that I don't like you and I don't like your errand boys. We speak a different language. I don't know why you can't just leave me alone."

"Because you have a record, Simeon—a string of precedents that is a sure guide to the way you are going to act in any given instance. Now, Tomorrow Julie may well have had a lot to do with those precedents, but her demise is not going to alter the pattern. On the contrary, if you love her as much as you say you do, you'll be more determined than ever to follow that line."

"What I do, Julie or no Julie, is my own business."

"Not when it touches on my interests."

"You can't be sure that it will."

"That's why I want to know what you have decided. I want to know that I'm right."

"Then consult your string of precedents. You have no place in my life, so stay out of it."

"No matter." Prinz turned away. "I have other ways of making sure. Spend a good night because the day will be a bad one."

To Withers, Prinz said: "Feed him."

By the time the food and the company were gone and Simeon had the emplacement to himself—unless he tried to get out—the cloud had formed a solid layer and the wind was rising.

His widom said: "Go nowhere. Try nothing."

He settled in a corner of his cell and turned up a warm chapter in his memory. Halfway through the night, the rain started. It did not disturb Simeon. He and Julie were lying at berth together, rocking gently like the boats they had known in the bay.

Rico Scarlatti breakfasted alone and on meagre fare. The bread was too soft, the marmalade was anaemic, and the English coffee never tasted quite right.

And now the weather had broken. Rain mists swept the saltings, as insubstantial as lace curtains, and all movement, it seemed, was downwards.

The rains he knew were of horizontal flow, made charming by their lack of respect for logic. Rain falls from the clouds to the earth, sure. But in Siena, it used a little artistry to keep you guessing. Not here. Here, only Prinz kept you guessing. And, by a round turn, Prinz prevented you from appreciating anything this place might have to give. Scarlatti wanted to meet Simeon for reasons of his own. And Prinz was keeping him away, because the reasons were no mystery to Prinz.

Scarlatti had been tempted to take issue with the man; to question the point of his own presence here. But he knew what Prinz's answer would have been. "You are here to keep a record."

"But how can I keep a record if I am not present. The terms of procedure demand my presence."

"There is no procedure as yet. We are talking. You are my trump card."

That was how it would go and Scarlatti would be no closer to his goal of devastating Prinz. Yet he could not talk of wasting his time or returning to Rome because then a chance might be lost, a contact cut. Worse than staying with Prinz was getting away from him.

Thus the waiting game was forced on Scarlatti and it resurrected in him the kind of futility he had felt in his early dealings with Shem. That, too, had made its mark on appetite and outlook.

Though they went their own way, the fortress on the estuary was so devoid of alternatives that they were almost constantly face to face. It was strange this morning that Prinz should have taken so long to emerge.

Scarlatti could not conceive of the man oversleeping. At times, he suspected Prinz of hanging head down from the rafters or taking his rest in a coffin—though he was too plump for phantom or flyer.

And when Prinz appeared now, he was wet. He dropped his raincoat on a folding chair, filled cup and plate in almost the same movement, and set about his meal with relish.

That much Scarlatti envied him, but it would not last for long.

"How is our prisoner this morning?" he asked. There was only one reason why Prinz should have sampled the exterior elements.

"Much as he was last night." Prinz was monosyllabic with bread.

"Which was?"

Prinz chewed on and swallowed. "Truculent. To me, it means only one thing. He intends to go against us."

"So you have it cut and dried. Could there not possibly be any middle ground? Perhaps he just doesn't like being pushed around."

"Look—when you have stuck your neck out as often as Simeon has, you can count yourself lucky if pushing around is all that you get."

"He wasn't doing anybody any harm. He's been out of circulation for fifteen months, you said. Isn't that evidence of a more passive mode of living?"

"His wife had a terminal condition. He was looking after her. Now, she's dead and he can start all over again."

"Suppose he doesn't want to do that."

"A person doesn't change that much."

"You put a lot of faith in unbreakable habits. In fact, you're not giving him a chance to show you anything one way or the other."

"I put faith in what I know. Simeon belongs to a type. His interference is causal rather than casual."

And that was very familiar. It was the accusation made against Shem in Garden Five—that he represented the cause of all evil in the world, wanton and willy-nilly, the manslayer.

Familiar also to Prinz, whose sudden silence and application to food was artificial.

Scarlatti pressed home the advantage. "I know the type." Perhaps he should have added: I know how they shake you up—remembering flying papers and flying Prinz when events moved to a violent climax in the hanging gardens of Tuscany. But that, perhaps, would show too much of his hand too soon.

"Shem was a new experience for me," said Prinz eventually. "Anybody can make a mistake once—but only a fool makes the same mistake twice. They ARE of a type. The difference is that this time I know what I'm fighting."

"I wouldn't be caught the same way again, either," said Scarlatti— and Prinz could think that as ambiguous as he liked. "Anyway, what are you going to do about Simeon?"

"I'm keeping him in suspense." Prinz could be ambiguous, too.

Three hours later, Pope Eugenio himself was at the other end of the telephone line, trusting his message to no lesser mortal.

"I want you back here," he said quickly and without grace. "Nothing you are doing there can be as important as the task I have."

Prinz was at a loss momentarily. He had come no further than midway through his work on Simeon. If he left it now, he could not be sure of success. On the other hand, the pope sounded perturbed and it was as well, at least, to hear the man out.

"What's the trouble?" he said, equalling Eugenio's lack of ceremony.

The receiver spat and fizzled as though all the static in Europe had been attracted to this one call.

"I didn't get that," Prinz had to say.

"—not something to be discussed on the telephone."

"Well, I'm afraid I am going to have to know a little more than that before I ditch what I'm doing here."

"Your Simeon is just an eccentric. I have singled out the real manslayers."

"A new guerrilla organisation?"

"Yes. Guerrillas of the mind."

"What?"

"Evangelists. They make promises no man can hope to keep.

"Then in what way are they dangerous?"

"People are listening. People are believing."

"I still don't understand the hazard . . . Are you saying the antichrist has changed its personality?"

"I am saying as little as possible on this telephone. I am instructing you to return here as soon as possible. If you want to keep matters cordial between your principals and myself, you will treat that instruction as urgent."

"But I haven't finished—"

"Simeon is not important. He is only an indulgence."

"That's not so, Your Holiness. Don't sell him short."

"No matter how much credit I give him, he is still only one man. I am dealing with whole movements and I want you to go where the need is greatest."

"Where is that?"

"Zimbabwe."

"But I thought we weren't talking about terrorists."

"These—proselytes—are everywhere. It happens that we have a

full Inquisition machinery at Lourenço Marques. That will be at your disposal and the preachers will be brought to you."

Eugenio said little more after that. It made no difference. He had left Prinz no room to manoeuvre. It was back to the Vatican with the hope that the point had been made firmly enough with Simeon.

He was still more worried about Simeon than any hot gospeller from the Dark Continent. The man was not responding to his various persuasions, but neither was he resisting them. He seemed remote and if that was some kind of defence mechanism, it would need time to pierce. Time Prinz no longer had.

On the most optimistic assessment, it meant that Simeon had no interest in the present confrontation, that he was hampered by bereavement, that he had withdrawn from all future contests.

On the most pessimistic accounting, it showed he had the beating of Prinz—an inner territory which interrogators could not penetrate, a superior mysticism.

And the comfort for Prinz in that was that Simeon would have to emerge from it before he could do any of the harm that Prinz feared. When he emerged, there would be obvious physical signs. For one thing, he would have to take himself into the arena. Once there, his presence would be so marked that even Eugenio would have to call for his relaxation in the flesh.

Since he would have to curtail the treatment, Prinz played safe and calculated for the second eventuality. He supposed he could leave Simeon to vegetate in Hurst Castle but that would prove nothing. To jump one way or the other, the man had to have freedom of movement. Give him this and he might provide evidence of intent that much faster.

Arthur Prinz marvelled yet again at his ability to make the best of every hand fate dealt him.

That rainbow had to be in his life somewhere. Simeon focussed on a fraction of spectrum glimpsed through a high window, the one fragment of colour to relieve the overall grey. He sifted memories like sand and found . . . that night when the four winds met and the whole cloud repertoire flowed, rolled, writhed, and tyre-tracked across the awesome sky . . .

Sweat beaded his brow now as the cords bit deep and his body weight hung dead upon wrist, elbow, and shoulder joints. He had scrabbled with his feet for some purchase in the ridges of the wall but there had been no respite. The angle was all wrong. He bloodied his toes for no good purpose.

And fastened onto a rainbow.

"I've never seen one so close." Julie's diminishing hands were pressed so hard on the arms of the wheelchair that Simeon fancied the knobs of bone must erupt through the skin. "I wish I could—"

Simeon found a strand of hair trailing along her cheek, tucked it back under the head scarf. One end of the rainbow rested but a short distance inland, the other dropped into the sea between this Milford beach and the island. If you could reach out an empty cup, it would come back brimming with coloured water, fresh as that.

When Julie wished, he usually kept quiet until she was out of it. But tonight, the sky was big, the pyrotechnic dusk so intense that he felt dwarfed, mutated, crippled into a condition comparable with Julie's own.

"Every day brings us something," said Julie. "The deer that flashed across our path in open country when the time was all wrong . . . The china and glass we bought for a line of melody, not even a song . . . And now this stupendous, incredible sunset with our very own rainbow. God is good."

If faith can move mountains, Simeon had thought, why not carcinomas? Isn't the lady more useful articulating her loyalty than heading for a hole in the ground? That, of course, had been before he discovered that even a hole in the ground would have been preferable to the great reducing fire.

"Don't you think so?"

"I'm sure of it," he obliged. Why be deterrent when he could offer nothing better?

"I have another wish." Julie had taken her eyes off the sky. The wish was that important. "To see you more interested."

"I am interested, Julie."

"I know." Julie had twisted around awkwardly in the chair so that she could see his face. The strain of it showed in her features. He shifted his position so that she could encompass him and the eloquent sky while still having support for her back. "You try, for my sake. I don't want that. I want you to try for your own sake. Let me just be sure of this one thing. It will make death so much easier to face."

"Julie—" In desperation. His voice broke. The words gave out.

"Simeon . . . I want to see you again. In my belief, that is more than a hope, it is a promise. You can have the same belief. It makes you talk about death like a night's sleep. It isn't outrageous."

"I've been let down so many times, Julie. I have the Midas gift in reverse. Everything I touch turns to dust. If I were to try this belief, I would ruin it for everyone."

"Have I turned to dust?"

Not yet, though Simeon savagely. Not quite yet. He said: "Not you. You never let me down. On the contrary—you're a source of joy to me. I just don't know how I managed to find you and then to keep you. I don't rest easy even now."

"You value me?"

"More than anything in the world."

"Nothing in the world has a value."

"You know what I mean, love. There are things that are untainted. More than . . . more than this sunset . . . You name the currency, you exceed it in worth."

"But you don't prize my advice."

The sky was losing its fire, degenerating from character to prettiness with the onset of night. The winds, having met, had gone their separate ways and the clouds had left cirrus in the centre of the stage. Julie shivered and that was a relief to Simeon. It meant he could cover his indecision with attention to her care.

"Well, do you?" she persisted.

He eased the chair back across the moistening grass to the tarmac. "I do. I always have. The record bears me out."

"Except in this. Now why not in this?"

"Julie . . . You've got it wrong. Truly."

"You love me?"

"You know that."

"Yes, I do. Perhaps it helps me to understand."

"Understand what?"

"Your RELUCTANCE. For goodness' sake, Simeon, let's make it meaningful. There isn't that much time."

"There's all the time in the—"

"The world?" Julie laughed. "Back to that old world again. How much IS all the time in the world, anyway? Maybe not so much. No —you can't accept my belief because you can't accept my death.

You don't want me to go. You want a miracle to make me well. If you say that, you would believe . . ."

"I . . . Well, is that so terrible? The disciples performed miracles."

"As a witness to the power of God. As a fulfilment of Scripture."

"But why couldn't that happen today?"

"Because today, DIFFERENT Scriptures are being fulfilled. Christ told us what to look for in the Sermon on the Mount— Matthew 24, Luke 21—wars and rumours of wars, food shortages, earthquakes, great tribulations as had never been seen throughout the earth—and the love of the greater number cooling off. When we saw these things, He said, we wouldn't have to worry about sickness or death because they would be only temporary things. That is the promise."

"And that time is now?"

"You only have to look around, Simeon. Do you really need to be convinced that something—stronger—than humanity is causing all this disease and deprivation? The Devil stalks the earth like a raging lion because he knows his time is short."

"And the Devil is causing death? Is this growth in you so spiritual?" Simeon bit hard on his tongue. He could have torn it from his throat. End of the comedy. No more pretence.

Tomorrow Julie's gaze was gentle. She read his thoughts like letters upon his forehead. "Thank you, Simeon—for not wasting any more time, for putting aside the barriers. Now we can really talk. . . . No, its cause is pathological; some impurity from something man has done to the world. Evil doesn't have to be seen as long as it can be heard in the mind. It shows its face to those who call for it. Otherwise, you have to read the signs."

Only a sliver of pink sky now, receding beyond the Purbeck peninsula—and a small fluttering figure on the path in front of them.

"Too small for a demon," said Julie. "They all have good physiques." She laughed again. Simeon had noticed over the weeks the rising pitch of her voice, as though, in some cruel paradox, her faculties moved towards childhood as her body moved towards conclusion.

They drew level with the struggling form. They recognised it as a swift. Some treacherous air current had brought it too close to landfall and now the very predominance of its marvellous wings kept it from launching itself back into the sky.

"I know what to do," said Simeon, almost thankful for a situation wherein he could make the statement. He gathered the bird gently in his hands, pursing his lips, whistling quietly through his teeth, trying to imitate the shrill note of the genre.

"Wait!" The bird's claws around his finger; Julie's claws on his arm. "Let's ring him."

"How do we do that? Why?"

"Some day I would like to know where he went. He and his friends go south this time of the year, you know. I'd like to—go with him."

"Paper and pen in my pocket," said Simeon. "Rubber band, too. Best I can do."

Julie searched and found, tore a small piece, wrote name and address minutely.

Simeon moved his hands in a caress over the bird, secured a leg between third and fourth finger, proffered it to Julie. She wrapped the note around the leg, found some reserve of strength to wind the band until the paper was firm. "Now," she said.

And Simeon tossed the swift into the air. It faltered, appeared about to fall, and then spread its great wings and veered away across the sward. Not far; just to a spar beneath the roof of a cliff-top shelter.

If Simeon and Julie had been able to push back across the grass, they would have found the swift had company. Come daylight, he would start for Africa with his fellows . . .

And the cell door opened to admit Arthur Prinz. He strolled to the wall, released the pulley.

"This time," he said with deliberation, "I am letting you down lightly."

"In any event." Simeon's legs would not take his weight and he crumpled to the floor. "You've made your point. Just—just let me out of here and I will promise, sign, or pledge anything you care to name that I will not go south to help the guerrillas."

"I'm glad," said Prinz. "But not surprised. You struck me as being far too intelligent to waste your time like that. Not to be misunderstood, I won't be sorry to see the back of you. Now I'll get you some help to our treatment room and some food, and tomorrow, I'll bid you farewell."

Simeon was examining the weals of the rope. Though he said nothing, he was mystified. There was blood and broken skin and yet—he had not been sick; he had not gone to pieces.

A present from Julie; a way out.

I believe in you, dead Julie. In you is my salvation. But that wasn't what she wanted, he recalled. It lay south and he would go south.

To look for a swift. And other things.

NEVER AN ASSASSIN
WHEN YOU WANT ONE

Harold Messenger fingered his phone and the intercom blared. Andrew Buthelezi waited for intercom contact and his telephone rang. Each, responding, found the other at the end. Messenger laughed at the idiocy of it but Buthelezi was more pressed with the urgency of his inquiry. "Harold, I want you up here without delay."

"I was coming anyway. We won't waste any more time with these things." Telephone and intercom went dead.

Next thing, they were together in Buthelezi's private office, which gave onto a scene ninety degrees removed from that of the conference room. The East River wandered away into the distance.

"I am expecting the Zimbabwe delegation," said Buthelezi. "They want to know how to phrase their application. Do I explain to them they don't qualify for our reasons?"

"No." Messenger was irritated. This was happening too fast. He had just taken a call from Zimbabwe—and found Prinz was the caller.

"What are you doing there?" he had asked.

"This is where the Inquisition action is, Harold," Prinz had said, taking a liberty ahead of anticipated praise.

"Inquisition? In ZIMBABWE?"

If the Vatican was into Zimbabwe already, what did that do to Messenger's reasoning? Eugenio had asked for Zimbabwe not to be accepted into the United Nations because of violations to the Church. The UN had agreed—on the basis that, since Zimbabwe was disqualified anyway while she was trading with Rhodesia, the UN had really conceded nothing.

Now, Prinz was saying that the Church of Rome was already installed in old Mozambique. More than that, she was operating a terror machine against Zimbabwe residents, apparently without interference from the local legislature. It was quite a riddle. And before he had had a chance to work it out, Buthelezi had summoned him for a meeting which required that he know EXACTLY what was going on.

"My man Prinz has just been on," he said. "I am not evading

your question, Andrew—I'm just trying to involve you in my line of thought. He was CALLING from Zimbabwe."

"I don't understand. What is he doing there?"

"My very question to him. He said that was—and I quote 'where the Inquisition action is.' "

"But how have they been able to set up in business in the very heart of the place they have been trying to blank out?"

"I was trying to solve that when you called and I still don't have an answer. When is this delegation due?"

Buthelezi's desk monitor buzzed. "Right now," he said.

There were three delegates, looking awkward and uncomfortable in European-cut suits. Messenger saw the pain in Buthelezi's face and knew the reason. Andrew would have preferred to see them in some kind of African dress. This only emphasised the fact that they had thrown out tradition for a niche in the modern world. Their last guise had been combat. Their next, they were still working out.

"I am Sandy Joachim," said the middle one. "Minister of Foreign Affairs. These are Matthew da Gama, minister with special responsibility for trade"—his left outrider—"and Eduardo Díaz, my chief of security"—on his right. The two proffered their hands. Messenger and Buthelezi returned the grip with all solemnity.

The Secretary-General indicated chairs and bade the party be seated. "Please understand me when I say that I can only give you a very limited amount of help," he said. "I am only an elected member as you seek to be elected members. The process of election remains democratic and must be a decision overall.

"That being so, all I can add is that if you believe we dispense justice and you believe your case is just, then you can be confident that the right decision will be taken."

"We were hoping," said Joachim, "that you might give us some advice on how to conduct our application."

"That doesn't matter," said Messenger. "No doubt you know that a working party of UN nominees studied the situation in Zimbabwe some months ago when your plea was first noted and a report has been prepared. The contents of that report bear far more weight than any representations you might make from the floor of the assembly. I am assured that you offered our investigators every co-operation at the time and no doubt that will go well for you."

Díaz coughed for attention. "Have you seen that report?"

"No," said Buthelezi quickly. He had seen enough canvasses to know what was coming next.

But Messenger didn't want a brake on the matter just yet. "I have seen it," he said. "The Secretary-General has not. That is just the way it works. The document is earmarked for his early consideration."

"And is it—good?" asked Joachim.

"Now I am sure you realise we cannot anticipate in that way," said Buthelezi.

"I am afraid," said Messenger, "it is incomplete."

"In what way?" asked Da Gama. "If there is anything we can tell you—it is our earnest desire to be frank."

Messenger knew that for a fact. Indeed, the intelligence which had so impressed Buthelezi about the rail traffic to and from Rhodesia had been volunteered by Da Gama himself in deposition, though whether it was naiveté or *sang-froid,* Messenger could not yet decide. His question had nothing to do with that.

"There is no mention," he said, "that the Roman Catholic church has established an ecclesiastical court in your federation. I find that a rather startling omission—in fact, I find it rather startling altogether, having in mind your one-time attitude to that Church."

All three of the delegates began to talk. Joachim eventually emerged as spokesman. "When we saw the United Nations getting involved with the Roman church," he said, "we thought it was the right thing to do."

Buthelezi let his breath out in a long sigh. Messenger was not sure what to do with the answer now that he had it. There was no doubt at all that it was innocent—but how much sophistication could be reasonably expected from people who had only now emerged from conditions of the severest oppression? He wanted more clarification.

"You mean—you invited the Vatican to move in?"

"No. They made a request and we did not refuse it."

"Was that a—popular move?"

"Those days are over, Mr. Messenger, and we are trying to forget them. In effect, the Vatican is helping us to do that."

"But the subjects of this Inquisition are your own people."

Díaz coughed again. Messenger began to wonder whether it was some kind of signal. Sure enough, the others let him speak. "These subjects are an embarrassment to us," he said. "As my colleague has stated, they are employing tactics we are trying to forget. They are extremists—sadly, former party colleagues who feel that the deal when made, was insufficient, that Portugal did not pay a high enough price for what she had taken over the centuries. We tried to persuade them that the real issue was our liberation and that the revenge motive was self-destructive especially to a young country. But they went their own ways. It makes very little difference whether we or the Church take them in charge."

"It's a bit of a—somersault—isn't it?" said Buthelezi, cautiously. But his care was for any lines Messenger had laid down. "Did the Church offer you any kind of return for allowing them into your country?"

"I think I can answer that," said Da Gama. "You, certainly, Mr. Messenger, have seen that a proportion of our trade is—shall we say —questionable. The matter of that traffic carried on tracks twenty-two and twenty-five at Lourenço Marques terminal—"

Messenger swore under his breath. And if they had admitted the traffic so ingenuously to the UN, then likely the pope must know. And if he knew, Messenger no longer retained an advantage. Then again, if he knew there already existed grounds for refusing Zimbabwe entry into the UN, why had he made that his price? Da Gama's next words made it clear.

"The Vatican promised to provide us with enough trade so that we could afford to rid ourselves of Rhodesian commitments. They had mineral holdings which could use Zimbabwe extensively, they said—as long as there was no guerrilla interference. That way, they said, we would have no trouble getting into the UN."

"But—" Buthelezi began. Messenger cursed again. If only Andrew could keep his mouth shut—

"But," he said. "This is what the Secretary-General wants you to understand." He hoped Andrew would get the message and excuse the interruption. "Working arrangements of this nature—existing links with recognized organisations—they should have been made known to us."

"And now they have," said Buthelezi. "I don't propose to take issue over it. Well, gentlemen, I don't know whether we have been able to set your minds at rest at all . . ."

Joachim stood up. The others followed. "For myself," he said, "I feel a lot easier for having been here. At least I know we are dealing with people who sympathise with our somewhat ambiguous situation. We are just getting on our feet as a country. There still exist certain indiscretions in our method of operation. When these are pointed out to us, we are very pleased to bring them into line. If there is one reason why membership of the UN is important to us, it is that we want to learn from professionals. Thank you for your time."

The handshakes were repeated, rather less formally. The delegation passed out into the soft Manhattan evening and Andrew Buthelezi said to Harold Messenger: "In the circumstances, I will allow you to shout me down."

Messenger had a grace to match his guile. "Forgive me, Andrew. The revelations were coming so fast that I was beginning to lose my cool."

"That will be the day," said Buthelezi. "But I could have lost mine . . . Now, what have we learned?"

"Most important thing is that Eugenio is as wise as we are about that disqualifying factor."

"Then why didn't he use it himself?"

"Because it was more important to him to be installed in their country."

"For what purpose?"

"That I don't know. But one thing is very interesting—he has told them he will HELP them get into the UN. Well, Eugenio may be clever, but he can't do both. I'm glad they don't know about the deal he made with us."

"I am, too," said Buthelezi. "That replaces the advantage we lost."

"Maybe," said Messenger. "But I still don't feel fully reimbursed. I thought I knew what Eugenio was playing at."

"You still have Prinz."

"Small mercies, Andrew. Very small mercies."

The Academy of Natural Sciences was in Eduardo Mondlane Plaza, a concrete tribute to the African surrealism that had fashioned the towers of Great Zimbabwe.

The dispute over artistry had gone to ground. Arab traders might have claimed intellectual responsibility for that particular fortress in days gone by but the truth of it lay with the Monomotapa and his vivid sense of fun. In any event, it had predated the Portuguese, which gave it considerable virtue as a precedent.

So here was soapstone newly cut from the sediments around King Solomon's Mines and transported south by men of sundry nations who thought that maybe they would get down to the Jewels of Opar if they Burrough-ed deep enough.

Said surrealism and civil engineering had produced a hybrid that was only ready by degrees. Taking the outside money that had been offered to them by speculators, the natives might have finished it. But when they saw a bank draught, they looked for a knife. There is a lot to be said for the intelligence of the underprivileged.

So the building progressed slowly. The man whose name, after all, now honoured this plaza, had always advocated integrity before expediency.

Nevertheless, the finer points were lost on Simeon, who was looking only for guidance. Julie had given him the *raison de venir,* but he did not believe for a minute that that was the total of it.

Prinz had told him to stay away and though, under questioning, he would have to resort to sentimentality approaching emotional instability, his eyes and senses were darting as sagely as any swift.

There was one matter he did not understand and neither of his sources—anxious as they were to inform him to the utmost—had even seen fit to mention it.

An anachronism existed. Icarus and Zed had spoken of Inquisition machinery here in Lourenço Marques being used against freedom fighters and yet the new Zimbabwe was a product of the success of the Mozambican liberation struggle. What kind of guerrillas were these who were still active after victory.

And if the Vatican were fighting them, how had she come to be allowed facilities for her own brand of terror in the bosom of a liberated state?

Zed and Icarus had spoken, too, of civil rights interests in Zimbabwe and Simeon had remarked on Christianity and bloodshed as strange bedfellows. But here were stranger yet . . . enemies face to face and also cheek to cheek. Furthermore, a man who tortured with the blessing of the United Nations. A man whose antiguerrilla function was overlooked in the new Zimbabwe.

First, the Vatican must have been able to make Zimbabwe an offer she could not refuse. Second, that offer must also hold good with the UN. What matter would interest all three parties?

Some partnership? Some . . . membership?

Simeon bought the only English-language paper he could find in the plaza shops. If that was the game, there could be a mention of it. The ubiquitous *Daily Telegraph* stated squarely that the application for UN membership was due for hearing within a few days. It was understood documents concerning the suitability of the state were with senior UN officials and Messrs. Joachim, Díaz, and Da Gama were attending high-level talks in New York. The paper was days old. The fact lent a necessary edge to Simeon's speculations.

Somehow, inside that mysterious deal, all interests were being served. Yet such an alliance was not possible with the facts as Simeon knew them. Somebody was not telling the truth. Well, Simeon had a fine choice of liars.

Icarus and Zed wanted him IN. Prinz wanted him OUT.

Prinz had talked with pains and indignities. The choice might prove to be more personal than prudent, but Simeon picked Prinz to be the deceiver. What, then, could be WRONG about the case personified by Prinz? Why didn't he want Simeon poking about in Zimbabwe?

Because the Vatican offer—and they could only have promised support—wasn't all it was cracked up to be?

He would take an educated guess—and he would take it before Prinz caught up with him, because that was only a matter of time.

At the academy, he gave his name and asked to see the director.

"I have good evidence," he told the official, "that Rome is going to let you down over the United Nations. She wants you kept out."

"What evidence?" The director was sceptical in the extreme.

Now there was movement at Simeon's back. Unsurprised, he found Randall and Withers at right and left hand.

"And where the swifts spend the winter," he said quickly. "I have followed one all the way from Britain."

The director had seen Randall and Withers before, scanning the patrons. They did not look like medical men, no matter how insane this most recent guest had sounded.

The way they manhandled Simeon through the automatic doors

and away from the building fulfilled his former guerrilla conception of a strong-arm role.

He was on to the Foreign Office before their car had pulled away.

Sami Ojukwe was conscious but keeping it to himself until he could work out his location. The taste inside his mouth was foul—traces of smoke, blood, vomit; a saliva record of his day. His head was a sheet of pain from front to back. To open his eyes would be agony. To keep them closed would make him sick. And now something was bouncing his body unmercifully. The whole world was turning beneath him and the effect was suicidal.

No guidance within, then; just an obsession with his ills. What lay outside?

He looked and saw a white ribbon of road unreeling behind him. Ridges of steel bodywork scored his back. He had been propped at the rear of a lorry, similar to these which had shipped out his brother and the rest of the congregation.

And that was the first piece of hope. If the vehicles had that much in common, they might even be accustomed to arriving at the same destination.

He began to take notice.

Likewise, Two-Pips began to take notice of him. The mercenary had a softer seat of sacking atop the rear wheel arch. In any event, he took the journey like a rodeo rider.

The sun had gone and the fleeting twilight was making white of the greys and beiges and black of the greens and others.

Two-Pips tapped Sami on the knee. "Nice to see you again."

Sami made no reply.

"Mind you, I didn't think it would be so soon. You must have gone some to get involved with the guerrillas—even to the point of going on a operation with them."

"I wasn't—" For some maniac reason, Sami could see humour in the situation. "Look, when the terrorists ran off, one of them took a shot at me for leading YOU to THEM. All I really want is—"

"To find your brother. I don't believe it. No innocent man could be that ham-fisted. Far more likely you joined up with some idea of waging a vendetta. Now suppose we try again. We have lots of time before we get where we are going."

"Where is that?"

"Not yet. Let me hear your story before I start doing you any more favours."

Now the unrolling road was at one with its environs. Parkland, jungle, scrubland were all grey.

"I wanted to find out where Nelson had been taken," said Sami. "I asked a missionary, Father Dominic, and he told me Lourenço Marques. I was trying to make my way there."

"That's fairly accurate, as far as it goes," conceded Two-Pips. "But Father Dominic seemed to think you were up to no good. He put your inquiry on the wire to Propaganda Fide."

"You mean to say you have been on the lookout for me?"

The mercenary chuckled. "Don't over-estimate your importance, Sami. If you hadn't been right there in the middle of two guerrilla operations today, you could have roamed around for months. But, as I say, any man with such a precious gift for getting in harm's way deserves my immediate attention."

"I wasn't there by choice."

"That's hard to swallow, Sami—particularly bearing in mind your state when I saw you last at your village. If ever anybody looked like taking the law into his own hands, it was you."

"My only concern was—"

"My guess is that you joined up with those bandits almost as soon as we drove off and that today you were getting your first taste of action. You were fortunate to survive."

There was darkness behind, and for all Sami knew, deeper darkness ahead.

"I was looking for my brother," he persisted.

"Try again, Sami."

"Look . . . I made my own way to the railway. I saw what happened there. It scared me so much that I ran back into the bush. Then I came across the rest of the gang. That is all. On my brother's life . . ."

"You're pretty free with your brother's life, considering."

"Considering what?"

"Considering that because of your public-spirited action, his life may not be worth very much."

Sami had thought he was punch-drunk by now, immune to any

more shocks. But this one still came up out of nowhere and set his
heart pumping.

"He's—DEAD?"

"Not as far as I know."

"But they told me he would just be locked up until—well, he
ceased to be such a disturbing influence in the village. I didn't even
know he was going to be taken away. What are you saying?"

"It's not up to me to say anything, Sami. But I have to tell you
that very few people come back from where I took your brother. As
a matter of fact, I am ordered to take you there, too. So anything
you say could help BOTH of you."

"But I can't make things up. That's how it happened. I don't
WANT to fight. That's why I am so anxious to find Nelson. I want to
do what HE'S doing."

Two-Pips lit a cigarette. When he inhaled, his gnarled face sprang
into satanic relief. Sami watched the glowing end of the cigarette and
wondered what came next.

"I could tell them that at Lourenço, I suppose," said the mercenary eventually.

"Tell them what?" Sami could not remember what he had said.
There had been too much activity in his mind since the words.

"That you want to do what Nelson is doing. That you want to be
with him. I suppose you know what that means."

"I—don't follow."

"Well, you know what is likely to happen to him."

"It was on my say-so that you came for him. I know exactly how
little he has done to get in your way in fighting these guerrillas. I
don't see how you can keep him for very long."

Two-Pips' face sparked into vision, was gone. "You're not up-to-
date."

"Has he done something else?"

"No."

"Then WHAT?"

"Nelson is a guerrilla in his own right. My peers tell me his is just
as bad as the gang we came across this afternoon, if not worse. A
SPIRITUAL guerrilla. He sabotages men's hearts and minds."

"But that is ridiculous."

"And you do the same."

"No, I—" Sami halted. He was for Nelson or against him. No middle ground. "Yes, I do the same."

"Is that an admission?"

"If it is what you want. What happens now?"

Two-Pips threw away his cigarette end. It made an arc across the night. "That is not up to me. The worst thing would be an auto-dafé."

"I don't know what that is."

"The cleansing fire."

"Fire?" Sami's day had been livid with fire.

"Fire cleanses. Fire refines. According to the priesthood. Now get some sleep."

As if Sami Ojukwe could sleep . . .

Simeon recovered his senses in a dank chamber which gave no indication of age or location; only the deep setting of the steel door evidenced an unusual thickness of wall.

He tested his faculties and found himself sound in wind and limb. Then he turned his attention to the door. It was not going to open from any efforts he made, so he rendered his presence raucous with shouts and blows and waited to see whether that would get the door ajar.

Shortly there were footsteps. A key turned and the door swung outwards, allowing the opener a broad view of the cell within.

Arthur Prinz entered. He showed no surprise at finding Simeon again and Simeon, for his part, did a fine job of hiding the dismay. Prinz, after all, was the man most likely. When they had taken their departures in Britain, nothing was more certain than that they must meet again, somewhere or other.

So here they were, nine thousand miles on, back in confrontation.

"You came after all, then," said Prinz. "You won't be told."

"Told what?"

"Come now, Simeon. You can't expect to keep on professing innocence."

"I came to Mozambique. So what? I had my reasons."

"Yes. The guerrillas."

"No, NOT the guerrillas. Look, Prinz, when are you and your

friends in the civil rights movement BOTH going to get this straight. I don't want anything to do with EITHER of you."

"Then how is it that you nevertheless turn up in a terrorist hotbed?"

"I followed the swifts."

"You what?"

"They migrated from England. I followed them."

Prinz's face was a model of incredulity. "You surely don't expect me to believe you came here . . . bird-watching. Why?"

"I wanted to see where they went."

"For what reason?"

"I promised Julie."

"Convenient . . . Convenient for cover, I mean. If somebody asks you what you are doing here, you can always say, 'I'm chasing birds.' Well, unfortunately, Simeon, a number of us know you rather too well for that."

"It's the truth."

"And I'm a Dutchman."

Simeon fell silent. Prinz, despite his certainty of Simeon's deception, was still not sure how to continue from here. He took a turn around the cell. "I don't know why you persist in such a transparent device, anyway."

"I persist because it is the truth. I want to co-operate. I want to get on with my search. I want to be free of this place, free of you, free of the other lot, free to live what's left of my own life."

"And that's an ambition for which I could feel considerable sympathy if I could only accept it. But dammit, man, the thing itself argues against any serious logic. How do you know your swifts came here? How could you tell them if you saw them? There's a native species which most people can't tell apart from the migrants."

"We ringed one."

"Of course, you ringed one."

"Julie and I. We did it properly, we didn't hurt the bird. We put our name and address. That was all. I mean, people know what is expected when you do that. It's like putting a note in a bottle. It can only mean one thing."

Prinz ended his circuit of the room. "And you got a response from Mozambique."

"No."

"Then what in the hell are you DOING here?"

"This is where the bird came."

"How do you know?"

"They always do. Records—kept over the years. Publications. It's no secret. British swifts come to Mozambique."

"But your particular swift. It could have been eaten over the Alps. It could have dropped dead on the way."

"No."

"How can you be so sure?"

"It was young, but not too young for the journey. It had plenty of fat for fuel."

"But . . ." Prinz was trying hard to get on terms with Simeon's thinking. Either the man was trying to unsettle him with a deliberate abstruseness or he was completely mad. "You've come all this way in the hope of finding one particular small bird. Surely you must know that is comparable with picking out one snowflake in a two-month blizzard. They get birds here from Europe, Asia, Madagascar, the Cape Verde Islands . . ."

"It's not impossible," said Simeon.

Prinz was laughing out loud. "You don't think so? I've a good mind to let you go and look."

"Can I?" Simeon took a step towards the door—a little too hasty for insanity, thought Prinz.

"Not yet," he said. "Because a thought occurs to me. You had tagged this bird with your address in Britain. What happens now if somebody tries to reach you there and you're here? You're not very convincing, Simeon. Maybe I should just lock the door and throw away the key."

"No—please!" Simeon pleading was a new effect. Prinz did not know whether to trust it.

"You didn't answer my question," he said. "Suppose somebody wanted to get in touch with you. While you were here, how would they do it?"

Simeon was staring fixedly at the floor as though the consequence had taken him unaware. "I don't know. It was stupid of me. I just—couldn't keep still. I couldn't be patient waiting for something that might never come. I had to make my own safeguards."

"And what about all the safeguards I gave you in England? What about all the warnings?"

"I didn't—think of them. I didn't put two and two together, I suppose."

"I could keep you here for a long time, you know."

"I didn't realise. The birds came to Mozambique, so I came after them. It was something Julie wanted . . . I didn't mean any harm . . ."

And Arthur Prinz could almost believe the man was unhinged. He saw confusion now, a lack of purpose. He remembered how Simeon had gripped the edge of the seat on that distant clifftop rather than leave it; how he had made pledges, rashly and in profusion, at Hurst Castle.

The man was soft in the head. It was no contest. A lesser person might have prescribed pity but Prinz was more honest with himself than that. The challenge was gone. He could not even feel he had won because Simeon had been crippled before they met.

In his pocket, there was even a reason for swallowing Simeon's explanation, but he had hoped to discard it.

"I am going to see to it," he said, "that you are returned to England. That way I cover all eventualities—I save you from going crazy in your hunt for an atom in a haystack, I save me from having to worry about you any more, and I save the situation by removing you from it. Will you go back to England for me?"

"I promise," said Simeon. "I'll wait for my messenger."

"No. I don't want you here again. Is that clear? If I find you here, there will be only one reason. You will just have to sit it out on your memorial seat until the bird comes back naturally next spring."

"It's a long time to wait." Simeon shifted uneasily.

"The alternative is worse."

"I won't have an answer for Julie . . ."

"You'll find it far easier to make your peace with Julie when you are closer to her."

Even so, Prinz ruled, it would do no harm to let Simeon see what might lie in store for him next time. The auto ground lay on the route to the airport and a function was scheduled for that afternoon.

The sun shone, the band played, and the heretics died. The point was made with force. Simeon did not stop vomiting until he was over the English Channel, by which time Frank Randall and Ronald Withers were quite convinced he no longer presented a threat.

They did not know that Simeon had already made his play.

Rico Scarlatti, terrorist bullets or no, was looking for some cool air on the verandah. Banned from Prinz's interview with Simeon by reason of sympathies expressed, he had been intrigued to see Prinz consigning Simeon to a car and giving him what looked palpably like a bland farewell.

For the rest of the day, Prinz had been missing. Scarlatti knew if he searched, Prinz would not be found. On the other hand, if he stayed silent long enough, Prinz would come to him—there were precious few others here with whom he could converse.

In the stillness of the evening, Arthur Prinz emerged on to the verandah and lowered his rotund frame into a rocking chair. He said, almost immediately, "Well, I think we've seen the last of Simeon."

Scarlatti started. "You haven't had him—"

"Good grief, no. I talked him out of it."

"I'm learning fast to know what that involved. Why wasn't I there? Either I keep records or I don't—"

"Not another demarcation dispute, Scarlatti. It wasn't an interrogation—right? When I say we talked, I mean just that."

"I thought you had finished that job in England. Obviously—"

"As a matter of fact, he talked HIMSELF out of my clutches. What do you think of that?"

"I take it with plenty of salt."

Prinz loosened his collar and lay back in the rocker. "Well, see how you savour this—he told me he was over here looking for a bird."

"A bird?"

"The feathered variety. Oh, don't worry about the other sort. He's still carrying that wife of his, that Julie."

"She must have meant his whole life."

"She nearly meant his death. She was the one who had him looking for swifts."

"I don't understand."

"A posthumous promise. They ringed a swift in England. He told her he would find out where it went for the winter. That brought him here."

"That's what he said?"

"Right. I suggested it was a fine cover story, he denied it."

"You believed the denial."

"Not at first. It seemed too incredible. How does he seriously think he can find one bird among the millions that come here for the winter. And then I began wondering whether Simeon himself would have tried to get away with such a tall tale—he's usually had more sense."

"Could he have been bluffing—trying to make you think it was so outrageous that it was bound to be the truth?"

"I considered that, too. But the fight's gone out of him. And when it goes out of him, it goes out of me. In his present state, he couldn't sabotage a picnic, let alone what we have going."

"You're sure?" Scarlatti still hadn't seen the man and he was sorrier than ever. He would have liked to form his own opinion. More than that, he would have liked to assure himself that Simeon was beyond danger—as vehicle or victim.

"It's in his eyes. Say what you like, do what you like, he's—elsewhere. So I've shown an uncharacteristic streak of humanity and sent him home."

"Well, congratulations."

"On my humanity? Believe me, if I hadn't received a little random corroboration of his story, he would never have got it past me."

"Corroboration—are you going to tell me you found the bird?"

"Not quite. But somebody did."

Prinz put his hand inside his jacket and drew forth an envelope. "This was inside the door of his apartment. It must have been delivered after he made up his mind to come to Zimbabwe. Randall and Withers discovered it when they found he had gone. They brought all his mail with them, which was quite intelligent."

"So you sent him home knowing that his swift had been traced here. I take back my congratulations. That wasn't at all human."

"The bird isn't here."

"But . . ."

"The letter had been posted from Italy."

"That's a bit far north, isn't it?"

"I'm afraid so."

Scarlatti felt a sudden chill. "What part of Italy?"

Prinz chuckled. "You'll never believe it."

"Tuscany?" The name itself was enough to freeze the lawman after the Garden Five fiasco. But there were other causes. "God, I know what they do to swifts in Tuscany."

"I, too. The trapper may have made a meal of the swift but I suppose he couldn't stomach the note. According to his letter, he just found the bird dead. Well, perhaps it was when he picked it out of his tower trap."

Scarlatti had his head bowed, almost in mourning.

"So you see," said Prinz, "I was actually showing humanity by keeping my mouth shut."

"You're a man in a million," said Scarlatti. "You're all heart."

"And there's more. I now have a way of settling my mind about Simeon once and for all. I can send him the note."

"But for what purpose if the bird is dead? You might just as well have given it to him while he was here."

"My friend, you still have quite a lot to learn about the criminal mind. If I had done that, I would have lost the chance to rule him out conclusively."

"If you send for him to come out here again, you STILL won't know whether he has come for that reason or some other."

"I won't GET him here."

"Not—Tuscany." Scarlatti's stomach was in a knot.

"It makes sense. If he goes there, I will believe his story entirely and will never trouble him again."

"The bird is dead." Scarlatti was having a job to retain his composure.

"Then I will have to tell a small lie. I know just the place where the test could be made. As a matter of fact, you know it, too." Prinz stood up, stretched, and laughed. "Isn't it funny how things work out?"

Never a terrorist when you want one, Scarlatti thought. He did not need to look any further for cool air. He was shivering.

LESSONS FOR THE HELPLESS

The miles flowed and the hours succeeded and Sami had no clear recollection of their passage so that something must have taken over his mind, excitement or exhaustion, fear or fever.

It was a different day—whether the next or the next but one, he could not be sure—and the transport was slowing on the outskirts of a city.

"Lourenço Marques," said Two-Pips, as though he had been poised for Sami's recovery just to tell him that. "You'll be seeing your brother soon."

"Then he's still alive?" The hope made a difference even though it might be short-lived.

"I didn't say that. You might be seeing him dead."

The pain in Sami's gut was sharp and ragged. It seemed the mercenary's ploy at friendship was over. Now he was back to hurting in as many different ways as he had words.

"It's unlikely, though."

"Are you building me up to knock me down again?" Sami did not care any more whether his tongue got him into trouble. Nothing could be worse than what he faced and he might at least come to it with some knowledge of having given as good as he got.

"Take it any way you like. I'm just stating a fact. There hasn't been an auto in the last few days and unless he has killed himself the chances are that he is alive."

"He wouldn't kill himself. He doesn't have the right."

"Every man has the right—to end his story where he wants to."

"Is that all life means to you? Start on one page and finish on another?"

"Sure. Cram in as many pages as you can between first and last. Pack each of those pages with as much incident as you can manage."

"And afterwards, who reads it? Who cares?"

"Nobody. Why do you still have this myth about people caring? The book is for a readership of one. While your life lasts, leaf back through it. But don't make the mistake of thinking that anybody else gives a damn about it. They're too busy compiling their own . . ."

A triple thickness of barbed-wire fences bordered the road and beyond lay hutments of corrugated iron, little different from the kraals of Sami's limited experience.

"Your new home." Two-Pips grinned at his own sparse humour. "Of course, it depends what comforts you're used to—"

"None," said Sami. "There's nothing to choose between the old home and the new one. They're both on the face of a miserable earth."

"In that case, you should prosper." And Two-Pips took himself off to the glassless window which let into the lorry-cab, muttering to the driver beyond.

The lorry swung left, unseating Sami in the inertia. It halted. A man with a rifle looked into the back, passed his eyes over Sami without a change of expression, and disappeared. The truck started forward and Sami saw the man replacing a heavy gate as he was carried further into the enclosure. He wondered if that were the end of the real world, of all things he might call familiar; although, when he reflected, his last normal vision had been many miles and many days away—Nelson and his flock at prayer. Then it had been the provocation. Now it provided a comfort that misted his eyes. He was glad Two-Pips had lost interest in him.

Another halt. This time, Two-Pips put a hand under Sami's armpit, levered him to his feet, and thrust him towards the sunlight.

Sami's legs were treacherous again. Too long in cramped positions had atrophied the muscles. He stayed on his feet with difficulty while tides of circulation ebbed and flowed from spine to heel.

He had hoped Nelson and the other villagers might be waiting to greet him, though why he should have expected any semblance of welcome in a place like this was beyond logic. Nevertheless, he was disappointed when his inspection of the dusty square showed only dusty white men in dishevelled jungle garb.

The rusting prefabrications lay to the right and left of him, giving no indication of their purpose or function. Ahead stood a sturdy, stone-built house from the colonial days with the unrenewed whitewash peeling and the geraniums, once fashionable, making a crimson and unkempt anachronism in the barrack setting.

Two-Pips pushed him towards the steps leading up to the verandah. Within the confines of the shade, a rocking chair swung forward and discharged its occupant.

He was plump, pink-faced, and clad in lightweight. He shuffled to the head of the steps and proffered his hand.

"Good afternoon. My name is Prinz. You will come to know me very well."

His grip held a chill that penetrated. Sami, who knew cold from fast-running streams and cold from malarial ravages, found this sensation more shocking than either.

Prinz completed the gesture. He looked for some sign of an intelligence he could understand among the narrow forehead, the craggy brows, the broad nose; some flicker of a defiance in the brown eyes. "Do you speak much English?"

"What the missionaries taught me. I was a good pupil."

"Then you have a lot to thank them for."

"I thanked them."

"In what way?"

"I betrayed my brother and his friends to them."

"And you consider that clears the debt."

"It's all I am prepared to pay."

"But you are not even prepared to pay that, Sami. My information is that you are here because you regret this small service and wish it undone."

"I regret it but I am not fool enough to think it can be undone. I am here to suffer whatever my people must suffer."

"There would be no need for any of you to suffer at all if you were only prepared to—shall we say—give credit where it is due. We are able to converse without difficulty because a servant of God has displayed the Christian quality of patience and long-suffering and brought you to a knowledge of my language—and yet you and those who benefited with you now turn around and tell these good people that they are false and their God is false."

"Not their God, their form of godly devotion."

"There is little difference. The one is implicit in the other. That is not my idea of paying a debt."

"We had no choice but to learn."

"It has taken you a long time to complain."

In dialogue, the exchange had become animated, but Prinz was not perturbed. "In any event, this is something we can discuss at length in the days ahead."

He went back to his rocking chair. Two-Pips marched Sami around the side of the house to a stockade.

At last, Sami could reveal his need for support.

But the stockade was empty. Alone in the massive cage, Sami threw back his head and wailed one word: "NELSON . . ."

When the Zimbabwe delegation held out their hands this time, there were pistols, small-calibre but unwavering.

Díaz chopped Messenger's wrist before he could get to the alarm button and that left Andrew Buthelezi and his aide a captive audience.

Joachim, for all his dilomatic polish, seemed no less adept in the circumstances. He waved the UN men into chairs and perched himself on the edge of the desk. He got his free hand around the intercom cable and pulled. When that jerked free from its wall socket, a red light flashed in the outer office and Messenger didn't have to worry about the alarm button.

Even knowing that, he wasn't easy. His wrist was still numb but he was working his fingers and there didn't seem to be anything broken. What made him unsure was the purpose of this armed and unscheduled visit.

On that point, Buthelezi seemed a little more familiar. "You don't need those," he said coolly. "We are quite prepared to listen."

"It's not your ears we want," said Joachim. "It's your hearts."

Messenger edged himself into the conversation. "This is going to achieve nothing. We've already explained that the issue of your membership lies with the general vote and not with ourselves."

"I no longer believe that," said Joachim. "You knew the Vatican was trying to cheat us and you said nothing. To me, that smacks of support. And I make no apology for this present method of approach. Our experiences with Western civilisations are fast bringing us round to the conviction that this is the only way to get what you want."

"By killing us?" Buthelezi was unmoved. "Surely you know you would be dead yourselves before you could get very far—unless, of course, you are a suicide squad."

Díaz laughed deep down. "We said we wanted your hearts. We meant the truth in those hearts. Frankly, we've been exposed so much to substitutes that we have quite a difficulty recognising the real thing. At least, when we were fighting for freedom, we knew the real thing."

Messenger was beginning to relax. For assasssins, these three were comfortingly rational. Momentarily, he envied the race recognition that had saved Buthelezi from sweat.

And then his own sweat started up again. The flashing light. By now, UN internal security was alert and planning. The outer office had seen three men go in. Assume three guns, each able to cover but one approach. Now figure out more than three modes of simultaneous access.

Doubtless, the window-cleaners' ramp was already winding up the wall with some very sham chamois aboard. Soft-footed guards would be lining up outside the door. He could almost hear the whir of blades as a helicopter quit the roof park with marksmen aboard and began its slow circuit of the executive floor. Shortly, the white telephone would sound twice and stop, which meant: "Lie flat because we're coming through the cupboard." Then maybe the chandelier would fall and shatter, discharging tear gas.

So the problem was not these people in here, but the forces outside. An exchange of enmity could end up with a lot more spilt blood than sense.

He said: "When you WERE fighting for freedom, you just kept an eye on long grass, trees, and sky. We don't have any of that in here but believe me, it doesn't mean no measures exist. And our security men are not used to the waiting game. There are half a dozen different ways they could take you without giving you a chance to hit back.

"And you started that machinery off yourself when you ripped out the cable. That wasn't a natural act and it triggered the alert. I would advise you to get your weapons out of sight before they can be observed. We can always say I tripped over the cable."

Now it was Da Gama's turn to look uneasy. He had his back pressed against the door and he had slipped the lock into place behind him. Now he listened in a dilemma. He fancied there had been a flurry of activity in the other office but now it seemed inordinately silent—no voices, no typing.

"They know," he said quietly. "I think they know."

Díaz said: "He's bluffing." But the hand that held his Beretta idled into the shadow at the hip of his jacket.

Joachim pushed himself off the desk and took one of the guest chairs. His revolver went into his pocket and so did his hand. "It is as well to be certain," he said. "These are different rules—that much is right. Da Gama, check the outer office."

"NO." Messenger came round the desk in a bound. "I don't want any—accidents. I'll open the door myself."

He moved across the suite. But now Buthelezi called him back. "I don't want any accidents, either. Leave the door shut."

The white telephone purred once. Messenger, halfway across the room, could not reach it.

It rang again. "Get DOWN," he shouted.

It rang a third time. And went on ringing until he had bellied across to the desk, stretched up, and hauled the receiver off the cradle.

"Hello. Yes, it's all right. I tripped over the wire. Maybe you could send an engineer."

The others were regaining their feet. A tap at the window. The cleaner who had ridden skyward with a Mauser in his bucket was watching the exercise impassively.

Buthelezi stepped across to the window and shucked open a pane. "Well, laugh," he said. "My fleet-footed Messenger got tangled up with the intercom and we've all been lying on the floor shivering."

The big gunsel was still chuckling when he dropped out of sight.

"At least," said Messenger, "you know we're not telling lies this time."

Joachim was back in his chair with both hands in view. "Except about the cable. I'm sorry for that. As you say, tactics tend to differ."

Da Gama had returned to the door, uncertain whether his orders had been changed. "Are we all right now?"

"Sit down, Matthew," said Joachim. "Take a load off your mind. These gentlemen will tell us whether we are all right or all wrong."

Andrew Buthelezi cleared his throat. "Perhaps I should do that, Harold."

"As you wish, Secretary-General."

The S.G. let himself down on the desk corner opposite that recently occupied by Joachim. "As I understand it, your complaint was that we had not told you of the Vatican's double-dealing. In truth, it was not until you told us you had Rome's support that we were aware of her duplicity ourselves. It required a little thought, a little discussion—a little PRIVATE discussion. You would not have been kept in the dark for much longer. Certainly, no such situation would have been allowed to proceed while you were enjoying UN hospitality. But tell me—how do you know now of the Vatican's intentions?"

"It seems not all the whites in Lourenço Marques are good Catholics."

"Not—" Buthelezi looked at Messenger.

"Prinz again," said Messenger. "What a man."

Díaz stirred. "Not Prinz," he said. "Unless he is using an alias. The man gave his name as Simeon."

"Simeon?" The UN men traded bewildered glances.

"Well, anyway," said Messenger quickly, "he informed you that Eugenio wasn't on the level. What then?"

"Nothing," said Joachim. "We may be backwoodsmen but we are learning fast. We are waiting for an opportune time to turn the fact to our advantage."

A knock on the door. A secretary with engineer Aldo Viazzanni at her elbow. "We'll be a minute," said Messenger. "*Ciao,* Aldo. *Momento.*

"Sir." The jobman smiled with gold-flecked teeth. Then he retreated to the outer office.

"I guess we can wind it up now," said Buthelezi. "If you are satisfied with the state of our hearts."

"Satisfied. Satisfied, too, that you will see our vulnerable position in isolation when you consider our application," said Joachim. "We are easy meat for any bounty hunter who comes amongst us."

"Just one thing," put in Messenger. "The Inquisition machinery in Lourenço Marques—is that still functioning?"

"For the moment. They continue to save us trouble with our own extremists. When it suits us, we shall—put THEM to the fire . . ."

"And these—acts of faith?"

"Still operative. They are quite an attraction. We make a lot of white money that way," said Díaz.

"And that doesn't bother you?"

"When the novelty wears off, we may start questioning the morality," said Joachim.

Buthelezi was chewing his lip. He barely nodded when the delegation took their leave.

Messenger said: "Something worrying you, Andrew?"

"Naïveté," said the S.G. "Naïveté that is sometimes articulated with a sophistication that takes your breath away. There is more to Zimbabwe than meets the eye."

"Then let's eat on it," said Messenger. "And I have to figure a way to get Prinz OUT!"

As they passed from the office, so Aldo Viazzanni passed in. He was well liked at Turtle Bay—a glittering smile, a hard worker. When he replaced the intercom wall socket, there was an extra component—a microphone. He was also a VERY good Catholic.

"The interrogation ended at 4:20 P.M.," said Arthur Prinz. "Let it be so recorded."

Rico Scarlatti made the entry on his pad. "Comments?" he asked mechanically.

"The subject remains unconvinced."

Scarlatti eyed the subject and Nelson Ojukwe smiled back—a valiant smile from a man not totally unshaken. But the hint of frailness was only physical.

"That at least would be the truth," said the African.

"It is not the only truth you have heard this afternoon." Actually, Prinz aspired to much the same kind of expression. The ecclesiastical function of the questioning meant little to him beyond the fact that he had to try and secure answers of a particular nature. It was a clash of whims. What really wore him down was to find that his technique was not producing results.

He did not abhor violence and indeed would come to it eventually, but his attitude was that of Eymeric, whose *Directorium* had laid the guidelines for Torquemada's definitive *Articles of the Inquisition*. Eymeric favoured the soft approach at the outset before applying such refinements as the *garrucha* and the *bostezo* and *toca*.

The hoist and the water torture were left for later in Nelson Ojukwe's case. Right now, Prinz had been tightening the cords on a spiritual rack for him. Without much success.

First of all, there had been the undressing of the victim with deliberate slowness and sadness, as though these servants feared for his life and his safety. When Nelson had laughed at the pantomime, there had been a close search of every inch of his skin for magic signs, names of angels.

The scrutiny was traditional but no less humiliating for that. Its purpose, as Prinz had explained to his corps of helpers, was to make sure the subject had no recourse to sorcery, since such access could render him insensible to pain and able to die without speaking.

He found the superstitious natives willing enough to accept that the man they searched might be in league with the occult. The friendly neighbourhood witch doctor was never that far away from their minds.

And as he explained to Nelson Ojukwe: "You are, after all, the antichrist."

Nelson, who had excellent physique and spirit despite his non-violent attitude to life, had found something else to amuse him in that.

Prinz was distraught that the first question recorded by Scarlatti should have to be: "Why are you laughing?"

The answer, similarly recorded in keeping with the *Articles* and the wishes of Eugenio, was: "I find it funny that YOU should call ME the antichrist."

"Then you are suggesting that I have the roles in reverse."

"It is not a suggestion, it is a statement of fact."

"That you are right and I am wrong."

"Yes."

"That God is with you and not with the Church."

"Emphatically."

"Then we have a long way to go, Mr. Ojukwe."

"For the record, I stay right where I am."

Rico Scarlatti had become engrossed in the exchange. It opened a door for him. He had teamed up with Prinz in the hope of destroying him and had found no weapon as yet outside of murder. The guerrillas who had provided Prinz's sport to date had been fluent—some more than others—and patriotic. But patriotism was not an emotion that moved Scarlatti.

He had heard all manner of doctrines—left wing, right wing, anarchistic—but could not feel sorry for such political animals. And when the doctrines tumbled with the onset of pain; when eagerness to impart information came under fear of death; when finally obscenity took charge of the tongue and all without raising a feeling within him, he had begun to wonder at the wisdom of his course.

The treatment was cruel, no denying that; cruel in any context. But the crimes had been just as cruel. While the situation stood at tit for tat, he could not consider it an injustice—even though, in his heart, he knew there had to be some grave miscarriage of faith at the basis of anything Prinz attempted.

So he had gone about his business in a shell, immune to torture, unmindful of curses, deaf to the ultimate offers of wives, daughters, even sons for the Inquisitor's pleasure in return for release.

When these people held virtue so cheaply, what removed them from sin? What made them special? How, through their wretched lives, could he pay back Prinz in the way that he wanted? Their victory would not have been a triumph for good—and he wanted no less.

Now Rico Scarlatti had come upon Nelson Ojukwe. Here was a man of nobility. His heart was forever with his people—his first and only offer to Prinz had been that the Inquisitor could do what he liked to Nelson if his flock could go free. And even the refusal of that had not deflated him. So be it. Nelson must now pray all the more that his little congregation could hold on to their integrity.

Paradoxically, it was Nelson's lack of concern for his life that had made it important to Scarlatti. At least, no paradox really. Shem had had the same selflessness and this, more than anything, was responsible for Scarlatti's involvement. Nelson Ojukwe touched the right chord. In fact—Scarlatti suspected—the only chord.

He wrote and he listened and he dared to think that his own salvation and Prinz's destruction might come through this man.

But in the corridor leading from the interrogation chamber to the open air, Prinz was thinking of somebody else.

"Ojukwe will have to wait," he said. "We are needed in Tuscany."

Scarlatti's spark dwindled and was gone. He had a fear of Garden Five. He needed Ojukwe for direction. Now Prinz was about to nail him on both counts.

"Do you want me to see if I can talk him round?" he asked, and was immediately ashamed of the poor deception.

Prinz made no advantage of the slip. "No. You would have to be there even if I didn't."

"I don't follow. Is there some doubt about your going?"

"Not really. Eugenio might make a fuss but I can see him off."

"Then why specify me?"

"Because you sent the letter."

"What letter?"

"About the bird being found—remember?"

"Yes. But I didn't . . ."

"Well, it bears your name, to be precise."

"Why?"

"I like to keep you involved."

"And do I have to pass myself off as this trapper?"

"You only have to see that he is there."

"Then why are you coming?"

"To see that you see that he is there. Frankly, much about this man Simeon puts me in mind of your old pal, Shem. I'd hate to be the cause of dividing your loyalties."

Scarlatti had been deep in thoughts of another kind and this sudden rush of revelations was dizzying. Even so, he knew that to be one of Prinz's favourite methods. And now he suspected that he was supposed to miss something.

"But that's not all, is it?" he said warily. "You're not taking on Eugenio just to play hide and seek in Tuscany."

"H-m-m," responded Prinz.

It meant nothing and Scarlatti resolved on extremes. "You're going to kill Simeon anyway," he said.

"If I can," said Prinz. "And I can."

"But why?" Scarlatti's thoughts were back on the salvation theme so smartly that he surprised himself.

"Because this world isn't big enough for both of us . . ."

The sea turned upon the zigzag shore, the sun hung by a thread, the sand martins glided and fed, but Simeon saw only flames and faces.

He tried to project the slaving memories of Tomorrow Julie but more recent scenes were immovable.

He even started on a prayer but found his focus blotted out by the intruders, not in terms of terror and contempt but in bland, blind moderation. Prinz's words on this seat weeks before came back in echoes . . . "massacres of missionaries" . . . "the appeal to reason is a waste of time . . ."

Simeon had seen savage justice, if justice was the word for it. "Legislation" was better and that left the responsibility with the lawmakers.

But had death been any less painful for the missionaries than it had been for the guerrillas? Was it any less final? According to Prinz, the situation had dictated the methods. But what had dictated the situation? Why, previous situations when the pressure had been on those who did not move fast enough to embrace the One Church, evangelism by force, colonising with the Bible in one hand and the sword in the other. And after that? Slave labour and fat colonists for four hundred years. It was a lot to wipe out and a missionary slain now, in the last decade, a church burned—these things could hardly be hailed as cardinal sins when, in truth, they were no more than reaction.

For either side, the criterion was life or death. While the one made life all important, the other made death honourable. And seeing that, the Church took lavish steps to ensure that the ending of these guerrillas should be a circus, a bullfight, a tourist attraction—a humiliation rather than an honour.

That too was conscious strategy. The auto-da-fé was not just a penalty; it was, as the title indicated, an act of faith for the Roman church.

It was complex but there could have been one greater dilemma. Julie had been the one for belief. While Simeon had the need to put his trust in something, his sinistral thinking had dictated that he go the roundabout way to join her. Thus, in Playa Nine, he had advocated a Universal Force for Good, a course of action that had incorporated the best, the most virtuous of all forms—and in Green Town, Illinois, he had relied on logic tempered with an emotional bond to his surroundings . . . and in the finish, another man, Judge Charles Woodman, had proved more logical and evidenced a greater affinity with a setting which was no closer than secondhand for Simeon anyway.

So here he was with only Julie and her concept to guide him through a problem she had never envisaged. The dilemma would have been if her concept had been more orthodox; if, in fact, she had found the intellectual visions she sought in any of the established modes of worship.

Having seen what he had seen, he could have ended up trying to carry on a moral argument across the grave. That, at least, he had been spared.

Julie had not thought matters would take this turn. When she had spoken to him of the plains of Megiddo, it was a request that he should continue her search for the cleansing medium, the answer to all questions, the right religion.

Or had she? Had she not also said . . . He struggled for total recall but it was impossible. The trespassers were still there in his mind howling for attention. Some day . . . some day he would find a direct confrontation between right and wrong. Something like that, she had said. And he would know. Yet he didn't know. And every time he tried to decide, these ghosts of the recent past, the effigies, the agony, sweet pink Prinz, blocked him, tripped him, blew his brains out.

Julie had said prayer would always help but they even had the answer to that. They crowded it out.

Who? Now who would have an interest in seeing that prayer did not work?

Click! Julie in vision was clouded, perhaps. But here, thank God, came Julie in words.

"Prayer," she had said, "is always an excellent proof to me of the existence of the Devil."

And when Simeon had started to say something about a contradiction, she had gone on: "You can concentrate on just about anything when you want to—so why should it suddenly become so difficult to keep your thoughts in order when you try to talk to God? Then, there's a barrage of distractions from things that don't matter —small noises, tomorrow's meals, yesterday's conversations. You could say 'So what?' to every one of them—but once you take that much notice, your prayer is over. Now what harm does a little prayer do. Is belief such an offence to logic that it must be smothered with trivia? Or is it that your spiritual directive enrages the arrogance of the one who really does seek to control thoughts on this planet? And since God would hardly interrupt Himself, it HAS to be the Devil."

At that time, Simeon might have accepted what she said but he could not echo the experience. The prospect of prayer left him tongue-tied and inadequate with all the darkness and immensity of space trapped within the confines of his lidded eyes. At that time.

But now he had words and he tried to use them. And Julie was right. She kept on being right.

On whose side, then, was the Devil? The scenes were unselective —did that mean he was on BOTH sides? If so, was this the Megiddo war? And if the question had to be asked, was that not answer in it-self?

The seat was wet under Simeon's grasp and the sun was dropping towards Hengistbury Head. The moisture could have been dew or the sweat of Simeon's struggle grown cool. Either way, it was time to move.

He quit the seat with a backward glance, crossed the grass to the road, and returned to his flat.

He kicked an envelope as he stepped through the door.

In the light of a lamp, he examined the Italian stamp and made out a Siena postmark.

The letter within was short, laboured, and without style. It said:

"I am requesting my friend the postmaster to write this letter for me because my English is not much.

"Yesterday in my bird tower by the river, I find a swift with a note on its leg with your address on the note.

"I have seen such notes before and my friend tells me that it means for me to write to you and say I have found the bird.

"If your wish is for me to return it I cannot be sure that it will fly back until the spring. If your wish is to collect it I am as above.

"I am keeping the bird fed and I am sure you will know this costs money but we can talk about that when we meet. So will you write to above and let me know your wish. Please write in English because my friend will tell me what you say and I look forward to meeting you soon.

"I am Rico Scarlatti. Anybody in my village will bring you to me."

Though Simeon scoured the Siena area in an atlas, he could find no mention of any village called Cinquegiardini. In Siena, they might know better.

Now he felt almost happy. It gave him something to do that was a pure link with Julie. At the same time, it took him out of the reach of the too many people who presently knew where he was.

He would not waste time on a letter. Tomorrow was empty and he would fill it with travel.

Sami Ojukwe was caught and held and he didn't even know whether Nelson was here. He had been taken by his own will but his release could not be engineered in the same way. If he was still out of touch with his brother, what now?

Two-Pips and his motley crew were gone, with supplies replenished and enough bottles to make the convoy jangle like a shaken chandelier as they left.

There had been no sign of any other prisoners and yet the man on the verandah had seemed more than some intermediate official. He had spoken of "no need for any of you to suffer." He had said, "You and those who benefited with you." These were strong hints that Sami was not alone. At best, they meant that he might see his brother and friends soon. At worst, it meant they had passed through the pink man's hands on the way elsewhere.

But the stockade stayed empty and the quick Mozambique dusk was hard upon the scene when Sami discerned two figures approaching. One was the fresh-faced man he had seen earlier. The other, a dark-haired European, a younger man.

Scarlatti had been otherwise engaged when Sami arrived. He viewed the convoy from a distance that lent anonymity although not enchantment. But Prinz's ebullience over dinner had been a sure sign that something had happened to please him.

The lawman was surprised to see the stockade with a population of one but when he commented upon it now, crossing the dusty square, Prinz silenced him with: "All in good time."

"The man's name is Sami Ojukwe," Prinz said in an undertone. "I am told he is a brother to our subject. Their present close proximity is not a point I intend to emphasise—not just yet."

"Give me a quick reason."

"What this man most wants to know is whether Nelson is here. I don't propose to set his mind at rest straightaway."

"Is that necessary?"

"In my opinion, yes. And my opinion holds sway."

With that, Scarlatti had to be content because they were now within easy earshot of the cage.

"Good evening, Sami Ojukwe," said Prinz. "I trust the accommodation is to your liking."

"Never having been used to much," said the prisoner, "I do not look for much."

"I thought you people were used to paradise."

"Not yet. We have to work for it but we know it is there—and soon."

"How soon?"

"When the signs are fulfilled and the number of evidences grows daily."

"Of this you are convinced?"

"Utterly."

"Then what possessed you to—what did you say?—betray your brother?"

"The Devil possessed me, as he did Judas."

"Some juju, you mean."

"No. The one Devil, Satan. I thought the witch doctors were the closest to him until I met you."

Scarlatti gasped and then had to bite on a chuckle. Here indeed was an Ojukwe. Prinz, however, was undeterred.

"Convenient," he said. "Convenient how you can blame all your shortcomings on the Devil. That way, you never need feel guilty for anything."

"I feel guilty."

"But you make no act of contrition."

"If you mean the taking of the sacrament, I certainly don't. But if you mean the taking of positive steps to right that wrong—well, I am here."

"What does that benefit you if your brother is not?"

"He's BEEN here. You TALK as though he has been here. Just tell me one thing—is he alive or dead?"

"What difference would it make? Death has no sting for you people. If he is dead, you set him on the path."

Scarlatti sensed the anguish that moved the man even though he could not see it in the gloom. But the sense was enough to include this Sami in the link he held with Nelson and even—since Prinz's letter revelation—with distant Simeon. Thus he wanted to provide relief.

"He's here," he said quickly, and damn the consequences.

Prinz let his breath out slowly. "Yes, he is here," he said. "He is undergoing a stiff interrogation and that is why you will not see him. My friend here is responsible for recording all his words during that questioning. He has a strong stomach and he does the job well. His name is Scarlatti. Learn to respect it."

He turned and walked away while Scarlatti faltered. There would be no further chance to see either of the brothers before he left for Tuscany. Somehow, he had to let them know, if not together then separately, that his heart was with them.

"Prinz is angry because he didn't want you to know," he told Sami.

Darkness notwithstanding, Sami's spittle caught him squarely in the face.

Crossing the compound slowly, while he wiped the moisture from his cheek, Scarlatti fell into deep despair. He had no contact at all with Simeon and could not be sure that he would get it. His role towards Nelson Ojukwe had been passive and non-committal, neither firm friend nor clear foe. And Sami had dismissed him as a tormentor. He could forget about links.

Re-entering the main building, he found his steps taking him towards the detention cell—a renovation of the basement that had once held a plentiful supply of Portuguese wines. He was already in trouble with Prinz and the prospect heartened him. Why not make some more trouble? He descended the steps, dismissed the guard, and roused the sleeping Nelson.

"Your brother is here," he said.

The older Ojukwe scanned his face, looking for tricks and lighting instead of something worth trusting. "Thank you for telling me."

"He—wants to be with you."

"And I suppose that cannot be."

"That is a measure of happiness larger than the one you are allowed."

"But if it was up to you—"

"I cannot say that. I cannot give you hope. I live with condemnation myself from day to day."

"Then God bless you for the risk you take to do a kindness."

Scarlatti returned up the steps ready to face any Prinz manoeuvre.

Nelson Ojukwe took himself over to the grating that gave the only access to air and light. He called: "SAMI."

Across the compound, his brother heard and the spittle turned bitter in his mouth.

In the late evening, a barrage upon Simeon's door. In the doorway, John Icarus and Adam Zed.

"Well, well." Simeon stood back to allow them across the threshold. Now that he knew where he was going, he did not care to volunteer too many comments in case he gave it away. He was bound for incommunicado and he wanted no company.

"What happened to you, man?" asked Icarus. "We came by with your papers and things, but no sign."

"I made my own way," said Simeon.

"To—Mozambique?"

Simeon could see no harm in revealing the Hurst Castle episode. It laid no obvious lines for these two to follow.

"I had a sample of Brother Prinz's hospitality at a little Bastille along the coast from here. I was more impressed by his methods than his arguments."

"That figures," said Icarus. "His arguments have little weight. Did he—use force?"

"A little. Nothing I couldn't take."

"So you took it. Didn't you wonder why it was applied?"

"He made it clear why it was applied. He didn't want me in Zimbabwe."

"And you haven't been there."

"I have."

"What?" Slow smiles of wonderment started on the Negro faces. "You mean you're on our side?"

"I'm on nobody's side but my own. I had a personal reason for going to Zimbabwe and I went. I was looking for a swift."

Zed laughed. "And did Prinz swallow that? Excuse the ornithological joke."

"I doubt it, but it was all he got out of me because it was all that was there."

Icarus was watching Simeon with his head on one side. "I think I'd have trouble taking that in myself," he said. "Not that I'm calling you a liar, Simeon. Just that you can't get away from the—handiness —of it. Tell us about your reason—do you mind?"

"Not at all. I can give it to you in a word. Julie."

Icarus set his head to rights. "How so?"

"We saw the swifts going south. It was one of the last things we did see together. I tagged one of them. Julie had a whimsy to know where it went. I didn't hear anything, so I read up on the subject. Most of our swifts seem to go to Mozambique."

"Then you had quite a task on," said Zed. "Impossible, I would have thought."

"That's what Prinz said."

"And I can see why—but how did he get to know you were there? Did you go to Lourenço and introduce yourself?"

"I went to Lourenço to see if anybody could point me in the right direction for the nesting grounds. His lap dogs, Randall and Withers, must have been looking for me." Now Simeon had to be careful. He could not tell them about the little mayhem he had made at the Academy of Natural Sciences without appearing to show an alignment to them. "I don't know why they should have been so close to the natural history museum, though."

Zed shifted himself from the straight chair to the bed to ease thin shanks. "Maybe we do."

Simeon looked from one dark face to another. Icarus was watching Zed. "Do we?" he asked.

"It's a theory. A possible explanation."

"Then give it."

"Hang loose. Let's put a little meat on it first. If I understand you rightly, when you tag, you put your name and address on the bird."

"Right."

"And the idea is that whoever finds the bird notifies you by letter."

"By letter, sure. I can't imagine them telephoning."

"Was there any mail here when you got back from Africa?"

"Nothing."

"Which is strange," put in Icarus excitedly, "because when we came by to check if you were home yet, the mailman was coming away from your door."

"Furthermore"—Adam Zed came to the rescue of his theory— "while we hung around on the cliff top to see if you would show, friend Randall paid you a call and went away quite satisfied, apparently, with what he had found. In short, they had a good idea where they could find you because they knew why you were there."

"But Prinz didn't believe me when I told him."

"He said it was a cover story."

"Yes, how did—?"

"Because it SOUNDS like a cover story, Simeon. The natural history museum was a chance they took and struck lucky."

"So—" Simeon hesitated. He was on the verge of mentioning the latest letter, but if he did that, he could forget about getaways. On the other hand, if there had been another letter, what was this one?

"I—" He shook his head helplessly. "I was going to run out on the whole thing . . . Believe me, I saw what you would have wanted me to see. Randall and Withers treated me to an auto on the way to the airport—just to burn it into my mind, so to speak. But I—just—can't see . . . how anybody can be right in this war."

"We never said we were right." Icarus stood up from the easy chair. "We said we were less wrong than they were. But if you want out, we won't stand in your way. Come, Zed."

"No . . . Wait a minute." Simeon threw caution to the winds. "I don't side with anybody—but I feel more at home with you two." He smiled wryly. Icarus and Zed regained their seats.

"I have had a letter today." He produced it and kept silent while Icarus read and then passed the sheet to Zed.

"Is this the out you had in mind?" asked Zed eventually.

"Tuscany, yes. What is it? Cinquegiardini?"

"H-m-m-m." Icarus played with his beard, curling a strand and leaving it wiry. "Well, you know where this came from—Prinz."

"Prinz?"

"And this Scarlatti is no Siena peasant, either," said Zed. "I've been trying to rumble him ever since I saw him here with Prinz. Cinquegiardini—huh—that's a nice irony."

"You're—talking beyond me," protested Simeon. "Is there something familiar about Rico Scarlatti?"

"Scarlatti and five gardens—at least, Garden Five. It was about a year ago in Tuscany. Scarlatti and Prinz ended up at each other's throats. A man was killed. I was wondering what they were doing back together."

"I still don't—"

"I'm not surprised," said Icarus. "Tell it straight, Adam, or let me."

"We only heard about it in scraps," said Zed. "It was a United Nations project—kind of rehabilitation—and it went wrong because this man, Shem, blundered into the experiment. He didn't mean to do any harm—in fact, he was trying his best to sort the people out—but Prinz got hold of him and put him on trial in Garden Five. Accused him of being responsible for most of the wrongs in the world. Called him the causal type. Scarlatti had to defend him."

"If Shem is dead, it can't have been much of a defence."

"Hear me out, Simeon. As a matter of fact, Scarlatti emerged as the hero of the piece. He threw Prinz into such a lather that the man panicked. That's when the guns started and Shem got his. No fault of Scarlatti's—some said Shem had himself killed deliberately. Others, that he did it because they were getting ready to shoot Scarlatti."

"Who? How did you hear?"

"Well, at the end of it, Scarlatti took off—running just like Shem had been when he wandered into the crazy complex. He even had Shem's sandals. It was quite a scene for anybody who lived through it. We heard it from a man called Willy the Blue. He was—sort of—our generation. There were others but they seemed to go their separate ways once they got out of the gardens. And he had a friend—Famous Gogan . . ."

"Gogan?" Simeon found himself shaking violently. "I know a Gogan. Are you saying he's—all right?"

"He's not dead, if that's what you mean. But we don't know where he is, either. Apparently, Willy never saw him after they all headed for the gate."

Simeon crossed to the cabinet and poured three stiffeners. There was an itch around his eyes. Then suddenly it was water on his face. Gogan.

"A year ago," he said.

"A little over now. About fourteen months."

"And for all you know, he could still be in this Garden Five?"

"Well, he could," said Icarus. "But why he should stay there when the rest trundled off, I don't know."

"Maybe I do." Simeon tested his drink and found it good.

Adam Zed sipped and pondered. "Are you saying you're going to Garden Five?"

"As sure as your life."

"I thought you wanted to be out. You know they have a trap set for you—and I can't even tell you what's on Scarlatti's mind unless he's just biding his time."

Simeon drank hearty. He was happy beyond measure. "Given the right reason, I stay in."

"And what's that?" Icarus toasted him solemnly.

"A long time ago, on a cliff top, in a different way, I tagged Gogan. Gogan is my swift."

Ready to face anything now was Scarlatti but more ready for some things than for others. Prinz in a poisonous mood would not have been as disconcerting as this Prinz, affable, pouring whisky, ladling ice, proffering glass.

The poison, it seemed, had been spent at the stockade, blackening Scarlatti's character. Perhaps he was pleased with the job he had done.

But . . .

"On reflection," he said, "I think yours was the wise move. Perhaps we will gain more by letting these brothers know the state of the game. Have you told Nelson as well? That would be necessary for equilibrium."

"I—" Scarlatti faltered. Prinz was bound to find out if he didn't know already. In any event, the signs were that he was going to turn the situation to some advantage. "I told him," said Scarlatti with determination. "I did it out of kindness and not to benefit some strategy of yours. I did it because I hate you, Prinz. I hate what you are doing and I intend to stop you."

The interrogator was unmoved. "The motive is unimportant. It does not alter the deed. You tell me nothing I don't know already. But to stop me you have to stay with me and while you stay with me you will be dominated because I am a stronger force than you. My capacity for evil outweighs your capacity for good."

"Are you admitting this Inquisition machine is evil?"

"All I admit is that I am involved not for the sake of Christendom but for the betterment of myself. It is not a reason the pope could sanction or even understand. Therefore it is evil. But I fulfil the demands he laid down and that is good. Light and dark are governed by the position of the sun. Did the Ojukwe brothers thank you?"

"They were pleased enough."

"You seem to have some kind of stain on the collar of your jacket."

Scarlatti reached for a handkerchief with as much aplomb as he could manage. "Some night bird."

"Really? It looks more like spittle."

Scarlatti finished wiping the denim. "All right . . . You led Sami to believe I was torturing his brother. He reacted in a way many brothers would."

"He—SPAT—at you? He didn't say 'Torture me instead'? Then maybe his faith doesn't have the same blamelessness as that of his brother. Maybe, indeed, they are better considered together so that the one can be a drain on the other. We'll try that."

Scarlatti's whisky lay untouched in his hand.

"Drink up," ordered Prinz. "We have an early start."

The lawman swilled tawny liquid round the glass. "On the brothers?"

"On Simeon."

"Then you'll be leaving some specific instructions."

"Not at all."

"So how do you count my move a wise one?"

"I said we might gain more by letting Nelson and Sami know the state of the game. We'll take them with us."

"WITH US! But . . ."

"I'll let them have a chat with Eugenio, thereby establishing our reason for being there. Then—and I'm quite sure His Holiness won't be watching every move—we'll continue to Tuscany."

"Why take them there?"

"They need a lesson in helplessness. There is no more capable teacher than Simeon. And you should make a fine example yourself."

Prinz was well pleased with all except Scarlatti's smile. He had thought the man would be diminished and demoralised and yet here he flourished.

"What's the matter with you?"

Scarlatti raised his glass. "Nothing. A man as wise as I am knows when to quit."

Prinz had wrought the unexpected—the forging of the links. Scarlatti would drink to that.

ALL ROADS LEAD TO...

Chat-chat went the voices in the Secretary-General's office and wing-wing went the microphone in the wall fitting, carrying their machinations to ears beyond.

For two days, Harold Messenger had been trying to get at Andrew Buthelezi for a definitive talk but had found his way blocked by appointments and procedures.

The S.G. had made himself scarce to do some thinking and only now was he ready for the request he knew Messenger was about to make.

"I'm pulling Prinz out," said Messenger. "Now that Joachim and Co. have passed back the news, I wouldn't give much for anybody's life in Lourenço and I owe Prinz that much."

He had expected Buthelezi's rapid confirmation, had even assumed it to the degree of speaking positively. The S.G.'s reaction surprised him. "I don't agree."

"But the man is in danger, surely."

"He is a representative of the United Nations. He only has to say that."

"And they only have to accept it. He's been acting as a torturer for Rome."

"Then in my opinion, he deserves what he gets."

"Andrew—?"

"I'm sorry, Harold. If there is any contention at all between us, it is over Prinz. You consider him to be your man. I can only think of him as the UN's man. Whatever he provides must be considered in that light, and frankly, the amount of liberty you give him displeases me."

"You have never said so."

"It has never mattered. He has never been—in my way—before."

"I don't understand."

"Well, you seem to have been so busy trying to sink the Vatican that you have overlooked the fact of our real interest in Zimbabwe. They have applied for membership. They have inferred a belief in our policies and purposes. But you are content to let them descend to wholesale persecution or whatever it is they now have lined up for the Catholics in their midst. Knowing what we know, we cannot allow such degeneration without making some effort to keep the peace. Prinz is so placed that he can lead that effort. Is there anything wrong with my reasoning?"

"Only that it seems to assume a certain lack of vision on the part of the natives—and you're the one who said there was more to them than meets the eye. Do you think they would be willing to accept Prinz in the role of mediator after what he has been doing there? And what has happened now isn't his personal fault. It was the pope who lied. I concede that a UN presence in Zimbabwe might be desirable. But I cannot feel that Prinz is the best person to provide that presence."

"Because he can no longer be regarded as a representative of this agency."

"Well, all right, Andrew—if that's what you want me to say."

"I considered you above petulance, Harold. The man is not a villain because I want him so; he stands convicted by his own actions—compromises and expediencies which you allowed. I am saying that I want to use him for an important UN task and you are telling me I cannot use him because of his reputation. It's your admission, not mine. Anyway, I want SOMEBODY there and I have always considered you an honourable man."

"Meaning that you want me there."

"Meaning I am surprised you haven't offered."

"I'm offering. Does that preserve my honour?"

"Thank you, Harold. I knew I had not underestimated you."

"Am I—allowed—to tell him I'm coming?"

"Why not? That would be normal procedure, would it not?"

Back in his own office, Messenger was still bristling with humiliation as he attempted to make the connection.

Then he had something else to think about. If the satellite lines had been busy, he would not have questioned it. He had been half expecting a two-hour delay. But for some reason—and the UN exchange could not explain it—telephoning out had become impossible.

Aldo Viazzanni was a devout Catholic. Sometimes, his enthusiasm ran away with him.

Rico Scarlatti came to Siena yearning for blindness. On all sides were matters familiar to him, structures he had written off, people he had saved.

In leaving, his one desire had been to stay. In returning, he wanted only escape. It was not just the nature of his mission. In a sense, he could believe that time had been in suspension for more than twelve months and here he was still in the same hands.

But the place itself had changed and he could no longer judge whether it was for better or worse. His commitments had been taken elsewhere. His very existence had been scrubbed from the Siena file. He was worse than a stranger. He knew where things were and when he got there, they weren't.

His old office overlooking the market square housed families. His old comrade, Cosimo Giotta, might well still be at police head-quarters but he could not bring himself to attempt a reunion. The man had not been entirely honest at their parting and even though his crime had been negligible, it would lie between them so that they could never achieve the closeness they had once had.

Scarlatti would be an embarrassment to Giotta and vice versa. Instead, Scarlatti was tied to a man he could not embarrass and there was no release until this situation was resolved one way or the other.

Randall and Withers had taken Scarlatti away; they brought him back. And Prinz, introducing the Ojukwe brothers to Eugenio, would meet the party at Garden Five.

If Simeon was moving according to Prinz's speculation, he must eventually arrive at the tourist information centre behind the Via della Campanile.

It was an area Scarlatti knew well for coffee shops, pizzerias, and ample facility for observing while not being observed. He had never seen Simeon but would have been willing to swear that he could recognise the man by vibration alone. That did not dissuade his attendants from sharing the scrutiny. Or from leaving a note detailing Scarlatti's name and location at the tourist bureau.

And Scarlatti, who had argued enough with Randall and Withers in that past which seemed telescoped into the present, now held his peace and drank his Chianti while they alternated between coffee and watery *birra nazionale* and waited for Simeon to pick up the message.

Simeon had found a flight direct to Florence and once there had discovered a coach that would run him through the night to Siena. He moved with the speed of urgency but that was just how it happens. His head was too full of contradictions for him to make a conscious effort at haste.

If he went fast, it was because he wanted to return fast. He expected to find nothing at Garden Five that would match or could touch what he had on his cliff-top perch with Julie. At the same time, the journey had assumed point with the knowledge that he might, at least, wipe out a debt he had carried for far too long—and one about which Julie had known and spoken.

If Gogan had been merely a fellow suitor for Julie's hand, Simeon would have dismissed him. As it was, in Playa Nine, Gogan had been the only suitor at that stage and Simeon had taken him out of the race for quite another reason . . . a seat on a rusty swing in a derelict playground overlooking the resort.

The swing had given Simeon the power of expression. At first he had considered it supernatural, then as opening some gate locked in childhood, then as a piece of worthless wood that he had burned for shared warmth on the night he had been wise enough to wed Julie.

But by that time, Gogan had been demolished. The conch which had been HIS power of speech, which had been doing for him no more nor less than the Thinking Seat had been doing for Simeon, had been blasted to fragments with a charge of calcium hydride placed by Simeon and detonated by sea water.

For a motive that was less than honourable because it was NOT Julie—just to keep Simeon unchallenged on his swing. And since that was a crutch that Simeon had thrown away, there now remained this dishonour, which should never have occurred. He wanted to make it up to Gogan because that was Julie's view and had become his own.

He could not be sure that Gogan did, indeed, stand at the end of this trail but the possibility was better than remote.

John Icarus and Adam Zed, travelling somewhere behind out of sight, and unsuspected by all but Simeon, had mentioned Scarlatti and said he seemed to be playing a game only too familiar to Simeon. That might have been an attraction, but not strong enough on its own.

Then there was Judge Woodman's parting wisdom at Green Town

—that next time (this time?), Simeon would be the prime mover, . . . the catalyst, the one who succeeded.

And Simeon went to face Prinz, the devil who had defiled the memorial bench with his attention to it. The man who had given him no chance to emerge as an opponent but had just wanted him out of the way—in much the same way that he had considered Gogan at the time.

The plains of Megiddo? It had been Julie's conviction that they would stand out in high relief, the good and the bad—and yet every time he examined the good, he found a fault, and every time he inspected the bad, he discovered a virtue.

Then again, if Satan had access to minds, could Simeon expect anything else?

Confusion was the currency of the Father of Lies. So Simeon could shrug off this fight on the argument that the issues were not clear—only to find that every contest would be the same while the Devil had the power to deceive.

In the flight to Florence, on the road to Siena, the thoughts had occupied him sleeping and waking and when he alighted upon the square with the first of the pigeons he was less certain of himself than when he had set out.

Though he regarded this as a personal mission, it was a comfort to know Zed and Icarus were backing him up. He expected no confrontation except his own but it might be interesting in the final analysis to see how the loyalties broke down.

Over coffee, rolls, and peach jam, before he headed for the tourist bureau, he realised he had spent less time than usual occupied with Julie. He hoped that the warm and golden memories which had cocooned him so well so far would not desert him when he needed them most.

"Julie," he said to the quiet morning before the Via della Campanile began its bustle, "I'm here for us and us alone. Let me not forget that."

The speech overheard by several, was understood by only one. Rico Scarlatti, bound for his vigil a few paces ahead of Randall and Withers, was pinned in mid-stride.

When he looked back, his escorts had gone to ground and Simeon, momentarily, was all his.

Harold Messenger had asked the Turtle Bay exchange to let him know as soon as the system was restored. In an hour, there had been no call.

"Our engineers seem to be having trouble locating the source," said the girl when he checked.

"Is it that obscure?"

"I wouldn't have thought so, Mr. Messenger. I don't know a great deal beyond the board but I do know that there are only certain things that can go wrong. Would you like me to buzz Mr. Viazzanni?"

Mr. Viazzanni. "Is he handling the repairs?"

"He and others."

A thought—maybe the obvious thought—came to Messenger. "No. I tell you what you do—you go outside the building and you call the telephone company direct. Give them my name. Tell them the situation. If they are in doubt, suggest they contact me—and they will find they can't get through."

"But what about our own . . . ?"

"I'll take my chance with the unions. I have important calls to make and delays mean deterioration in a vital situation."

"I understand, Mr. Messenger."

Like hell you do, thought Messenger, as he replaced his handpiece.

Aldo Viazzanni. A faithful employee for years. Until, maybe, a question that divided his faith. Of course, it was possible the breakdown was natural. All the same, it was timely. If a small check yielded nothing, there was no reason why news of it should go out of the building. In any event, communications had to be restored promptly for all sorts of arguments apart from his own.

What nagged was the link he could not help making in his mind. The telephones were off, he suspected, because somebody did not want calls going out.

Not until that somebody had gained a little headway himself. But how could he know what was going on—unless access had been made to Messenger's conversation with Buthelezi?

Well, the broken intercom wire had been a chance, perhaps, for Viazzanni to place a device. It had been fortunate but unforeseeable. If that was so, Viazzanni must have been seeking opportunities for quite a while. Was this the only intrusion?

And describing the chance as unpredictable brought him up short again—because it had been created by the Zimbabwe trio. Was that accidental? If Messenger's suspicion, as stated, was that Joachim and Co. had opened the way for Viazzanni, then he might as well put his brain to bed. It was ridiculous.

But . . . but . . . but . . . Unless! Unless Viazzanni knew the state the delegates were in when they went to the Secretary-General's office. Unless he knew what they had been told by their government.

And all that needed was another microphone in one of the guest suites—a far simpler installation.

Messenger's internal phone jabbered. "Two gentlemen from Bell Telephonics," said the switchboard girl.

"I'll meet them in the hall," he said quickly.

He was waiting when the elevator door slid wide. Before it could close, he had ushered them back in and digitised a three-floor drop to the accommodation section. He knocked and got no reply from the suite the Zimbabwe group were using. All out looking for a phone, he thought.

He opened the door and said quietly: "Somewhere in this room is a microphone. I don't want it removed, I just want details of location. I guess you can see why I don't ask my own staff to deal with this. One of them placed it."

One of the engineers, big and redheaded, made some tired comment about Watergate, but he let it go.

"When you've finished here," he added, "please come up to the Secretary-General's office."

"Is nowhere sacred?" asked the redhead.

Messenger left them to their work and took himself back to Buthelezi.

He stood in the centre of the S.G.'s office and spread his arms. "This place is bugged," he said. "Every word we say can be heard and I don't care who knows that we know."

Buthelezi was wide-eyed. "Harold, you're putting me on."

"No way. If I wasn't wary of setting off all our alarms again, I'd show you myself. As it is, it's taken care of. I have outside help."

"Outside help? What's the matter with our security people?"

"They can't fix telephones. Have you tried yours lately?"

"No."

"There's something wrong with them—although I expect them to go right at any minute."

"You have lost me yet again, Harold."

"Just remember that we are being heard and our words acted upon. At any time now, our anonymous listener will start covering his tracks."

"And is he really anonymous?"

"No. I suspect Aldo Viazzanni."

"Aldo? But he's been here for years. A loyal man."

"Loyal to his creed."

"His creed?'

"His creed is in Latin."

"Well, I'll . . ."

"Anyway, I have two experts on their way up here to examine his recent workmanship. They'll be here as soon as they've located the bug in the Zimbabwe delegation's quarters."

"There, too?"

"There and I don't know how many other places. I think we can get Aldo up here to tell us."

The desk set trilled. The switchboard girl. "We're working again, sir. Just as suddenly as we went off. I can't understand it."

"The power of prayer," said Messenger, and the girl rang off giggling.

The intercom buzzed. "Two gentlemen from Bell Telephonics," said the voice of the outer office.

"Straight in," said Messenger. The men entered and Messenger indicated the intercom's wall fitting. "Careful how you deal with that. It's rigged to set off all kinds of alerts."

The redhead was on his knees, using a screw driver like a bomb disposal expert. He had the casing off before Messenger could articulate the thought. "But it doesn't mind keeping open house," he said. "Do you want this removed?"

Messenger and Buthelezi bent to examine the foreign object.

"Italian," said the second engineer. "They're almost as good as the Japs used to be."

Messenger went back to the telephone. "I want Aldo Viazzanni up here," he said. "Tell him it's to do with the job he did two days ago."

Andrew Buthelezi felt distinctly out of breath. He heard Messenger's words and saw two strange men crawling around his office.

"You—were in the guest quarters," he said eventually. "What did you find?"

"There was a microphone, all right. In the telephone mouthpiece. Not exactly an unexpected place," said the redhead.

"Except when you're not expecting it," said Messenger. "I'm obliged to you gentlemen. If you would like to send in your accounts for special consultation, please spare us no expense."

The engineers quit the room well satisfied with the arrangement.

"They'll go straight and tell the world about it," said Buthelezi.

"Somebody already told the world about it. Where is Viazzanni?"

Back to the telephone. "He's not answering, sir," assured the exchange. "His bleep is haywire, too."

Buthelezi was at the window, his concern drawn to the antlike convergence of people on the plaza below. They were moving inward from the outer edges with indecent haste. Something to see. He called Messenger to share the view. "Maybe that's the reason."

As he spoke, the door sprang wide and a secretary entered. "Mr. Viazzanni, sir . . . He . . . He . . . JUMPED . . . from a seventeenth-storey window."

"Jumped?" Messenger had to be sure whether the fact indicated guilt or disposal.

"Jumped, sir. No one else was near him."

"Well, at least we can telephone for an ambulance," said Messenger.

"Seventeen storeys?" Buthelezi pursed his lips. "AFTER we call a priest, Harold. At least let's observe Aldo's priorities."

The door closed as the secretary retreated to the task.

Second admonition—and all right, Viazzanni was done listening. But Messenger was annoyed. He was even more annoyed when he had finished his call to the number Prinz had given him in Lourenço Marques.

Prinz, it seemed, was also gone. And he had taken two native prisoners with him. Gone to Rome.

That much he had to report to Buthelezi. "Now," he concluded, "where do I go? To Lourenço? Or after Prinz? I do know where Prinz is."

"You also know where Lourenço is."

"If Prinz has gone, perhaps the whole Inquisition machinery has moved on. I ought to find out—from HIM."

"So change planes in Rome. But I'm telling you—I don't want Prinz on my payroll after this business. And if his actions lead us to even worse consequences, Harold, I am afraid you will be out of work, too. But before you do anything else, you see Joachim and his brothers. You tell them the situation—and you apologise for that damned microphone."

"I'll—see to it," said Messenger weakly. He wasn't used to turning on a spit. And Prinz would pay for that.

Rico Scarlatti in Siena with but an instant to make his move and weld his link. Now what staccato term would say it all?

"I'm Scarlatti," he said. "I'm with Prinz."

"Or against him?" asked Simeon quickly. The lawman had been expecting bewilderment, a sudden show of panic.

"I'm out to get him." And how much longer before Randall and Withers surrendered their cover.

"Are you alone?" asked Simeon.

"No."

"I don't see anybody."

"If you did, you would recognise them."

"Ah, yes." Simeon was looking beyond Scarlatti. Randall and Withers had obviously decided not to let the conversation run for too long unchecked. "Mr. Withers and Mr. Randall. What a small world this is and how it keeps turning. And that means, I suppose, the letter about my swift was a complete fabrication. I thought Mr. Scarlatti here looked a little too intelligent to produce an illiterate message like that. Now I see that he is precisely intelligent enough to enjoy the company he keeps."

"It wasn't absolutely untrue." Scarlatti was bothered that Simeon could be so convincing. Perhaps it was what he really believed. "There was a genuine letter from Siena which these two men intercepted. Prinz figured it for a chance too good to miss."

"A chance to what? To see whether I was really concerned for the bird? Well, I'm here. Have I proved my case? Can I go now?"

Frank Randall had stationed himself behind Simeon. Ronald Withers was looking decidedly tense. Simeon regarded the cordon with distaste. "So in the end it comes to the same thing. Prinz wants to work me over again. Tell me, what's the matter with all these Zimbabwe guerrillas? Aren't they giving him his money's worth?"

"He has a PERSONAL interest in you," said Randall.

"He envies you your spirituality," supplied Scarlatti. "Guerrilla motives are very superficial. He prefers some deeper wellspring to tap."

"But why Cinquegiardini?"

"It made a certain kind of sense to him," said Scarlatti.

"And you?"

The lawman wasn't sure of the full weight of the question. Was it supposed to be a hint of some knowledge of the link between him and Garden Five? How could Simeon know about that? More likely he was just confirming that Prinz's thoughts were Scarlatti's thoughts.

"Well, I knew the area," said Scarlatti carefully. "I had some experience of it."

"You had some part in choosing it?"

"I didn't sign the letter."

"But your name was on it," put in Withers as a safeguard.

"I have an Italian name. Prinz was being humourous."

"I'm not concerned with the ins and outs of it," said Simeon. "All I want to know is what you intend to do with me. The day is young. Can we get where we are going today?"

He had more enthusiasm for the journey than Scarlatti could muster and that proved one thing—Prinz's assessment of Simeon's broken condition was way off the beam. The fact that Prinz could be wrong about SOMEthing heartened Scarlatti and made him that much readier for Garden Five.

Simeon, for his part, was anxious to make some progress or at least to change his surroundings. The Italian might have been in the company of Randall and Withers for so long that he found it hard to conceive of shaking them off. The only way was to get right into the middle of the scenario so that Prinz thought the bait was safely enclosed. Only then might Simeon and Scarlatti be afforded the chance to talk freely; when Prinz's will seemed inevitable.

At first contact, he was not overly impressed with the Italian. According to the Icarus-Zed story, Shem had not been, either.

Perhaps Scarlatti was a slow burner. If anybody in the world could sympathise with slow burners, it was Simeon.

"Cinquegiardini," said Simeon, as Randall took the car onto the road south in an uncanny re-enactment of that earlier journey. Scarlatti travelled as front passenger and Simeon occupied the back with Withers. "That's Five Gardens, isn't it?"

"Right." Withers was producing his cigarette case. Scarlatti had not seen it since the last drive south and the fact did little to calm him.

"And are there?"

"What?"

"Five gardens."

"There were," supplied Withers. "We are only concerned with the fifth."

"What happened to the other four?"

"They were destroyed," said Scarlatti. "They were being used for a UN people/environment experiment that went awry."

"Who destroyed them? The people or the environment?"

"That's too many questions," said Randall.

"It doesn't matter," said Withers. "Let him hear it all. A man was killed because he disrupted a very fine and peaceable mode of living."

"Shem," said Simeon.

Scarlatti started. "You—KNOW—about Shem?"

The others were also shifting uneasily. They had been told Simeon would be perplexed by fast movement. But already he seemed to be ahead of them.

"I heard about it. I had some friends who were involved."

"You DID?" Scarlatti didn't bother to hide his eagerness. "Who were they?"

"Just people. Who bothers to ask names? We shared a bottle."

"Young or old?"

"I would say young."

"Willy the Blue? Famous Gogan?"

"You could name them and I wouldn't know." But now Simeon was worried. Did Scarlatti know for a fact that Gogan was elsewhere? And if so, was this trip to Garden Five no more than a lethal waste of time?

"I never knew what became of them," said Scarlatti, and it was good to speak openly of those days. "When I ran clear of the gardens, I heard feet behind for hours, even days, but they trailed off to the last one. They all found somewhere to go. I was the only one who elected Rome."

"And nobody was left there—"

"The place is empty," broke in Randall. "Just us, Prinz, and a couple of Bible-punchers he brought along for the laugh."

"Bible-punchers?" Simeon's surprise was genuine, but it wasn't an unpleasant surprise—in fact, they might be a better find than Famous Gogan. Immediately, his mind filed a correction. Gogan was important for a particular reason. They might have value for other reasons. He should not judge one idea above another—and he still had a debt to Gogan.

"I told you Prinz was interested in spirituality," said Scarlatti. "They are part of that."

"Prinz is also working for the Vatican. Are they part of that, too? Are they the antichrist?"

"You bet," said Randall.

"Because Prinz told me the guerrillas were that."

"These are spiritual guerrillas," said Scarlatti, with his tongue in his cheek.

"Ah . . . Then the purge of the insurgents has taken a new turn. I take your meaning of spirituality."

"I think Scarlatti has said too much," put in Randall. "I think he's talking out of turn."

"No matter," said Withers. "Who is hearing him? Only us. He knows we'll relay the conversation to Prinz. I don't guess he is saying anything untoward."

Simeon said: "Do I sense some kind of division here?"

"Come on, Simeon." Randall talked without taking his eyes off the road. "If you heard about the Garden Five incident, you must know where Scarlatti fitted in. You must also know that for him to occupy his present position requires a certain amount of credulity from us. We have driven this way before, with him in much the same predicament that you are in yourself. The situation last time was unresolved. This time, there are no mistakes and no misjudgements and only one possible result."

The cool dismissal angered Scarlatti, the ready belief that he was impotent and incapable of preventing a hazard.

"Last time was NOT unresolved," he said. "Prinz was lucky to escape with his life. If he had been dealing with people as ruthless as he is, he would not have survived at all."

"But survive he does," said Withers, "and survive he will as long as you look on killing as immoral. Are you saying you want to finish him?"

"There are worse things than death," said Scarlatti. "And some of them a lot more just than unjust."

"Whatever you have to offer"—Withers folded back his jacket, showed Scarlatti the handgun in its armpit holster—"you can offer it from alongside Simeon and Nelson and Sami Ojukwe. Mr. Prinz is happy to give you what you want."

"And I'm happy to accept," said Scarlatti.

But he didn't sound very happy and Simeon was glad Zed and Icarus knew their way to Garden Five. For another reason, too. He did not know how long it would be before anybody else remembered that he hadn't shared a bottle with anybody but Tomorrow Julie since before Shem's piece of history.

When Harold Messenger paged the glasshouse, Sandy Joachim was revealed but his compatriots, Díaz and Da Gama, were away on errands, he said.

"I'll come to your suite," said Messenger. "There is something I want to show you and something I want to say. I'll be with you momentarily."

Joachim met him at the door of the suite with an empty glass. Messenger took it with grace and consulted the decanter. When he had taken a generous shot, he grounded the glass on an occasional table and made for the telephone. He unscrewed the mouthpiece and called Joachim to observe.

"Microphone," he said. "Placed by one of our engineers—NOT on my instructions. It seems he took his orders from the Vatican."

"I see it," said Joachim, and there he had the advantage because Messenger was lost in a maze of wires and connections. "One of the new Italian type."

Messenger confessed. "You're seeing what I'm not seeing," he said. "I wouldn't know it if it stood up and bit me."

"We were offered some," said Joachim. "It's surprising the propositions that come your way when people are trying to win your minds."

"Well, I'm sorry. It should not have happened—and I should say that isn't all the bad news we have."

"Your man Prinz has taken off," said Joachim. "It's all right, I know. He plays a devious game, that man, but he is likely to catch himself out one of these days. You thought we thought he was only in Lourenço for the Vatican."

"He was—but on loan from us. That is not to say we sanctioned everything that he did there. Certain matters have only lately come to our knowledge. Anyway, the vital thing is that he has two of your nationals with him in Rome."

"Bible-punchers."

"BIBLE-punchers?"

"Religious nuts. He's welcome to them."

"You mean you're not concerned for their safety?"

"Not at all. They're a force of disorder as far as we are concerned. They refuse to join the Zimbabwe Federation Party or any other party; they talk constantly of our government being overthrown by a heavenly government, they talk about the end of the world and—worst of all—they seem to single out the laziest, most impressionable of our people and take them away from the work that is vital to our continued existence. Time enough to think about God when we've got our country straight—"

"I'm sorry again. I really had no idea—"

"So if Prinz wanted to interrogate anybody, he couldn't have done us a better service."

"But they are your people."

"They would deny that—emphatically. They are what you would call a pain in the neck."

"Then I'm apologising for nothing—"

Joachim turned the telephone receiver in his hand. "I thought you were apologising for that."

"For the fact it is there, not for being the perpetrator."

"I understand—but if you are going to say we are violating basic human rights and a fundamental UN policy about freedom of worship by not caring about these—holy hostages—I would tell you politely to mind your own business. In the terms of your own constitution, what goes on inside our own country is our own affair. It is only when we cross borders that we have to worry about rights. You have to concede, Mr. Messenger, we in Zimbabwe are far more civilised than the first and second worlds would like to believe. We learned sophistication from the masters even if we were fighting them at the time. If the Portuguese taught us one thing, it was not to waste time on misplaced sentiment."

Perhaps Harold Messenger was weary of too many reproofs. Perhaps the instinct was nobler than that. But he found himself disliking Joachim's arrogance and wondering whether there was anything to choose among the sides and stands that had tilted and swung him so dizzyingly in the last few days. He even began to question his own outlook. He had been content enough up to now knowing that he was involved in doing the best that could be done in difficult circumstances. For years he had been moved by the idea of nations united. Now, suddenly, he had started to wonder whether the framework in which he operated was capable of carrying the idea. But these were thoughts too profound for the present exchange.

"That statute about people worshipping in their own way," he said. "That is not thwarted by borders."

"The trouble with these people," said Joachim, "and what takes them clear of the statute, is the fact that they try to force everyone else to worship their god in the same way. They are an apostasy."

"Or an antichrist?" The question was mischievous.

"That's what the Catholics call them. I suppose it isn't too far removed from our own view—huh, that's funny."

"But your quarrel with the Catholics isn't doctrinal."

"Hell, no. They double-crossed us—that's all. We don't feel any strong moral indignation that they should take these evangelists with them. They can bore each other to death with theological discussions."

"And what about this man who told you about the double-cross—this Simeon."

"I don't know. He came and went. My information is that two of Prinz's men took him off, and not too gently. Later, he was seen looking decidedly ill at one of the Inquisition's autos, and even later, boarding a plane for Britain with the same two men."

"But why did he tell you?"

"We never found out."

"Did you try?"

"He was no sooner there than he was gone. He may contact us again some time."

"So you know nothing about him."

"My brother-in-law at the Academy of Natural Sciences said he made an inquiry about migrating birds. Before he could be specific, he had been removed."

"And nobody knows where he came from and where he went."

"No . . . It's only a suggestion, but it would make sense to me to follow up Prinz. That way you might come across Simeon again."

"I intend to follow him. I intend to have quite a long talk with him but I have to move to Lourenço to—see the situation there."

"What situation?"

"Well, we want to try and make the Roman exodus a peaceful one. No bad feeling. No bloodshed."

"Look . . . We're good boys, Mr. Messenger. We stopped eating people a long time ago—it's a pretty impure meat, you know. We've no intention of harming these people. We just want them out. No, you just take off after Prinz and Scarlatti and these two huckleberry friends of theirs."

Scarlatti! Now, Scarlatti rang a bell. "Scarlatti?"

"He was some kind of assistant to Prinz though there were murmurings that their relationship was—strange."

"Strange—you mean bent?"

"No. Mysterious. More than it appeared. I don't know, Messenger —I only get it third or fourth-hand. Why don't you go after them? Believe me, there's no need for peacemakers in Lourenço."

Joachim still had the receiver in his hand. "Do you want this in or out?"

"Tear it out."

"And then lie on the floor?'

"What?" Messenger was slow taking the point and even slower to smile.

Joachim extracted the tiny unit with a surgeon's skill and placed it on the palm of his hand. "You talked in the past tense about the man who rigged this. Have you fired him?"

"He fired himself—straight out of a seventeenth-floor window."

"Civilisation." Joachim was back to condescension. "You certainly make suicide easy for yourselves. The highest things we have are treetops and by the time you've climbed up there, you've changed your mind . . . You know—I reckon you have a cheek suggesting you should go to Lourenço Marques to tell US not to shed blood . . ."

Messenger fled to the information bank.

Thus they came to Rome and although Sami wavered before the Byzantine magnificence of the papal demesnes, Nelson walked with sure step and head held high.

"Straight down the monster's throat," he told Sami in their native patois, which confounded Prinz. "Now let us see if we can choke it."

Prinz had given them fresh clothing, clean but ill-fitting, and had taught them the ways of the bathroom. Hygienic they were, by God's law, but some of the devices were confusing.

They had not seen Scarlatti since he had carried warmth between them in Lourenço and they did not mention him for fear of indicting him.

They wondered where he had gone but were not given time to dwell on it. Prinz had them at the Vatican, creased and laundered, within two hours of their arrival.

He learned that Eugenio was waiting to see them—but he was not expecting what he found in the pontiff's chambers.

Eugenio was standing with a crucifix thrust at arm's length before him. When the natives entered, he bowed his head and uttered a flood of Latin. Then, crossing himself, he was ready.

"They are—quite safe," said Prinz, at a loss.

"To you perhaps," countered the pope. "But you are no spiritual leader. These devils may leap into my mind."

"What?" Prinz was ready to scorn until he remembered his present company. The sight must be ridiculous enough to them without any additions from him. "I—I trust my safety is also embodied in your exhortation," he went on. "My hesitation was an absence of appreciation and not a lack of credibility. Now, truly, the antichrist comes within reach of the fountainhead. Forgive me, Your Holiness, for being so remiss. I shall remove them."

"Certainly not! And have them believe I do not have the power to face them? That would be playing right into the hands of their dark master. No—bring them closer. Let me look at them."

Prinz hustled the Ojukwe brothers forward, though they moved without reluctance.

"That cross will not protect you," said Nelson suddenly. "Or that Latin gobbledygook. Do you really think magic comes into it?"

Eugenio was not perturbed. "You cannot tell me anything. My faith is my stronghold and you do not even speak the language of that faith. You are no threat to me. The crucifix is a weapon of strength and not defence. Before this, your master cowers."

Prinz had been trying hard to find his own place in the context of the exchange, but it was too bizarre. Eugenio might talk of faith but Prinz thought he recognised hysteria. Was the man so fixed in his ideas that he saw these two as demons?

He watched the brothers for some indication of their own reactions. But Nelson was, if anything, the one in control of the situation and Sami seemed in much the same quandary as himself.

Nelson indicated the crucifix. "For a Roman, you know little enough about Roman traditions," he said. "In Jerusalem at the time of Christ, the occupying force used stakes for impalements and there is no record of crosspieces at all. The Greek Scriptures of your New Testament use the word '*stauros,*' which means stake. The horizontal spar is something your Holy Roman Empire picked up along the way —probably from the Druids—and sanctified the sacrament. That's why I say it won't help you. It lacks integrity."

"Lies," responded Eugenio. "Antichrist propaganda. Defiling the Cross would be a pretty obvious strategy. I hope, Prinz, you see the kind of abomination we are facing."

"Indeed," said Prinz, though he saw only two Africans, one with a measure of education. He continued more disturbed by Eugenio's reception than by the evil inherent in the men he had brought to the Vatican. Could ill-acquaintance with religion render him that insensitive to influences?

"You seem unconcerned," said Eugenio, "and I can't understand it. Is this the kind of enthusiasm you bring to the mission I assigned you?"

That at least sparked a positive response and Prinz was relieved. "There's nothing wrong with the way I do my job. I brought them to you because I thought you might be interested to see the face of your enemy. You indicated as much in advance."

"I KNOW the face of my enemy. I encouraged your presence because I must be always ready to stand before that enemy. But it is in my power to destroy them—and that is what I want done."

"Without trial?"

"I have tried them."

"You have barely spoken to them."

"It needs very little dialogue to reveal their convictions. They are prepared to do it from the outset. You heard for yourself—"

"The one man has not spoken. Have you also tried Sami Ojukwe?"

"He is here. That is the first evidence against him."

Mention of his name jerked Sami from the objective state which the rapid exchange in a foreign tongue had forced upon him. He knew what evidence meant and if there was any doubt that his degree of guilt was as great as that of his brother, he wanted it out of the way. "I will give you more," he said. "I will give you plenty. I identify you as that great harlot of the Book of Revelation, the one known also as Babylon, the one that has been misleading the nations since primitive times.

"Your ancestors built a vile tower on the plains of Shinar, they peopled Sodom and Gomorrah, they killed Christ, they fed the people darkness for twenty centuries . . . and you haven't changed. Will that guarantee me the same fate as my brother? Because I can give you more—"

Eugenio had withdrawn the crucifix until it was pressed to his chest. "Enter me not. *Nomine patris, filii et spiritus sanctis* . . ."

"And do you want me to say something about the Trinity?" Sami hammered on. "About the triads and pantheons of the lands you conquered with sword and Cross; about the compromise that prompted the Decree of Nicaea . . ."

"ENOUGH!" It was Nelson who called the restraint. "When they will not concede the few things, they will not heed the many. We have done enough to earn our deaths. Leave it there."

And Sami subsided.

Prinz waited for the pope to begin some kind of answer. Of the four men in the room, Prinz was probably now the calmest. In fact, he was even enjoying his position as an observer to a struggle in realms beyond his means. And he retained his good nature, he knew, because of his superficiality.

But Eugenio's next words were for him. "You see, I hope, why these men must die."

"I see why you want them killed."

"And as soon as possible."

"Then . . ." The gravity of the task was lost on Prinz because his mind was moving already in other directions. He had been short of an official reason for going to Garden Five although he would have arrived there, nevertheless, with Eugenio thinking he was on his way back to Zimbabwe. Why not now tell the pope some of his plans and stay out of trouble? There was always the danger that the one extra lie was the one that caught you out.

"As a matter of fact," he said, "I have United Nations business of a similar nature in Tuscany. There is no reason at all why I should not—kill THREE birds with one stone. The virtue in that is that these men will be separated from the sympathy of fellow believers. They will die a lonely death, unable to communicate their—disease —to any others."

"Splendid." Eugenio had made a spectacular recovery. "Forgive me if I was a little short with you earlier. I am only a man and sometimes supernatural pressures weigh heavily."

"I can understand that," said Prinz.

He was heading north with Eugenio's blessing before the pontiff emerged, pale and shaken, from a telephone conversation with the Zimbabwe Foreign Office.

The federation, suddenly hostile to the Vatican's presence in their midst, had taken decisive and bloody steps. Furthermore, they had opened the doors on the prisoners of the Inquisition and freed the antichrist across the face of the earth.

Pope Eugenio could not believe that Prinz had had no foreknowledge of that. It made sense of too many of his actions. End of blessing.

John Icarus and Adam Zed had seen Simeon safely on his way and had elected to stay a day behind. It was an election made not so much by strategy as by circumstance. If they had wanted to travel contemporaneously but unconnectedly, they would have had to use a different medium. If they had wanted an exact parallel, the services were but once a day.

Trains and boats would have put them a day behind, anyway, and the question became academic.

As it turned out, they were grateful they had remained static for the extra hours. Otherwise, they could well have missed the news broadcast which contained this item:

"More than a dozen Roman Catholic missionaries and fieldworkers are reported to have been killed in a new outbreak of violence in the newly formed Federation of Zimbabwe.

"Observers recall similar atrocities carried out by guerrilla movements in the days before independence was granted by Portugal to the former colonies which now make up Zimbabwe but can see no apparent reason for the renewed terror.

"Up to this time, the Church and the new government of Zimbabwe have seemingly been working in collaboration to restrict the activities of dissidents within the federation.

"A Vatican spokesman would neither confirm nor deny that there had been a breakdown in this mutual arrangement. The Zimbabwe Foreign Office said a statement was being prepared . . ."

"Wow!" said Zed. "Does this mean the eclipse of Arthur Prinz? Stand by for our next bulletin . . ."

Icarus was not amused. "Or does it mean that Simeon is off on a wild swift chase? We need more information and we'll have to see if our mentors have it."

The approach to higher authority was elaborate—unnecessarily so, thought Icarus and Zed. It would have been handier, in their book, if they could have consulted with the nearest Protestant archbishop. Unfortunately, there was no power of delegation to that degree. The World Council of Churches had offices adjacent to the Carnegie Peace Palace, which housed the International Court of Justice at The Hague, and from there all blessings flowed.

Even so, there were local agencies—branches of USEFUL, a good-works co-ordinating group which parallelled Charitas in the Roman Church's functions. USEFUL was useful in that it also contained the initials U, S, and F. Put them together—as only a few intimates did—and you came up with the Unam Sanctam Fighters, presently responsible in total for the directions of men like Icarus and Zed.

If anybody had up-to-date information, they did. Icarus rang USEFUL.

But his brow was no less furrowed when he narrated the latest to Zed.

"Prinz got out all right," he said. "And Scarlatti. And two Mozambican evangelists. They flew to Rome."

"Then our plan is as was."

"That's what I thought. But USF aren't so sure. It seems there's a matter of policy involved."

"Policy?"

"They didn't explain. They just told me to hang fire and call them back this evening."

"Policy . . . Well, there aren't that many possibilities, surely. Are they losing interest in Simeon?"

"I don't know. They knew exactly what we were doing and they sanctioned the arrangements we made. As far as we are concerned, nothing has changed. Simeon, Scarlatti. Prinz . . . they're all en route for Garden Five. Now why the delay?"

The men fell silent, each busy with his own interpretation. Outside, a yellow November lay gentle upon the Hampshire woodlands.

Icarus saw the glory of it first and tried to work it into his equation. As a minor character in the drama about to unfold, perhaps he was not permitted the luxury of emotion. Nevertheless, he felt a distinct regret to be leaving this quiet place and plunging headlong into the mechanics of his calling. For the first time, he knew a little of what it had cost Simeon to make his move—and a little, too, about a love so great that it could render the cost payable. If anything happened to Simeon because he wasn't there . . .

"It seems to me"—Zed broke in on Icarus's thoughts and he was sorry with one breath, thankful with the next; he could not get too close to the subject if he was to do any good—"it seems to me that the only change in the situation is those two envangelists. What are they—Rome's or ours?"

"USEFUL didn't say."

"Not so useful. But do you think that could be the holdup?"

"Depends whether they are travelling under duress—like, as Prinz's hostages—or whether they are Vatican staff members he was able to take with him."

"Black or white?"

"What?"

"Well—African or Caucasian?"

"I said Mozambican."

"And the word was evangelists?"

"Yes."

"Not missionaries?"

"No. Look—what are you trying to say, man?"

"Fringe religion. Are they our concern or not? That's the policy."

"Adam, it's speculation." Icarus had to admit, though, that the thought made a lot of sense. "But that would still be no reason to hold us back. We're on a rescue operation. So we rescue them as well —so what? Does that commit us to something?"

"Only if . . ."

"Only if what? For crying out loud, Adam—"

"If these—religionists—are as much against our church as they are against Eugenio's."

"Damn it all, saving a couple of extra lives isn't going to plunge us all into the fiery lake."

"Putting our own lives on the line to do that? Maybe USEFUL doesn't think they're worth it."

"I'll tell you, Adam—it bothers me considerably to think we are being prevented from keeping an eye on Simeon because of abstracts like that."

Zed joined Icarus at the window. "I'm just glad," he said, "that we have a man in Garden Five already."

When Rico Scarlatti had left these hanging gardens he had been running, in the style and in the presence of Shem. He had been sure of achieving great things—of adding one victory at least to the encounter that had cost Shem his life.

And now he returned in the manner that had prevailed before he had known Shem—as oppressed, as a victim of circumstances he did not understand, as a tool of Arthur Prinz. This time, he could not plead ignorance. This time, too, he had Simeon for company.

The rank and bitter realisation as he passed along the remembered white road brought tears to his eyes. He had advanced not one step —which meant that Shem's blood cried out from the ground.

"And now," he said, "I can try to be myself"—although he wasn't even sure that himself was any creature worthy of recognition.

"I know how you feel," said Simeon.

"What—being myself?"

"No. Just trying. People keep telling me I have a reputation but I can't believe it. If I did anything, it was—through Julie. And now she's gone . . ." Simeon's voice trailed off. There was a lump in his throat he could not swallow.

"So here we go," said Scarlatti. "Two failures for the price of one. Welcome to my world."

"Welcome to MINE."

The same wrought-iron gate which had lain open invitingly for running Shem still stood ajar. The Giambologna fountain was gone to make a bigger sweep of drive, and a path lay straight and true to Garden Five.

Scarlatti, rolling down the car window for a desperate smoke scent of laurel, breathed only petrol fumes and hot tarmac.

"And welcome to ours," said Ronald Withers.

At their left hand, the lake sparkled—the lake beside which Dayan and Rapoport had played their games of computer détente. A little way out, the steep and leafy island where Che had been imprisoned with his books of the knowledge of life and death—and where murder had come to him just when Shem had caused him to begin to see light.

That at least was unchanged. The befogged bower where Mitchell, Brennan, and Kortovsky had collected dew for their mythical moon journey was indistinguishable, overgrown with fruitage and bougain-villaea and free of shrouds. Garden Four, the setting for Willy the Blue and Famous Gogan and Lucia with their fellow bearers of bar-ren banners was anybody's guess.

Scarlatti had paid the complex little attention when he made his exit the year before and his followers had trodden heavy-footed across beds of rare flowers. And the man who knew all the gardens best—well, such was the state of Scarlatti's recollection that he ex-pected to find Shem's body still sprawled on the lawn like a broken doll.

But he was saved from that. The lawn before the house was as even as before and unoccupied. Except for a wooden bench with high back and squared-off arms.

Simeon saw it and knew it. And screamed.

Either Arthur Prinz had tied a knot in the software or the United Nations was excessively gentle in self-reproach. Whichever, Harold Messenger found in an hour of application that every reference to Rico Scarlatti led him to another reference.

From Scarlatti, he got: Try Garden Five, or Algol to effect; for Garden Five, he drew: Try United Nations Temperate Environmental Control Agency; for UNTECA, the response was: Try UN ancillary agencies; for Arthur Prinz, it was: Try Personnel.

No doubt he could have beaten down the machine's guard eventually and made it confess, but that would take time he did not have.

In the car to the airport, on the plane to Fiumicino, he gave the job to his memory.

Arthur Prinz had filed a report on the project's demise which laid the blame squarely at the upturned toes of a dissident called Shem, who had found his own way into the Tuscany gardens and proceeded to participate in the matrices there apparent. The result, said Prinz, was entirely to be expected. The worldly one had come like a wolf among sheep upon the garden people, who had only their genes to trouble them. He had imposed influence after influence to get them thoroughly bewildered.

Shem's presence alone would have been enough but he had not been content with that. His ultimate crime had been to bring the whole garden complex into disrepute—and in such an emotive way that the confusion had found its manifestation in bloodshed. Shem's blood, it was true—but when the objective of the scenario was no bloodshed, this incident had been sufficiently serious to derange and misdirect all the carefully cultured minds hitherto occupied with genial and worth-while matters.

Rico Scarlatti had been Prinz's idea when he could see things going awry—though how soon that was after the appearance of Shem, Prinz's account did not show . . . and Messenger couldn't help wondering whether it had been an afterthought at all, or whether Scarlatti had been up Prinz's sleeve as a very early precaution. So Scarlatti had become involved as a legal and democratic representative of the vagrant Shem. He had striven most conscientiously to show his client in a sympathetic light—only to be seized with the same irrationality that had struck other garden members.

It had been during a particularly intense piece of testimony that Shem had snapped, displaying the kind of madness Prinz had suspected from the beginning. He had launched himself at the tribunal. Scarlatti had tried to stop him and been beaten unconscious for his efforts. An attendant guard had tried to wing Shem in the leg to curtail his headlong flight, only to have the defendant stumble at that point and take the full charge in his chest.

The event had been so traumatic that the UNTECA subjects had quit the gardens in disarray and dispersed beyond the means of any immediate force to locate them.

In the circumstances—and because reports of the incident would have been likely to become more mythical with each telling—Prinz had wound up the project and presented himself for a full, frank, and meaningful explanation.

He had never been asked to elaborate on his report because there were other more pressing matters to hand.

Now, going over it in his mind, and allowing for faults of recollection, Messenger still had to admit that questions should have been asked at the time. Knowing Prinz, too, he had to suspect the purity of the account.

But here was Scarlatti involved in another Prinz venture, presumably under no pressure, and that looked like a commendation—or at least an indication that the Garden Five episode had not caused any lasting rift between them. Then again, was Scarlatti's intention so simple and straightforward? Or was there some kind of revenge motive operating?

Messenger was regrettably aware of being on the very outside of this thing and the sooner he got INSIDE it, the better.

He bade the cabbie who had brought him from Fiumicino to put him off at St. Peter's Square. He wasted little subtlety on the Vatican secretarial corps, and when he found Prinz and two Africans had been and gone, heading north, he was quickly away.

By the time he got to the piazza exit the Swiss Guards already had a message for him. Pope Eugenio would be pleased to give him an audience as a matter of urgency.

His reply paid little regard to protocol. His own business, he said, was the more urgent. He had come to see Prinz and was leaving now in pursuit of that ambition. He would be glad to wait on Eugenio when the present matter was concluded.

What he didn't add but what he was already considering was that the next audience should be on his home ground—and more in the nature of an *audienźia* . . .

Still, he needed the answers that only Prinz could give him before he began building that particular pyre.

North, the office staff had said, and north meant Tuscany. His assumption that it also meant Garden Five would have won him no plaudits as a visionary, as he was quick to announce to himself.

Prinz, for all his machinations, had very little fertile imagination. And maybe he was heading for the same place in the hope that the same thing would happen. But who was in Shem's role this time?

Could it be Simeon?

And why should Simeon be so determined to become a victim?

And why should he, Messenger, be so sure that this would be history faithfully repeated?

His conviction was that Prinz was up to his old game—but the result did not have to be uncontrollable.

A little has brought me a long way, Messenger reflected as he motored into Tuscany.

And more than Simeon, more than Scarlatti, more even than Prinz himself, one question dominated his curiosity.

In whose name?

Whom was Prinz citing as his authority? The Vatican? The UN?

Harold Messenger would have been surprised. And others were just finding out.

Before the car could come to a standstill, Simeon was out and running across the lawn, racing the shadows cast by encroaching cumulus.

Nobody spoke and nobody stopped him. Scarlatti, for his part, was trying to understand the meaning of the action. He saw Simeon reach the bench, pause before it in apparent disbelief, and then begin a rigorous manual inspection across its timber spars.

For Randall and Withers, there was no such mystery.

"Another triumph for Prinz's ingenuity." Withers was smiling broadly and even his hatchet-faced colleague was twitching his lips.

"What does that mean?" demanded Scarlatti.

"We brought him a little keepsake from his Hampshire cliff top. He put the bench there in memory of Tomorrow Julie," said Randall. "And we took it away."

"We thought he would feel more at home if he had something familiar close by," added Withers.

"You don't miss a trick, do you?" Scarlatti stepped out on to the lawn, ready to take a swing at anybody who got in his way. But me, he thought, I miss tricks all the time. I was a good lawman because I could solve other people's problems—it's so much easier than solving your own. I failed Shem and now I write off Simeon as not being what I expected. He's a casualty and his wound has nothing to do with Prinz. Prinz capitalises—he has no greater power than that.

By that time, he was at the bench and Simeon was seated in its centre, gripping its seat with the hands of death.

"The whoresons just told me," said Scarlatti. "Prinz must hate you as much as he hates me."

He had been afraid Simeon's reserve would be gone, that he would have liquefied.

But the man was hanging on, face twisted in anguish. For a full minute, it was as though he had not heard Scarlatti. He fought a lone battle with his feelings and then suddenly relaxed. "Well, they can't do worse than this," he said, "And I think I have the beating of it."

He loosened his grip on the wood and took to tracing its lines in the manner of a caress. "There's something . . ." he began.

Then Randall and Withers were at hand and Prinz was striding across the grass with the Ojukwe brothers.

"Sami and Nelson Ojukwe," said Scarlatti to anticipate any uncertainty. "Two more of Prinz's victims. They're evangelists from Zimbabwe. As far as I can tell, they belong to no particular church. Their faith is self-sufficient."

"Spiritual guerrillas," recalled Simeon. "Like you and me. So Prinz has had a go at them, too."

"Not very successfully. They have an assurance that transcends Prinz's particular currency."

Prinz caught the tail end of the comment. "Assurance," he said. "Blind obedience to a power they believe greater than themselves.

Well, I can be that power. And as for being spiritual—it seems we
got out just in time. Your black brothers took an axe to the rest of
the mission staff."

"What?" Scarlatti wondered why he felt like laughing. "You mean
THESE people?"

"What's the difference?

"Only that while we were there, those black brothers were letting
you take an axe to the evangelists. What happened?"

Prinz did not answer directly. He brought Sami and Nelson into
the compass of the inner group. "Scarlatti you know," he said. "This
man is Simeon. If you want to blame anybody for the bloodshed in
your country, blame him."

Simeon was surprised. "Why me?"

"Because you told them in Zimbabwe that the Vatican was double-
crossing them. That's what you were doing at the Academy of Natural Sciences and all this talk about swifts and all the rest of it was
boloney. You weren't there for Tomorrow Julie any more than I
was. Well"—Prinz kicked at the bench, scoring the stained surface
and showing blood-red wood beneath it—"you're HERE for her, all
right."

Simeon took a deep breath and let it out slowly. His face was
ashen and he looked ready to crumple. His hands were still working
on the timbers. The first spots of rain splashed between his fingers
and in seconds the rain had become torrential. Randall, Withers, and
Prinz herded Scarlatti and the Africans across the lawn. They
seemed ready to let Simeon stay where he was and Scarlatti made no
effort to stop with him. In that event, he reasoned, their captors
might well have insisted that Simeon go, too.

By the time they reached the steps to the villa the rain had
changed its angle of fall through ninety degrees. The flow now was
horizontal and visibility was all but gone.

"What about Simeon?" asked Withers.

"Let him get wet," said Prinz. "He's not leaving—not now."

He slung a gratuitous arm around Scarlatti's shoulders and pro-
pelled him up the steps. "I'm glad you've made up your mind at last,
although I knew from the outset that you were only waiting to pick
your moment. You wanted revenge, Rico, and you're not the type.
Revenge is my game."

At the villa door, Scarlatti shook himself free and turned. Garden Five was blotted out by the downpour.

"Don't count me out yet, Prinz," he said. "I'll die myself before I lose another client here."

Harold Messenger kept the needle below seventy as he moved up the knee of Italy. There was an urgency to cover the ground but the overriding need was to reach his destination.

So when the civil guard vehicle which had been creeping up behind him suddenly put its klaxon into strident action, he was happy he had not infringed any speed maximum. He slowed slightly, edged to his right, and made way for the authorities.

They came level, drew in front, and then flashed him to stop. While the driver kept the tail neatly in the path of his bonnet, the guard in the passenger seat trained a carbine on him and he decided quickly that two layers of automobile glass would not stop the charge. He obeyed the instruction.

The barrel of the gun stayed steady as he came to a standstill, as the guard driver stepped from the official vehicle and gestured Messenger into his own passenger seat, as the driver replaced him behind the wheel.

Only then did the man with the carbine drop the weapon out of sight and shift across to the civil guard vehicle controls.

Messenger asked the questions, but there was no word from his driver until both vehicles were heading back towards Rome.

"For what reason?" repeated Messenger.

"It seems, *signore,* that there was an appointment you failed to keep."

"I had to move on rather quickly. I tendered my apologies to His Holiness."

"My information is that this was not a matter that could reasonably be left in abeyance. I am sure you realise we are bound to accept our principal's assessment of the importance of that meeting."

Messenger sat back and chewed his lip. His treatment of Eugenio had been cavalier, in his own estimation, but should have been acceptable from the provisions he had made. Was Eugenio recalling him just for the hell of it? And if so, how many valuable hours was he going to need to work out his whim?

Certainly, Messenger could not be delayed for long. There was no telling how much time or how little Prinz needed for his intentions.

"I trust the pontiff understands that circumstances dictated a rapid change of plan and that it is not meant to imply any indifference to his wishes."

"I would not know anything about that, *signore*. We were merely asked to find your car and ensure your return. There is certainly no reason to believe that you should not be able to continue with your business in a little while. In fact, to that end, I am instructed to restore this vehicle to your control once the engagement at the Vatican has been kept."

It was a waste of time asking the man further. He had been fed only the barest essentials for pursuit and furnishing him with any more details, even those he might glean from the nature of the questions, was a threat to discretion.

Messenger turned his attention to Eugenio's motives in effecting such a rapid recall. General discussion on the UN-Vatican entente could have waited. It had to be something more immediate than that.

And the most immediate thing was Zimbabwe. Messenger thought he had moved pretty fast ahead of the Lourenço Marques storm but he could not outpace a telephone call. Did Eugenio already know the federation were sending his crew packing? And if he did, then what should he be seeking? While Zimbabwe stayed outside the UN, there was no jurisdiction which Messenger could impose. If some kind of protection were needed, surely it was more expedient to apply directly to the Security Council than to try and trace an official travelling alone on a long and busy Italian road.

But then perhaps that also had been done and this enforced interview was to point out to Messenger where his duty should be. And if he didn't fancy taking that pointer from Andrew Buthelezi, how much worse to have it come from Eugenio. All in all, Messenger was in a fine and fighting mood by the time the guards presented him at the portals of the Holy City.

Eugenio, however, was not. In fact, he appeared to have been weeping.

"My people in Zimbabwe have been wiped out," he said, in place of a greeting. "I hold you responsible."

Messenger was thunderstruck. "Your Holiness—I—I had no idea . . . I was given a guarantee by a Zimbabwe delegation in New York that mission staff would receive safe conduct. I can't understand why they should have told me that if—"

"Your understanding is of no concern to me. More than a dozen of my priests and workers butchered and those spinners of evil freed to go about their devilwork. That is my concern. That—and placing the blame."

"Forgive me, Pontiff, but I do not follow you."

"Your man. Prinz. I thought he was working for me but there was obviously a large part of his operation which was kept concealed. In the event, he outsmarted himself, enraged the people of Zimbabwe . . . and precipitated the slaughter of many of my missionary staff."

"I am sure there is some mistake. No member of the UN would deliberately trigger such a situation."

"Deliberately or not, he was here only hours ago with two of those —demons—from Zimbabwe and he said nothing—NOTHING— about it."

"Then he did not KNOW."

"I cannot believe that. It is his doing."

"Your Holiness—" Messenger's sympathy was draining. This was, after all, where the initial lie had been fathered. He did not see why the UN should now bear the papal burden. Nevertheless, he held his patience remembering that he had to get away.

"Your Holiness . . . I think I myself may be able to fill out little of what happened. But let me say straightaway that this is only an explanation and not an acceptance of any responsibility . . . In fact, it may turn out to be quite the opposite . . . If there has been violence in Zimbabwe, then events moved faster than any of us anticipated and in a way we did not expect. We knew your staff were to be removed from Lourenço Marques as *personae non grata* because Zimbabwe officials had discovered a certain—inconsistency of intent. You had told them that you would support their application for membership in the UN. You had told others, of course, that you were AGAINST their membership—even to the point of making it a provision of our present entente. Well, they somehow got wind of this and decided that NO Vatican face in Zimbabwe was better than TWO Vatican faces. That is the reason for their action. Why they should have preferred bloodshed to a diplomatic dismissal, I don't know."

"And how did they find out? Because Prinz told them."

"First things first, Pontiff. Are you admitting that that is the case? Because if you have been double-dealing, I'm afraid there is little you can call on us or anybody else to do."

"I admit nothing. My first loyalty—and my only loyalty in the final analysis—is to those who give the Church spiritual support. If I sometimes have to employ the methods that are used against me, then it is on the head of the creator of those methods and not on my head."

"Are we—talking about Prinz again?"

"No. Yes. We are talking about Satan and anybody who works on his behalf."

"But Prinz was working on your behalf."

"Until he turned Zimbabwe against us."

"He did not do that."

"How do you know?"

"Because I was given the name of the person who passed on the information and the name means nothing to me."

"What is that name?"

"It would not be prudent to tell you."

"I suspect it may not be possible to tell me—a desperate invention to save Arthur Prinz's precious skin. Well, there is holy blood on his hands and I will find him."

"Believe what you like. Do what you like. I am not giving you any names."

"I do not know what your urgent errand was in Tuscany but, take it from me, you will not travel alone. You may enjoy the privacy of your car, the privacy of your thoughts. But you cannot prevent my agents from following you."

Messenger needed time to think his way around that. "Is that why you called me back? So that I would lose any advantage of distance?"

"I called you back because I thought I might be treated to some honesty and some genuine concern for misfortune that has occurred solely because of the involvement of your representative in Vatican matters. Since I find no evidence of either quality forthcoming, I must make contingency plans."

"My concern, Eugenio, is for the people who were killed because they thought you were powerful enough to protect them. My honesty is for the people who might recognise it."

"Then it is over between us."

"And thank God for that."

"You—you talk of thanking God but He is not behind the schemes to undermine the Vatican's rulership. I have already named that one. Give your thanks to him—and now you are free to go and join your fellow workers of disorder."

"Thank YOU."

"I do not want your—" Eugenio began, but he could not survive the twinkle in Messenger's eye.

Messenger's car was waiting and when he had shaken off the shackles of suburban Rome, he put his foot down to the boards.

He had lost too much time already—and it might give the four men in the trailing car a little hardship.

In that respect, the ambition was not successful. Two-Pips could drive like the devil and a good road made a welcome change.

The water teemed from east to west and Simeon sat within, like a rock among rapids. There was no drowning in this torrent. For all its force, it carried air. He found he could breathe without difficulty, feel, see, even enjoy. And think.

Now that the pressure for meaning was off momentarily, he could examine this seat which had chilled him so.

There was no denying its familiarity, but identification could never be total. The name plate at the centre of the back rest had been removed. All evidence of its existence was present—the rectangle of lighter shade in the wood, screw holes at the four corners of it.

But why remove it? Was he to be denied even Julie's name? That was an elaboration Prinz could have skipped. No amount of woodwork could erase Julie's name, and the real shock had been to find the bench here, anyway. That surely was the Prinz touch.

But why no name?

Simeon, alone in the downpour with visibility gone, had tried recognition by touch. The excess of moisture had thwarted that.

And since he could not be sure this was his bench and therefore not sure that it was not, his mind had put up a theory which explained everything.

The name plate had been removed because it did not bear Julie's name. The bench was a fake.

He shouted it. "FAKE! FAKE! Prinz, I rumbled you."

It was more relief than strategy and he was glad the rainfall blanketed his sound. Nobody heard.

But somebody came. A figure, indistinct, as seen through thick glass, circling in towards the bench.

The glass thinned. The figure took on features.

"Gogan?" said Simeon with his stomach in a knot. "Is it you?"

Then Simeon had company on the bench and this sitter didn't bother him at all.

"I don't believe it," said Famous Gogan. "Man, that ID was too rapid."

"I was hoping," said Simeon. "That's the only miracle. How are you?"

It was a question that covered a lot of ground. He did not even know whether Gogan's thoughts were on reunion or revenge. He had not seen the poet from Playa Nine since he had filled the man's conch shell with calcium hydride, veiled by a thin layer of sand, and let him carry it off to the beach for a ritual cleansing.

The idea had been to wreck a desalination plant which had been poisoning the water and flattening the tides with an irresponsible run-off that heightened local sea salt content by 800 per cent.

Gogan, placing his shell near the water's edge so that the first of the new waves could wash it clean of the sand, had found that the advancing water brought him the opposite of exultation.

When moisture met calcium hydride, the result was explosive. Gogan's shell, his confidence, his very fabric had been shattered and spread to the four winds.

Complete demoralisation in a manner that Arthur Prinz would have admired. And Simeon's motive had been straight out of madness. He had done it to preserve his Thinking Seat—his rusting swing on the cliff top where Gogan had talked just once with Tomorrow Julie. And Simeon's jealousy had been for the swing and not for Julie.

Simeon had carried his sin for five years without knowing how to absolve it. When John Icarus and Adam Zed had mentioned Gogan in this garden context, all other hazards and machinations had gone by the board.

Simeon had called Gogan his swift and it was an analogy made in the certain knowledge that Julie would have agreed. When they had found the togetherness that had dispelled Simeon's need for a Thinking Seat, their shared discomfort had been over Gogan—Julie because she had encouraged Gogan's attention in order to draw Simeon's, Simeon because he had destroyed the man for a reason that was not honourable.

Time passed, distance grew. Now, in this unlikely setting, against all the odds, they were suddenly face to face—and Simeon did not know to what extent Gogan still suffered from his action.

"How are you?" he said.

"Better than I was." The reply laid a responsibility on Simeon for the condition. "I mean, better than I was BEFORE I met you."

Simeon was bewildered. "You can't be saying that what I did to you had a GOOD effect," he said. "For all these years, I've been wanting to ask you to—"

And when it came to the phrase, Simeon was hung up. "—forgive me," sounded less than masculine. It sounded more like—Julie? "To forgive me," he said. "What I did was bestial. You and I, so much alike that we had to watch each other's every move. And I blew up your life line."

Gogan had been bearded and beatnikian. There was little change in his appearance except that the world had veered towards that mode, in any event. But the hair had silver strands which Simeon could not remember and the lines were etched deep where they were not hidden by beard.

"Well, I won't say I didn't feel it," said Gogan. "And I won't say I wouldn't have killed you right up until—maybe a year ago, as recent as that. But something happened right here that gave me a deal more insight into the plight of invalids like us. Now, I can't consider anybody deserving of death."

"Shem," said Simeon. "I've heard a little about it. He sounds like somebody who would have done us both good. I wish I'd known him."

"I'm glad I knew him. Sure, he started off out of direction like most of us and in a way he never had a chance to get straight. But it was watching what the authorities did to him that put the rest of us right. How did you hear?"

"Some people I know—John Icarus and Adam Zed. Civil rights workers—"

"The names mean nothing to me. But then, I've been here for a year or more—"

"And Scarlatti."

"Yes, of course, I've seen Scarlatti. But I would have thought he could have told you everything you needed to know about Shem."

"He hasn't had the chance—and now we're both in the same boat."

"What do you mean?"

"We're prisoners."

"But that's no sweat, man. Why don't you make a break?"

"Why are YOU still here?"

"I—had reasons."

"I had reasons, too. You are one of them. I can't speak for Scarlatti but I think he's out to get Prinz one way or another and he won't leave until he's done that."

"Prisoners of conscience— Look, I don't know how long this rain is going to last. We ought to make some kind of plan. I have a pad they would never find."

"I don't want to go missing."

"But I thought we were going to talk. We may not get another chance. Look . . . come back and have a few words. You can always turn up again."

"If I'm not there, they may take it out on Scarlatti."

"Believe me, they'll do nothing without you. This is all for your benefit."

"How do you know that? We just got here."

"I knew you were coming."

"You mean you were—told?"

"Not in so many words. But I knew this place wouldn't be left alone forever. Scarlatti survived that last episode and so did Prinz. There had to be a score-breaker. It's why I stayed."

Something of the mission went out of Simeon. He had pictured Gogan disabled, incapable of moving out of the garden because he, Simeon, had robbed the man of direction. Now Gogan was making it clear he had well-thought-out reasons for staying.

"But—I don't understand the attraction for you. You said you had found no man deserving of death. What are you waiting to see?"

"Just—developments." Gogan was brusque. "Now are you coming with me or are you going to wait for them to bring you a towel?"

The downpour was diminishing. The grey outline of the house was making a solid imprint beyond the wall of rain, now righting itself through ninety degrees of an arc.

"They'll think I've gone for good."

"You can't get out of here without their knowledge. The most they will do is search. You want to be caught eventually, fine—but first let's have a little meaningful discussion, huh? It's been a long time."

So they went—back across the squelching sward like oversized rabbits. Gogan slowed them both down before a Buontalenti cascade, presently in full spate. He indicated a recess beyond the water stairway and they plunged through the fall without a second thought. It would have been difficult to be more wet, anyway.

Gogan put his weight to a sandstone block and the section of wall swung on a pivot, exposing a chamber beyond.

"You'll see more inside," said Gogan. "It used to be quite a place for a tryst and it serves me well now."

Talk of romance and still no mention of Julie. For Simeon, that made something not quite right.

Andrew Buthelezi was troubled. The Food and Agriculture Organisation had been keeping a casual monitor on Harold Messenger in Rome and now the text of their report was that he had not returned to Fiumicino to continue his flight to Lourenço Marques. This meant only one thing to Buthelezi—Messenger was off in pursuit of Prinz. Despite his job, despite the S.G.s express wishes.

Lourenço was uncovered. Somehow, Buthelezi had to make his own reparations—and the first necessity was to try and catch Joachim, Díaz, and Da Gama before they headed for home.

There, fortune was on his side. The three of them were reached at their suite. They came to his office without protest or delay. Phrasing his approach was another matter.

"I'm . . . glad I caught you before you left," he said, already missing Messenger's easy presence. "Your stay was—eventful. I guess you have seen the best and the worst of us—"

Joachim took him off the hook. "As a matter of fact, it is a sojourn we have enjoyed immensely—much more so than if it had been formal. We HAVE seen the best and worst of the UN and perhaps most intending members don't have that privilege—not in such a short space of time. But we have seen how you dealt with matters which concerned us and how you put our feelings first. It was all . . . rather endearing, if you will excuse the term. I would have liked to thank Mr. Messenger but I take it he has left."

"Left?"

"For Rome. We had a talk a little while ago. He was anxious to locate your man Prinz but a little perturbed at having to go to Lourenço Marques. I told him there was no need for peacemakers in Lourenço. Frankly, I was a little rude because I was irritated that he should think there was such a need.

"After that man who jumped out of the window, I said, I reckoned the UN had a cheek telling us not to shed blood . . . I—I wanted to apologise for that. My true feelings are as I have outlined them to you."

"At all costs, you managed to convince him that Lourenço wasn't important," said Buthelezi. "He's disappeared—presumably on the trail of Prinz."

"In Rome?

"To begin with. And then, wherever Prinz went."

"We can pick up the trail," said Matthew Díaz. "We have our interests in Mr. Prinz."

That jolted Buthelezi. "For what reason? I thought once he was out of your country, he was out of your minds."

"He has committed crimes."

"What crimes?"

"He has abducted two nationals."

"Messenger told me that. He also told me you didn't much care about them because they were—the apostasy."

"That was my comment," put in Joachim. "I'm afraid my chief of security had to remind me that whatever these people were, they were our subjects. I sometimes forget we live in a glasshouse. If it were to be discovered that we rated one of our people any less than another, I am afraid anarchy would not be far away."

What would Messenger have made of that? It was a *volte-face* made convincing with good argument.

"So you have shifted Prinz from servant of Zimbabwe to criminal."

Díaz let his breath out in a whistle. "When is a white man ever

OUR servant? We trusted the white Vatican and this is the result. Prinz was laughing at our folly the whole time he was there."

"Then . . ." From vague promptings in his own subconscious, Buthelezi was beginning to perceive a light. "Then Prinz's real crime is that he is white."

"Brother," said Da Gama, "it seems to me you have been away from the veldt for too long. You make that sound like a criticism of our thinking and yet you know it is no different from the way in which the whites consider us. Prinz's crime is NOT that he is white, but that he has dared to sully blacks."

Buthelezi pushed his chair back angrily and rounded his desk. "Hypocrisy and double-talk are wrong in any colour. When you thought Prinz was doing you a bit of good, you didn't care how many of your—subjects—he took out of circulation. Now it seems that there might be a little national pride involved, he suddenly emerges as a scapegoat. Believe me, it was for reasons just like this that I LEFT the veldt. I DON'T accept that these two poor evangelisers have become important to you. I say that you are just out to get Prinz. And I ask—what else is there that you have not told me?"

Joachim stood up and held Buthelezi's gaze unflinchingly. "In case you should think we have only the words and not the stomach to hold our own in this world, which is more of a jungle than any you will find in our continent, when I told Messenger there was no need for peacemakers, I neglected to add that it was too late for such refinements. We have made our own peace. Only Prinz prevents our solution from being 100 per cent effective."

Buthelezi felt sick. For so many years, he had worked at the ideal of man unified, of one heart beating at the centre of a world free from pain, hunger, disease. If giving was all it took to establish peace on earth, then the UN had the answer, he had thought. The oneness would come from shared gratitude.

But it really wasn't that simple—because people were not prepared to show gratitude, let alone share it. The goal was too optimistic. And his faith in the goal had kept him remote from the reality which now faced him, eyeball to eyeball.

Zimbabwe had been wronged—by one of the powers that should have set her right. Zimbabwe wanted revenge and it would require a superior reasoning to convince her that she did not have justice on her side.

"I could ask you to leave Prinz alone," said Buthelezi. "But you would argue that I was making the plea out of loyalty to an employee. I could tell you it was in the interests of world peace, but you would only say, 'What difference does the life of one amoral man make? And surely, is not such a man as much of a danger to the UN as he is an affront to Zimbabwe?' To that, I could only agree—and add that so long as the dedication of my organisation is to saving lives, I would plead for ANY man's life."

Joachim took his eyes away. For some reason, he found sincerity the most difficult to face. "But mostly for Messenger's life," he said, to infer an ulterior motive even if there was not one. "Don't worry. I will give you a guarantee that we will leave Messenger alone."

"I didn't—" Buthelezi recovered quickly. He had paid the price for letting his feelings show but that would not happen again—not with these people. "If that is anything like the guarantee you gave Messenger about the Vatican staff then I feel considerably less than reassured."

"Well, I don't know what else I can say."

"Nothing, Joachim. Your words mean nothing."

"Then how can I convince you with my actions?"

Buthelezi was back at his desk, checking papers and consigning them to files. "I take it you are going home via Rome."

"That's—true," said Díaz.

"And that while in Rome, you will take steps to locate Prinz."

"Also true."

"Then I will go with you—wherever you go."

"For Prinz?" asked Joachim.

"For Messenger, for Scarlatti, for Simeon, for the evangelists, for everybody we find at the end of the trail."

"I warn you it will make no difference to the result," said Joachim.

"We'll see," said Andrew Buthelezi. "We'll see . . ."

A fire burned well, providing warmth and illumination. Fat rustled in a pan and a bacon aroma reminded Simeon that he had not eaten.

"Cosy," he said. "I had no idea cave-living could be so sumptuous."

"I tell you, man, those romantics had the right idea," said Gogan. "Now this is me precisely."

"Romantics?"

"*Giardini segreti.* Don't you know NOTHING? Made for lovers. Are you still celibate?"

Simeon could not answer. Was Gogan harking back to his days of Thinking Seat impotence? Or—

"Did you ever make it with that Tomorrow Julie?" Gogan persisted.

Then he didn't know about— The question was tasteless in Simeon's circumstances, but perhaps not in Gogan's. At least now Simeon could speak.

"I married her," he said.

"Grief, I'm sorry. I didn't mean . . ."

"It's all right. You didn't know. Maybe if I'd shown that much sense sooner, I wouldn't have . . . well, done what I did to you . . . Yes, we had five good years. Julie died a couple of months ago."

"Sweet lord, Simeon, I . . . I'm demolished."

"That bench out there on the lawn. They want me to believe it's the memorial I had placed on the cliff top in England where she died. They know I have an attachment to it. But I think they're fooling."

"Fooling?" Famous Gogan looked bewildered. He addressed himself to the pan, scooped the contents on to two platters and brought them to Simeon. He gave one, kept one, sat down beside Simeon.

"I'm moving ahead too fast," said Simeon. "You see, I don't think that IS the bench. There's no name plate on it—just the mark where any inscription might have been. That's their way of breaking me down. It worked right up until the time they left me alone. Then I began to feel . . . differences. They won't catch me that way again."

But Gogan was remote. "Julie dead, Simeon, I didn't do it, I swear."

The concern was bizarre and it took Simeon aback. On the bench, in the rain, Gogan had seemed refreshingly normal and unscarred and yet here he was, exercising a clear persecution mania. Yet if a man were to be irrational all the time, what would irrational be?

"Of course not," said Simeon. "We never saw you for those five years although we talked about you and wondered what had become

of you. It was an honourable marriage, Gogan. Julie taught me how
to live my life. I suppose I taught her things, too. You probably remember her as . . . unfulfilled. Well, we fulfilled each other. And
then we found she had stomach cancer—and for fifteen months she
taught me how to live with her death . . . If somebody had been
planning my destruction, they couldn't have done the job better."

"Do you believe that?"

"Believe what?"

"That somebody could plan to destroy you. I don't mean by assas-
sination—I mean . . . supernaturally."

"Somebody like the Devil?"

"It's not so hard to swallow, man."

"Not at all—in fact, I find it far easier to take in now than I would
have have done five years ago. But I wouldn't have thought YOU
would entertain such notions."

"Entertain them, I can't get RID of them. They're my curse."

"Julie used to think that. She could see an active force for evil in
the world. When I was with her, it was clear to me, too."

"And without her?"

"That's MY curse. I don't know. I mean, I DO know—I just
haven't got used to the idea of them being my convictions and not
hers. Julie could put it all into black and white. I see too many
shades of grey. Like this business. I've got two civil rights workers
telling me to take note of what the Catholic church is doing in Zimbabwe because what the Vatican calls the antichrist is actually the
proper Christian attitude. Then I've got the representatives of Rome
telling me that what they are doing is right because these spiritual
guerrillas they are persecuting are the ones leading the world astray.
On top of that, I have the kind of forceful argument that is being
used against me, which I feel is wrong but which Prinz says is right,
because it is important that I should understand and keep out. Now
I have just learned that the Zimbabwe authorities have killed off the
Vatican representatives in their midst—and I have seen no malice in
two of these so-called terrorists. And somehow, because I promised
Julie, I have to decide which of them is right, or if any of them is
right, or if I am capable of knowing right when I see it. I have to find
what Julie called 'the plains of Megiddo.' Julie is serene. She was so
sweet and genuine that she can rely on a place in whatever the spirit-

ual future holds. My hope, my . . . paradise . . . would be to see her again. So I have to pick the winning side."

"Are they here?" Gogan was enthusiastic. "These plains—are they here? Because I knew there was something holding me."

Simeon reached for bread and mopped his plate. "I don't know— because I came with the intention of getting you OUT."

"Out?"

"To face the world. I was afraid I had sabotaged your self-confidence for all time. I thought maybe you were nervous. Julie and I were both anxious to make it up to you if we ever got the chance. When Icarus and Zed said you had been here—well, it seemed like a—a heaven-sent opportunity."

"Heaven plays her part." Gogan took Simeon's platter and set it down before the fire where an urn of water was warming.

"But I can't see . . . All these people. All these options."

"You'll know what to do when the time comes. You did in Playa Nine."

Gogan let Simeon chew that over. Emotions kaleidoscoped on his spent features in the fitful graphics of the fire.

And perhaps that was the real seat of Simeon's doubt. He recalled Green Town, Illinois, and Judge Charles Woodman. It had been Woodman who pulled the sure stroke that took steam out of the Green Town crisis. Woodman, by logic alone.

And the judge had assured him: "Next time, you will be the catalyst. You will be the man who frees the rabbits."

The Japanese had been so anxious to have it believed the two hundred California whites which had landed up in Green Town were disease carriers and so careful to see that their backup idea—two hundred Hiroshima survivors—had arrived in the town exactly on the bobtails of the bunnies. Woodman, when he saw the incredible assembly of American fringe lunatics gathered to greet the twin offensives, had perceived that the whole idea was to make the United States look foolish to herself. And that being so, the rabbits were no more disease carriers than they were personal friends of Richard Adams. Thus, he had released them from their cages in an action which had saved the situation by making people stop and think.

At the time, the extrapolation had seemed a supreme intellectual feat. Now it seemed merely and maddeningly irrelevant because it gave nothing to show the way out of this labyrinth.

"When the time comes," Simeon echoed. "The time has to be NOW. I can pin-point the evil. But there's too much GOODNESS."

The climax, however, was not as immediate as he feared. The options were still arriving, but he did not know that.

Famous Gogan knew it. Famous Gogan had secrets.

DON'T YOU GO
DOOMSDAY
ON ME, TOO

Simeon was gone and that gave life a twinkle for Arthur Prinz. He had given the philosopher a chance and the boy had taken it. At last, a contest was shaping up.

Randall and Withers were nervous of reprisals. "I said we should not have left him," volunteered Withers.

"Nonsense," reassured Prinz. "The situation is exactly as I wanted it."

"But—"

"I TOLD you. He won't leave the garden until his job is done—whatever he deems it to be. In the meantime, I think we can afford to have a little fun at his expense. I calculate it will bring him out of hiding. We'll see to it in the morning."

"In the MORNING?" queried Randall.

"Certainly. Let him have a night in this chill and he'll be that much more ready to come in out of the cold tomorrow."

"You're taking a chance, aren't you?" asked Withers.

"Look." Prinz's tone went hard. "If I could draw him to Mozambique—if I could draw him to Tuscany—don't you think I know I can keep him here?"

"I just can't figure out where he is," said Withers.

"He's HERE. He will come when I call."

Night fell and sleep came easily to Prinz. The same was not true of Scarlatti or the Ojukwe brothers. They rested little, each in the confinement of his own thoughts. They had misgivings—Scarlatti of future, Sami of faith, Nelson of fraternity.

Scarlatti could only mull over Simeon's now evident absence and wonder what it would mean in the nameless game on which they had now embarked. Sami spent much of the night in prayer, seeking a certainty that the performance would match the sum of his promises.

Nelson prayed, too—not for himself, because he was set in his course and sure of it, but for Sami, who had so recently shown the failings of Judas Iscariot.

There had been little opportunity to assess the state of Sami's heart and Nelson pleaded now that the boy should have the courage to act in accordance with his faith.

Night went. Morning came—a clear morning with ample dewfall which would have raised a mist to remember in the old-format Garden Two. As it was, the mist clung like lace to the hem of the lake and left the lawn unshrouded for Prinz's intentions.

He saw Scarlatti first. He said: "You know Simeon has disappeared."

"Has he?" Scarlatti was going to make Prinz work for every single response.

"Does that mean you're surprised? Maybe you thought you were all for one and one for all. Simeon has copped out."

"Then we might as well all go home," said Scarlatti. "Where's YOUR home, Prinz? Is there any place in the world left for you?"

Prinz chuckled. "I told you in Mozambique what I was going to do. Simeon is not beyond recall. A pity, though, that you couldn't have had a few more words with him. It must be a major disappointment for you, throwing up everything only to find that your hero has cleared off."

"I'll survive it—particularly since you tell me he hasn't gone for good. If I have learned anything at all from you, Prinz, it is how you operate. Right now, you're playing your fish . . . Simeon and all the rest of us. But don't look to get a bite out of me so easily."

"We'll see." And Prinz was gone to his next call.

His line with Nelson Ojuke was similar. "I don't know whether you were hoping to find some rapport with Simeon," he said, "but I'm sorry to say the man is missing."

"My rapport is with God," said Nelson Ojukwe. "And I'm glad to say that He is still very much around."

On to Sami Ojukwe. "A good night?" asked Prinz. "I'm afraid this northern weather may not be to your taste."

"I'm with my brother," said Sami triumphantly. "I don't care if it rains lizards."

If Prinz had not decided his strategy already, he might have been disheartened by the negative reaction to his attempts to raise terror. Indeed, he was bound to remark—although only to himself—that the three of them had toughened up considerably since they had entered the garden.

He found it hard to believe that Simeon had effected the change.

Nevertheless, the sun was climbing and the missing member, wherever he was, must surely be awake and taking notice by now. Time to start, then.

He called his assistants and they herded the three captives out into the centre of the lawn.

There he got busy with rope and by the time he had finished there was no easy way of separating bodies from bench—and no room for Simeon.

Only when he was adjusting the last knots did he notice the rectangle of lighter wood on the backrest.

The name plate was gone.

Try as he might, he could not remember when he had seen it last.

Shortly, he cursed his concern. If it was gone, the explanation was simple. Simeon had it—and probably torn fingernails, also, from removing the screws. When he thought of the extra suffering, his earlier good spirits were restored.

John Icarus and Adam Zed were on the road. Their second call to USEFUL had revealed the Hague stalemate still unresolved. By mutual and unspoken consent, Icarus and Zed were for giving the bishops no more time.

And as Zed had said, travelling didn't alter anything. The irresolution was over what to do when they GOT to Garden Five.

They were in Siena before they bothered to seek further instructions. They were on the road south, twenty-four hours behind Simeon and party before they began to piece the directions together.

No longer a simple matter, The Hague had said. On the way to being a full-scale spiritual confrontation at Garden Five. A reiterated bitter opposition to One Faith—and a warning that priority of concern should be given to "those exercising a Protestant persuasion if and when the conflict assumes the character of a small Armageddon."

That in itself was a contradiction in terms if it was not a clear paradox. One (Catholic) Faith versus One (Protestant) Faith and no middle ground. "Armageddon" was an emotive and overused epithet. Christ had said: "He who is not with me is against me." That was a qualification cited by either side. But no room for doubt, compromise, manoeuvre?

"Somebody's paranoic about this," said Icarus, as he piloted the USF hired car across the Tuscan landscape. "Can there be that many angles that we don't know?"

"We're not lacking details," said Zed. "It's the kind of ecclesiastical staying power that keeps trotting out the millennium—that's what we don't have."

"In other words, you think they're overreacting."

"Of COURSE. What difference is it going to make to the rest of the world what goes on in Garden Five?"

"Every fire has to start somewhere."

"John, don't YOU go doomsday on me, too."

Zed still favoured his own theory about the status of the evangelists Prinz had in tow. "I think all they're telling us is to watch out for distractions. If these two Mozambican Bible-punchers try to complicate matters by belting out their own variations, we have to keep our wits about us."

"And suppose they are right and the rest of us are wrong?"

"Good grief, John! I'm glad this car isn't wired for sound—what are you saying? You're making excuses and we haven't even got there yet."

But Icarus was unrepentant. "I don't like dogmatism. I'm used to finding it on the Roman side, but when it comes from USF it disconcerts me. I thought our motivation was keeping this a free world. Ensuring that people have their proper rights—including the right to be wrong. Now the bishops say, 'You can't be wrong, you must be right. We are right. You must be with us' . . . Priority for 'those' exercising a Protestant persuasion.' What else could it possibly mean?"

"So you're saying it's even all right to be a *Unam Sanctam* follower."

"Sure—if you have all the facts before you and that is the choice you make."

"Then what the devil are YOU doing here?"

"Seeing that nobody has to make the choice WITHOUT the facts."

"What about the right of the uninformed man to stick his neck out?"

"Okay, okay," conceded Icarus. "But nobody in Garden Five is going to be uninformed. So . . . We look after Simeon and Scarlatti, the Vatican looks after Prinz and company—"

"Not now," put in Zed. "Not after Lourenço. I reckon it won't take Eugenio long to tag Prinz as the architect of that little tragedy."

"All right—the UN looks after Prinz and friends. But who—?"

"Who represents *Unam Sanctam?* Who are we fighting?"

"No. Who looks after the Mozambicans?" Icarus wove the car through the narrow streets of Roccastrada and knew an answer was nearing.

When the downpour had blotted Harold Messenger's path, the light was already going. The torrent was more than his windscreen wipers could take and he slowed the vehicle to a crawl. Before visibility went altogether, he found a lay-by and switched off the engine.

He rolled down the window, blessing the rain for a place of concealment, waiting to hear his pursuers pass by.

But no car came. Even when the rain stopped and the premature dusk had been fulfilled and the clouds broke up to reveal stars, there was silence on the road.

And maybe he had been dreaming or at least romanticising when he spotted a car full of men travelling behind. Eugenio had promised him a tail and circumstances had done the rest. No doubt the suspect sedan had turned off way back and was long since at its innocuous destination.

He did not know the route to Garden Five well enough to try it in the darkness. He rolled up the window and prepared for sleep.

Rest was elusive. The day had been too full of surprises. Zimbabwe, for one thing. He had taken Joachim and the other delegates at their word and now found that word untrue. He wondered where they were and how Buthelezi was coping. He wondered at the wisdom of having put his job on the line. Surely, the S.G. could see now that Messenger's detour had made little difference to the Lourenço Marques situation—and that being so, perhaps his standing was out of jeopardy.

Then he thought about Eugenio and the confrontation and the remarks that had been passed. He did not regret any of them, but he did give a thought to how the estrangement would lie with the UN.

Despite all this and an encroaching hunger, he was almost happy with the way things had turned out. Pangs and conditions aside, contentment with the new schism got him through the night.

Now with the sun up and the way clear, he was travelling again. He even whistled a little.

Until he scanned the road to his rear. The driver of the friendly foursome trailing him waved a good morning.

There they stayed, speed or manoeuvre, along the final miles of white dust road. He considered passing by the elaborate wrought-iron gate of the garden but dismissed the plan immediately.

Little chance of shaking them off now if night and cloudburst could not do it. Besides, they probably knew the location as well as he did.

So he made the turn into the drive and stopped. They followed suit —and faster. The chummy driver was at Messenger's door before he could get out. And the rifle in his hand was anything but chummy.

"All right," the man said quietly. "We'll take it from here."

"Then you take me, too," said Messenger. "And just remember that Mr. Prinz's first loyalty is to me and mine to him."

"I'll keep it in mind," said Two-Pips.

His companions dispersed in several directions and he waited for Messenger to fall into step with him.

They did not see the third car, which came from the north, turned across the road towards the gate, and suddenly veered away, kicking up dust.

"What the hell was THAT all about?" said John Icarus.

Simeon awoke in guilt. Sleep had stolen upon him unobtrusively as he relaxed before Gogan's fire. When his eyelids had grown heavy and persistently so, the struggle was lost. Even his most anxious concerns were only half articulated before they were forgotten and shutters came down one by one on the cells of his brain. The fire did what no amount of composure could have done.

And here was a new day and Simeon was sick of himself. Many hours had come and gone without his presence. The other captives could be dead for all he knew.

Across the cavern, Gogan was stirring.

Simeon shook him awake. "I have to go. Is there only one access to this place?"

Gogan was nodding his head. He plunged his hands into the urn that had stood by the fire and took water to his face. "One access."

"Well, I don't want to give it away. Maybe you should—"

Gogan put his weight to the wall and daylight splashed upon the cave floor.

"Hell's teeth," said Simeon. "How long did I sleep?"

"All night," supplied Gogan. "And you were ready for it. How did you expect to face today?"

He was gone through the opening and back in ten seconds. "All clear."

"Any movement?"

"I didn't go far enough to see. We'll find out now."

They ran in the lee of high box hedges, they paused in the shadows of statuary. They penetrated a bank of azaleas and beyond lay the lawn. Gogan halted Simeon with a grip on his arm.

There was movement and plenty of it around the bench at the lawn centre. Gogan could feel Simeon's resistance but he kept the grip firm. "Now COOL it. Let's reason it out. What are they doing and why?"

"Scarlatti and the two Ojukwe brothers," said Simeon. "They seem to be tied to the bench. And Prinz is—"

His nose caught a scent that went direct to the mucous membrane and bounced back with tears. He sniffed. "It's PARAFFIN."

As he watched, Randall and Withers were circling the bench with jerry cans, tossing the liquid contents over woodwork and wriggling men. "They're going to—"

He jerked free of Gogan's grasp. He heard a scratching noise and saw fire in Prinz's fist.

He burst from the bush, yelling.

His cry froze Rico Scarlatti to the marrow, conjured up nightmares in the sunlight. Simeon ran, screaming: "No, no, no-no-no-no!"

And Scarlatti screamed back: "It's WATER!"

Simeon faltered, lost his stride, and stumbled even as a rifle shot rent the garden sounds and sent birds into panic. He went face-down into grass stinking of spirits, a section of the wide circle Prinz had treated before his bench charade.

Scarlatti watched the proceedings through a haze. The shout, the shot, the fall—all spectres of history reiterated.

Then Simeon gave it all the lie. He rose to his knees and looked around. Scarlatti wanted to catch his eye but Simeon's attention was elsewhere. He was watching the man who came forward from the drive with rifle at the slant.

If that be noon, there strode another rifleman at three o'clock. And a third at nine o'clock. And—Simeon spun about—a fourth at six o'clock, the way he had come, propelling Famous Gogan ahead of the barrel.

Scarlatti looked for Arthur Prinz—and found him shaking like a leaf.

Andrew Buthelezi had spent the night airborne—Kennedy, Shannon, Fiumicino—and his face was familiar enough to draw VIP treatment for himself and his party at any port of call.

When it was learned that the UN Secretary-General was heading for Rome, there were not too many matters likely to make up his agenda. Wires hummed, assignments were laid.

Breakfast time at Fiumicino, the paparazzi were waiting—and because Buthelezi's mission had become such a personal matter, they took him by surprise. He had overlooked the machinery of the press and the rather better-known issue that lay between himself and the pope.

He was not ready for interviews or statements and again could have done with Messenger's attendant polish. To the speculators of the news media, Buthelezi taking three Africans to Rome made a particular kind of sense.

They expected conciliation. They had no idea—and Buthelezi was thankful—that he was aiming for salvation and the Zimbabwe trio were intending revenge.

Since reticence only made the media more determined, Buthelezi mounted a quick conference and told the correspondents something in the nature of what they wanted to hear.

"What," asked one, "is the UN's attitude to the massacre in Zimbabwe?"

"I am still awaiting authentic information," Buthelezi said. "Reports are conflicting. Until I have a clear picture, I cannot comment."

"Then what are you doing here?" asked another.

"Seeking that clear picture. This is one of the two cities where I am likely to obtain it. On my instructions, my aide, Harold Messenger, should be on his way to Lourenço Marques. We will be in earliest consultation."

And who were his companions?

Buthelezi introduced them by name and said they had been in delegation lobbying the UN when first reports of the incident had come through. "Naturally, they are as anxious as I am to have a proper account," he said.

"Are you here to see Pope Eugenio?"

"Among other people," said Buthelezi. "That is not my first plan."

"What IS your first plan?"

"I will issue a statement when I have prepared it."

"I ask again, what is your FIRST plan?"

"And I answer again that a statement will be made at the right time. This is an emotive situation being relayed to me by exciteable people—the Italians no less than the Africans. I am sure you will appreciate that my assessment of it must be conducted with caution and not under extreme conditions. I am sure you will also appreciate that if I were to detail my locations and movements too closely, the pacific environment I seek would be impossible. I am not trying to hamper you in your endeavours, gentlemen, and I trust you will grant me a little more time to succeed in mine. Thank you."

Buthelezi stepped back into the private VIP lounge, beckoning Joachim, Díaz, and Da Gama to follow. While the four refreshed themselves with coffee and rolls, officials checked over their documentation.

Joachim and the others had been made tacit by the speed of events and Buthelezi was not sorry. It gave him a little time to think, though that time yielded no clear path for him. Messenger, he thought, was safe enough at the moment. But bullets were no respecters of person and if the denouement were allowed to so deteriorate, he might lose a good man who was trying to protect a bad one.

Whatever happened to Arthur Prinz was only the consequence of the kind of dance he had led in life. Buthelezi had never been able to understand people like Prinz whose drive was so relentless that even position could still not remove them from gutter fighting.

He was surprised that somebody as straightforward as Messenger could have a need for an obvious trickster. On the other hand, perhaps it was the information gained by such devious means that gave Messenger the assurance to do the job.

The others were ready to leave the airport and were wondering how they might run the gauntlet of the newsmen. Despite their negative participation, they had not enjoyed Buthelezi's conference. They had seen him dealing with a force they could not altogether understand and if there had been any vibrations at all, they had been bad not for the deceivers but for the shedders of blood.

All the same, they felt no shame for the Zimbabwe action. It was pay-back. The Vatican had dictated the terms and the Portuguese before them. The Europeans were the masters of double-talk but the Africans had found a way of reducing the argument to its simplest form. It disturbed them that people in general could not accept such simplicity. But then, the men who had fired questions beyond this lounge door were Europeans, too, and perhaps the only language they understood was duplicity.

When the Africans tried duplicity, they were bad at it. Their lies were transparent and their intentions misunderstood. When they set out to mirror the tactics they met, they heard words like "treachery," and they fast came round to the belief that the meaning of the word varied with the identity of the speaker.

Thus they had no doubts about what they were going to do when they found Arthur Prinz. They would take him back to Lourenço and there he would be able to study Zimbabwe justice—for as long as his strength held out.

Arthur Prinz . . . They were well rested and well fed and ready now to move on.

"Where do we go from here?" asked Sandy Joachim.

"Searching Rome is a waste of time," said Buthelezi. "I know where Prinz was heading and he has had time enough to get there. Our best direction is north."

"I suggest you could be taking us away from Prinz and not towards him," said Matthew Díaz.

"You can suggest what you like. My main concern is my aide, Harold Messenger. If his intention was not to track down Prinz, he would not be in Italy at all. I am satisfied—and you should be—that he is very close to the man and my proposal will take us very close to Messenger."

Díaz sat back and splayed his hands. "If the others follow that reasoning, it is good enough for me."

"And how should we get to Mr. Messenger?" asked Joachim.

"The UN had an establishment in Tuscany, a little way north of here, in the recent past. Prinz was connected with it. There is good reason for thinking he has gone back there."

"How do we move?" Da Gama was still thinking of gauntlets and loaded questions.

"We go UP!" Buthelezi pointed skyward. "First via the stairs and then via a helicopter."

He led the way to the roof and wondered why the others were suddenly dragging their feet. A craft in plain livery was warming up and the pilot tapped his cap to Buthelezi.

Joachim, Da Gama, and Díaz advanced with evident ill-ease. The Secretary-General fed each of them up the steps and into the glass interior.

When they were seated and belted, the trauma seemed to have passed.

Da Gama even chuckled. "The last time I saw one of these things," he said, "I was under it and running like hell."

"The last time I saw one," said Díaz, "it was putting down napalm and I lost a brother."

"Well, now," said Joachim, "the roles are reversed. Now WE are the death dropping out of the sky."

The helicopter rose, banked north, and then headed across the morning at a speed which made Buthelezi despair.

John Icarus brought the car to rest fifty yards south of the gate. "Out!" he said.

"What?"

"Out for Pete's sake and get the bonnet up."

"Oh." Adam Zed had been still trying to work some sense into the scene that confronted them on the threshold of Garden Five—the group of men and guns fanning out on either side of the drive. Now he quit the car in haste, uncovered the engine, loosened some leads, and waited for Icarus to join him.

When they both had their heads ducked into the shade and their nostrils full of the scent of hot oil, Icarus said: "Do you think they saw us?"

Zed sneaked a glance along the way they had come. The gate was

still in sight but nobody had emerged. "If they did, they're not showing it."

Icarus fiddled with plugs and deliberately dirtied his hands. "What
do you make of it?"

"Beyond me, man. Who are they? Prinz we know. Simeon,
Scarlatti, Randall, Withers—it was none of them. And weapons. I
didn't think we would need our irons, John."

"All right." Icarus reached through the driver's window and drew
forth a cloth. He wiped his hands. "We are dealing with unknowns.
In this situation, how many unknowns can there be? We can discount ourselves and the people we know—and we can discount any
rescue effort for the Africans that Prinz has in tow."

"Why?"

"Because these gunsels were WHITE. And from the way they
moved, they knew their business. What does that make them?"

"Militia?"

"What KIND of militia?"

"Well, I can't think a careful man like Prinz has broken any
LOCAL laws."

"Wise up, Adam. WHITE men with GUNS . . ."

"Mercenaries?"

"Right. But why? Us they don't know about. Would anybody go to
that much trouble to rub out two Bible eccentrics?"

"And that"—Zed took the cloth from Icarus and made reparations to his own hands—"only leaves Prinz. You know, we could let
them finish the job for us."

"We what?"

"It's all right, John, I'm not serious. Hell, suppose it was Simeon
they were after—he draws trouble like a corpse draws flies. I reckon
we have to go and look."

Zed started to close the bonnet. Icarus stopped the downward descent. "Your logic is fine," he said. "You neglect one thing. We may
want to make a quick getaway so reconnect those leads, for crying
out loud."

Zed obliged and then followed Icarus into the shadow of the wall.
Together, they moved towards the gate. A cautious glance revealed
no observers. They went through the opening and bellied down in
the undergrowth.

As they hit the earth, they heard shouts and a single shot.

"Damn," said Icarus. "They've either started or finished."

"Let's hope started." Zed pushed forward through the vegetation, moving on hands and knees. Icarus followed, regretting the ungainly attire. If they had known they would be crawling into Garden Five, they could have come better dressed. They could have come better equipped all round.

They were trying to go quietly but stiff laurel leaves gave them opposition for every yard. At this stage, they wondered how much time they could spare for caution. They wanted to reach the action quickly—but they wanted more to be able to control their participation once they reached it.

"With luck, we still have an ace in the hole," hissed Icarus.

"Sure, but where's the hole?"

"He gave me a location."

They entered the last thickness of azaleas. Zed parted branches with care and looked out at the lawn and the activity thereon. A crowded bench, Simeon picking himself up from the ground, Prinz, Randall, Withers, all frozen in their stances. The mercenaries closing in from four directions. And two other figures, one of whom caused him to curse.

"Forget about aces," he said. "They have Famous Gogan already."

Andrew Buthelezi, watching the unfurling landscape, saw an oasis of green spring out of the Tuscan terrain.

"Take it down," he said. "As low as you can. I don't want us spotted just yet."

"What does it matter?" Joachim was craning forward, trying to pick out their destination. "Our arrival is a fact of life. Whatever Prinz is doing will be interrupted. Why waste time on strategies—unless time-wasting is a strategy in itself."

Buthelezi kept his eyes on the lowering hand of the altimeter. When he was satisfied the craft could handle any snag undulation in the road, he settled back and said calmly: "I have interests in that garden, too. I'm not ferrying you to the spot to wipe everything out."

"We don't WANT everything," said Díaz. "Just Prinz."

The pilot dropped the helicopter even lower so that its shadow traversed the white road like some squat bug.

"I don't know that I'll even give you Prinz," said Buthelezi. "When your minds are already made up, I don't call that due process of law."

"It's too late to argue about concepts," put in Díaz. "The facts speak for themselves—a mountain of dead. And Prinz, whether he never struck a blow, bears a percentage of the responsibility for those deaths. He was a willing member of the Inquisition machinery."

"If there are—percentages—of responsibility, there should be degrees of penalty. You give the same to everybody—execution. And you're right . . . it IS too late."

The *Guadeloupe* was making its final descent. In the last seconds of elevation, Buthelezi saw the sweep of the drive and more vehicles than he had expected.

There was ground under his feet before he could exercise his mind on the curious fact. Now he could see only the exterior wall of Garden Five and one car parked a little way down the road.

He had expected the presence of Messenger, Prinz, Scarlatti, even Simeon, but the garden looked more densely populated than that.

"Let's go," he said. "Jack—when we're clear, make tracks. I'll call you if I need you."

The pilot raised his thumb. "Anything you say, Mr. Buthelezi. I hope your—business—works out."

That was Jack Peterson's discharge but he knew what it meant. You can't drop four guys in the middle of nowhere and expect them to find their own way back—and you can't always rely on other people's transport.

He would go but he would not be far away. If he got a call, he would be there directly. If he didn't get a call, he would make it even faster.

The four gunmen closed in like mandibles and Messenger and Gogan hastened before them, not really knowing why. Famous Gogan was looking for a familiar face. Harold Messenger saw too many.

"Prinz," he said. "What the hell have you done this time?"

The man was calmer now, working on escape routes. Messenger suddenly out of the blue was a shock to the system and a sure sign that if he wanted to keep his UN posting intact he would have to lie like he had never lied before. And the means which made that impossible was following a few feet behind, smiling a recognition.

"Mr. Prinz," said Two-Pips. "Small world. One week, I am delivering souls to you, the next I am seeking yours."

Prinz fought for balance on the slippery morass of wholesale treachery and then found himself a handhold. "Who sent you?"

"Why, the pope. Your employer."

"And it's over the Zimbabwe business."

"Astute, Mr. Prinz. I know of no other—although somebody as ubiquitous as your good self could quite easily have any number of interests on the go. Yes—the Zimbabwe business."

"Then I can GIVE you the very man who fouled up our operation in Zimbabwe."

Prinz got hold of Simeon by the arm and thrust him at the mercenary. "HE told them we were double-crossing them. That's what started the bloodshed."

Two-Pips gave Simeon no more than a fleeting glance. "The name we have is yours, Mr. Prinz. No other price has been quoted to me and I am a very literal person."

"What about Scarlatti? He was involved—" Prinz was running through the list now in desperation.

"One name," said Two-Pips. "One wage. We are professionals and we do NOTHING for nothing. If Pope Eugenio wants accomplices, he will have to put out a new contract."

Simeon could face guns and angry men but his own silence he could not bear. Since Green Town, he had been looking for the chance to assert himself. Here, he had despaired at the size of the gathering. Now, even Prinz had gone elsewhere with his accusations.

"What he says is right," he began. "I blew the whistle on your—arrangement—in Zimbabwe and I'm damned if I'm going to be sorry. Furthermore, if Sami and Nelson Ojukwe want to know why Prinz brought them here, it is because I was here—and for that, I AM sorry . . ."

"Shut up," said Two-Pips. "I hate to hear people being noble but that's not the reason. Shut up, all of you."

At first, to untrained ears, there was just the bird song reviving after the shot. But the mercenaries were tense. Then the Ojukwe brothers picked out the alien sound. Sami recognised it and was aware of a paradox—a mind full of flames and a gut full of ice. The

others had it now, a drone that was turning fast into the dry, flat rev-
olution of a helicopter.

But the sky was empty. While the sound reached a peak and subsided, there was no vision to partner it.

"The road," said Two-Pips. "Let's get this crowd under cover and
we'll investigate."

The nine prisoners were pushed and bundled towards the house
without ceremony, up the steps, through the doors, which were
closed behind them.

The hall was cramped, dank, and strewn with leaves. The chill had
stayed with it from yesterday's storm or some storm before that.

It was the first time Simeon had been inside but he gave the hall
little attention. He found a window with a view of the drive.

He had expected to see Two-Pips and friends en route to the gate
but instead the pathway and attendant shrubs were deserted. Only
momentarily. As he watched, the mercenaries emerged from the
thickets and massed at the gate.

"Please, God," he said. "An empty road and no more people."

It was a peculiar kind of prayer.

From their shelter, John Icarus and Adam Zed had followed proceedings that gave scant hope of improvement or easy resolution.
They retreated to the dark side of the azalea bank.

"What now?" asked Zed.

"We get back to the car—fast."

"But what about our people? We can't just—drive off."

"Who said anything about driving off? The one advantage we have
at the moment is that we are free agents. Let's keep it that way."

The point had been made. They beat their way back through the
undergrowth and did not pause for breath until they were within the
vehicle.

"Right," said Icarus. "What do we know now that we didn't know
before?"

"That they have Gogan."

"Apart from that."

"Well . . . It looks as though control of the situation has changed
hands. Those mercenaries are rounding up EVERYBODY. Do they
WANT everybody?"

"Gogan, Simeon, Scarlatti, Prinz, Randall, Withers, two evangelists, four bounty hunters, and one other," counted Icarus. "Did you manage to see his face?"

"I didn't even manage to count him. Was there somebody else?"

"He went in with the mercenaries. He had no gun—and I don't think he had much choice."

"Two cars," contributed Zed. "I saw two cars."

"The bounty hunters in one, the loner in the other. There's something familiar—I'm certain we know him."

A sudden wind sprang up among the trees that topped the garden wall. Loose gravel kicked up and bounced along the back and sides of the car.

Icarus looked round. "Here's MORE company."

The *Guadeloupe* grounded on the road fifty feet behind them. Engine snapped off and rotor blades slowed their circulation.

"NOW do we go or stay?" Zed had his eye on the car's ignition, looking for the key. Icarus was fumbling through his pockets. "I must have dropped . . ."

"Then FORGET it," said Zed. He climbed out of the car, turned towards the helicopter, and waited. He didn't take his eyes off the craft as Icarus kicked open his own door and emerged.

Four coloured men were descending from the *Guadeloupe*.

"BLACK mercenaries?" asked Zed in a tone which could have been mischief or disbelief.

For long seconds the two and the four traded glances and made assessments. "At least, they're our shade." said Zed. "Near enough."

Icarus started away from the car and Zed fell into step. They kept their hands away from their sides—not raised but not able to make any sudden or suspicious move.

"We come in peace," said one of the four.

"Join the club," said Icarus. "I know you. You're Andrew Buthelezi and that makes a lot of sense. The man inside is Harold Messenger."

"So he IS here." Buthelezi steered towards the gate.

"Hang loose," said Zed. "Before you move, you'd better hear the odds. Your man Messenger just arrived with four whites who look like jungle fighters."

"With them?" Buthelezi looked puzzled.

"At the same time as," said Icarus. "Tell me—did he know where he was going?"

"Well, yes, but . . ."

"Maybe the others didn't and they were trailing him."

"Who are they?"

"Your guess is as good as ours. We've only had time for a quick reconnaissance."

"Who are you?"

"That depends on who YOU are," put in Zed.

Icarus silenced him. "Mr. Buthelezi is from the United Nations and so is Messenger. If anybody can help us sort out this mess, they can."

"You still haven't answered my question," Buthelezi reminded him.

"John Icarus . . . Adam Zed. Our employer is the World Council of Churches."

"What?" Buthelezi had to laugh. "Well, I knew the Vatican was involved but I had no idea the Protestants had mobilised. What brought you in?"

"A man called Simeon. We knew the Romans were seeking his support, so we put forward our own case. And that was a long time and a lot of twists ago. What about Arthur Prinz? Isn't he supposed to be working for you AND the Vatican?"

"On paper, yes. In fact, I think the UN is party to very little of what he does. Mostly, I think, he is working for himself. Simeon, you said. Is HE in there, too?"

"All God's children," said Zed. "They're all inside."

Buthelezi started a reply as the *Guadeloupe* came back to life. Slipstream plastered the talkers clothes to them and robbed them of words. As the craft climbed away into the noon sky, the Secretary-General tried again. "He was the one who put the cat among the pigeons in Zimbabwe—oh, forgive me. These three gentlemen are from Zimbabwe—Foreign Minister, Mr. Sandy Joachim, Head of Security, Mr. Eduardo Díaz and Head of Trade, Mr. Matthew de Gama. They are here to—stake a claim on Mr. Prinz."

"And to thank Mr. Simeon," said Sandy Joachim. "Do I understand he may be in some kind of trouble?"

"We may ALL be in some kind of trouble," said Icarus. "And as for your Mr. Prinz—I suspect there may not be enough pieces of him to go round."

"You say these—mercenaries—followed Harold Messenger. Well, he came from Rome."

"Then Eugenio sent them. Maybe the pope thinks Prinz knows more about Zimbabwe than he told him. Maybe he has a little Inquisition fire burning for Prinz—that would be a nice irony."

"Not," said Díaz, "if we can help it. Prinz owes his first explanations to us and if it means taking him from under the noses of this white trash—well, we've fought them before . . ."

Buthelezi bowed his head. Icarus and Zed, relieved at having found allies, had failed to allow for a difference of motives even among the occupants of the helicopter. While divisions exist, thought Icarus, we are no better off—probably worse.

"We can't face them if we can't agree among ourselves," he said. "Let's just say for now that our common opposition is the boys with the guns. If and when we get rid of them, we can consider claims and counterclaims. Meanwhile this is a hell of a place to hold a conference . . ."

"Would you like," said Two-Pips from behind his rifle, "to come inside?"

His companions-at-arms added emphasis to the invitation.

Simeon watched the gate, waiting for the worst. Scarlatti shouldered his way into the seer's attention.

"One thing about death-wishes," he said, "is that they tend to get you killed. And I know because that fact cost me the last case I fought—right here. So pardon me if I don't enthuse over your confessions in the garden just now. It's just as well for all of us that Two-Pips subscribes to the profit motive."

"Two-Pips—is that his name?"

Scarlatti nodded back over his shoulder. "That's the name Sami and Nelson gave him when he raided their village and carted them off to Lourenço Marques. Now you should listen to those Ojukwes before you start throwing your life away. And what on earth are you doing over here, anyway? We ought to be formulating some kind of plan."

"I'm watching. If I see what I expect to see, don't bother making any plans. They'll be a waste of breath."

"And what do you expect?"

"More people. More reasons to clog up the works."

"I don't understand, Simeon. The more of us there are, the less power they have. Each extra captive diminishes their resources by that percentage. Four of them watching . . . nine . . . of us—"

"FIFTEEN," said Simeon savagely. He could see movement along the path. The mercenaries were returning with six men ahead of them. Simeon saw tincture but no features, went on watching.

"But fifteen is a MAGNIFICENT number. How can four keep a proper surveillance on fifteen? What's the matter with you, Simeon?"

Scarlatti turned back into the clustered hall. "It seems we have some more company—six of them."

When the window got too crowded, Simeon elbowed his way clear. Scarlatti went after him, still needing an answer.

"What's bad news about a 15–4 ratio? We can have them running around like nobody's business."

"WE can."

"Why NOT we?"

"Oh, what the hell?" Simeon found the staircase and sat down. "I want Julie. I don't know where I am."

Scarlatti took himself off. On the one hand, temperament irritated him when he was trying to think. On the other, perhaps Simeon was best left alone to get a grip on himself. In a while, Simeon covered his face with his hands.

Scarlatti looked for Arthur Prinz—and found a surprise that unsettled him because it undermined the bitterness that had brought him across two continents.

Prinz was haggard—wordless, bent, face to face with too many versions of his own death.

Nelson Ojukwe, who had found no curiosity sufficient to take him to the window, instead lowered himself to the stairs by the side of Simeon.

"I don't know Julie," he said. "Please tell me about her."

Simeon made no sound.

"Someone you love, obviously," persisted Nelson.

"She's dead." Simeon's voice was muffled. He dropped his fingers and Nelson could see runnels of moisture on his cheeks. "If she was alive, I wouldn't be here."

"Are you sure of that?"

"Damn sure."

"You mean when she was alive she—kept you out of trouble."

Simeon took a good look at the man because there had been some familiarity governing the choice of words. "How much do you know about me?"

"Little enough. While you were missing last night, we were able to talk to Scarlatti. He told us what kind of a man you are."

"Then you know I am no stranger to trouble and neither was To-morrow Julie."

"Trouble has usually managed to find you. From what Scarlatti said, it seems you have never been a willing participant."

"That's true enough." Simeon rubbed his hands along his thighs to get them dry. "But I must admit that I walked into this with my eyes open. Julie told me before she died that—oh, it's silly. We had a beautiful relationship. Some of the things we said had meaning only to us."

"I would be most honoured to hear what your Julie said that led you here."

"She talked of the plains of Megiddo. They're mentioned in the Bible book of Revelation. You probably know better than I do—"

"I know," said Nelson. "I know well. So Julie saw this place as Megiddo."

"Not here—somewhere. The place where good confronts evil and wins. She asked me to find it for her. It was MY belief that the place was here. I don't know if I'm right. Does it look that way to you?"

"Very much so. Perhaps not to the point of the Final Battle—the Armageddon of the Bible—being sited here. But things are happening which someone without knowledge of the Revelation might not have thought possible. As I understand it, the Established Church is recognised as something of a villain in all this. That makes a special kind of sense to me. The people who have brought about that position are yourself and —"

"And us," said Harold Messenger. "I'm sorry I didn't introduce myself earlier. There wasn't much time. Messenger, special aide to the Secretary-General of the United Nations. For better or worse, we now know EXACTLY where we stand in relation to the Vatican on world matters. Thanks to Simeon—and thanks, in a left-handed way, to Arthur Prinz."

Simeon had been beginning to relax in his conversation with the evangelist. He had been talking about Julie and it helped. He had remembered something that had become clouded in the rapid passage of events. He had recalled that his whole motivation was geared to a reunion with Julie when that battle had been fought.

And here came the United Nations—flag-waving, tub-thumping, saving the world. Simeon remembered something else, too.

"You put this garden complex here," he said. "Maybe you can tell us some way out of it."

"If a physical exit was all that was required, we could be gone in a moment," said Messenger. "As it is there is other business to be done. But don't entertain any worries about the outcome because we have powerful influence. Tell me, Mr. Ojukwe, do you have a place for us in your—Revelation?"

The new captives were entering the hall and it looked as though dialectic was at an end. Nelson took a piece of paper from a pocket, scribbled briefly, and handed it to Messenger.

The aide saw only, "I Thessalonians, Chap. V, vv. 1–3." Then a voice he knew well said: "Harold?"

He tucked it out of sight and forgot it as he swivelled to meet Andrew Buthelezi. It was a nasty moment.

For Simeon, too. He was looking at John Icarus and Adam Zed. And they were talking animatedly to Famous Gogan.

In the hubbub and the jostle, Simeon knew what he had to do, even down to the last detail. The notion took his breath away, dried his tears, made him jubilant because it even stood his own earlier thinking on its head.

There must be no bloodshed . . . otherwise, his stance would be no more virtuous than that of Two-Pips. The problem was, which of those who had presented themselves as friends only to be proved collaborators . . . which of them could be trusted to act without malice?

Somehow, Nelson Ojukwe and his younger brother had become remote from the prevailing situation in Simeon's mind. He put them ABOVE it.

Harold Messenger had spoken of other business to be done and that meant he and his superior, Andrew Buthelezi, already had plans made which could conflict with Simeon's vision. The influence they could command between them was the biggest barrier to the important realisation of Simeon, the catalyst.

Arthur Prinz himself was a write-off—no trophy to any vigilante or bounty hunter. Since his last tactics had failed on the lawn, he had crumbled visibly with the weight of judgement that could not be deferred.

Whatever he had been, he would never be again and Simeon, for all that the scars were still emblazoned upon his wrists, could feel only sympathy now.

The Devil was gone from Arthur Prinz. Instead, Simeon saw Satan brooding behind the eyes of all these others whose motives were no different from those of the four men who were, at least, honest enough to carry guns openly and announce their intention.

And that just left Icarus, Zed, and—it seemed—a colleague of theirs called Famous Gogan. They did not like Prinz but as yet had given no hint in word or deed that they were ready to inflict harm on him.

Even Scarlatti carried a latent revenge wish and Simeon could not be sure it would not surface, given the opportunity.

So Icarus, Zed, Gogan, or nobody.

As yet, Two-Pips was making no attempt to impose any kind of order. Conversation was plentiful, though in several groups.

Simeon quit the stairs and threaded his way to the USF men. Then took him into their small, tight circle with shame on their faces.

"Well," he said, just to relieve their particular tension, "everybody's gotta have an angle. Perhaps I should have realised that Gogan here was too good to be true."

"I'm sorry," said Icarus. "I could say we had it so arranged for your protection but that would be a euphemism. Whatever we did was to counteract Vatican moves as they affected you. That's how we assessed Prinz. Now, it seems, he has it coming from all directions. These hoods are from Eugenio, three of the guys we came in with are for taking him back to Zimbabwe to burn and the other is UN— and they probably have their own ideas."

"What about you? Do you want to hang him?"

"Hadn't thought about it," said Adam Zed. "And that's the truth.

We're against Rome and if Rome is no longer backing him, then I guess that puts him outside our concern."

They scanned the room and found Prinz hunched in a corner. Randall and Withers were ministering to him with something approaching affection.

Two more, thought Simeon. Two more to be trusted.

"If I started something," he asked, "would you help me?"

"Started what?" Icarus wanted to know. "I'm not volunteering for martyrdom."

"The way I have in mind, nobody dies. Nobody even gets scathed. The thing is, we have to be disarming."

He smiled and passed on. Time was short and he still lacked bodies. He viewed the Zimbabwe latecomers. If nothing else, they owed him a favour.

He made his approach. "I'm Simeon," he said.

"Simeon." Sandy Joachim's interest showed up straightaway. "You were the one who put us wise to the Catholic plans. On behalf of the federation, I want to thank you . . . Gentlemen"—Díaz and Da Gama gave their attention—"This is Mr. Simeon. We didn't really expect to find you here. On the other hand, we're not surprised. You're obviously at the centre of many good things. If there's anything we can do—"

"There is. I'm sure you'll agree that, whatever our plans are for Arthur Prinz, we're all up a baobab tree while these gunmen hold control. I have a plan to get rid of them but I need help. I make only one stipulation: my strategy is nonviolent and I want it appreciated as such. We have a certain advantage of numbers here. I want you to stay close to just one of these mercenaries. But let it not be the one nearest Icarus and Zed, the men who came in with you. And let it not be the one nearest those two men you see with Arthur Prinz. Wait for my word."

Just one more arrangement to make and Simeon wondered how long it would be before Two-Pips decided how to deal with the fifteen problems in hand.

He came to Prinz's corner. The man was breathless and sweating profusely. If he still recognised Simeon, he did not show it.

"There's only one way to save Prinz's life," said Simeon quickly, to Withers and Randall "and you have to believe me. While these men hold the guns, nobody's life is worth a candle. I want you to apply your famous persuasive powers to one of them. But not too hard."

Simeon was back on his seat on the stairs with five seconds to spare.

Two-Pips looked around for an alarm. He had already expended one shell and he had to keep an eye on ammunition, particularly when the crowd was getting more like an Afrikaner pool party by the minute.

What he wanted was a noise that would grab the attention of the audience. He up-ended his rifle and smashed the butt through a window.

The resounding tinkle did the trick.

"Now look," he said. "You're multiplying faster than rabbits and it's about time we took some heat out of the situation. We are here to collect one man. Our plan is to take him and go. The rest of you can make your own way to wherever you want to be."

Faster than rabbits . . . Simeon could not believe his ears, could not mistake the chord struck within him. Judge Woodman had said: "Next time, you'll be the man who frees the rabbits."

Swifts, rabbits, what a wildlife safari this was turning out to be.

But somebody had asked a question. Sandy Joachim. "Who is this one man?"

"Forgive me. Our latest arrivals are not *au fait* with the operation. The man we want is Arthur Prinz."

"Then you can't have him," said Joachim. "He's ours."

Two-Pips was grinning. "And who, sir, are you?"

"From Zimbabwe," said Joachim. "We punish our own criminals."

Two-Pips' smile did not vary by a watt. "Then you have a right to know what will happen to him. He is off to see the pope."

"That is not possible. Zimbabwe has first claim."

"And I have second," said Andrew Buthelezi. "The man has the protection of my agency, the United Nations."

"United, indeed." Two-Pips gave his rifle to a colleague, pushed past Simeon without caring much where he put his feet, and took a place of prominence on the stairs. "I never expected so much trouble over so little worth. Does this mean there are two of you who care what happens to this—killer?"

"More than two." Simeon stood up, brushing off mud from the mercenary's boot. "More than two because I say that we ALL get out of this place alive. You're not giving US the chance—it's the other way around. Get your crew together and ship out."

Two-Pips was taken aback. "Are you dictating terms to us? You of all people should be glad enough to see Prinz getting his deserts. What's the matter with you? In any event, I'm sorry to disappoint you all but Prinz is money to me and that's what makes my claim superior to any of yours, I will KILL to get him."

Icarus and Zed had moved behind the man who held Two-Pips' rifle. Díaz and Da Gama were waiting near the third man. Randall and Withers had moved unobtrusively to the sides of the fourth. In the crush of bodies, the manoeuvres had gone unnoticed except by Simeon. He observed with satisfaction.

"But you don't have a gun," he said.

And suddenly, neither did any of the mercenaries. Two-Pips glanced from face to face in haste. He saw men who had conquered the jungle with him massaging arms, wrists, shoulders. None of them could meet his gaze.

"Now go," said Simeon. "Get into your car, get onto the road, get back to the Vatican, and don't return. We have more eyes than you do."

Two-Pips descended the stairs and pushed his way through the melee. At the door, Andrew Buthelezi prodded him with the butt of his own rifle.

"If Eugenio wants to know who took away his prize," he said, "my name is Andrew Buthelezi and I am Secretary-General of the United Nations."

"I know you." Two-Pips spat on the floor. "Jumped-up niggers. I've shot you a thousand times and rifles come easy. Keep watching your back."

He hustled his troops down the steps before him and failed to take his own advice. It gave Sami Ojukwe a chance to plant a good Christian boot right where it would do the most good.

Sami wondered whether the job he felt on seeing Two-Pips spread-eagled was altogether holy. But perhaps he might be permitted one small excess.

The rifles had found their way into the hands of Randall and

Withers, Díaz and Zed. But most of the entourage accompanied the jungle fighters to the gate.

On the way back, Joachim fell into step with Buthelezi.

"Now it's just you and me," he said.

But though they combed the house, Arthur Prinz was gone.

Simeon had skipped the exeunt because he had pressing plans involving Arthur Prinz's safety. Such arrangements were barely completed before Joachim, Buthelezi, and the others sought him out.

"Prinz has disappeared," said Joachim. "Did you see anything?"

"Of course he didn't," said Buthelezi. "At least, he won't say so. Where is Prinz, Simeon?"

"Out of your reach," said Simeon.

"Impossible. He wasn't fit to travel anywhere."

"Don't underestimate him. When you have one slim chance to evade death, you can go like the wind."

"In which direction?" Díaz still had his gun and looked set to use it, whatever the range.

"He has transport," said Simeon. "And a head start."

An engine revved in the road beyond the gate. In a moment, Joachim and Co. were retracing their steps at speed.

Simeon watched the cloud of dust along the drive with wry amusement and Harold Messenger watched Simeon with a little of the same. He edged closer to the seer. "All right—I don't buy it, either. Look at Randall and Withers—they're still here and cool. Would they be that way if their boss was making a break?"

"If they were good enough servants. You won't find him, any of you. The UN, the Church, the Zimbabwe nationalists. You may use different forms of words but you all want him dead. I said no bloodshed. Too many of us are doomed by our weaknesses already. Prinz fed too well at the tree of the knowledge of life and death. But you see the state of him now—his days of terrorising are over. Why not mark that fact with a little mercy?"

"We don't want to kill him," stressed Buthelezi. "For crying out loud, we are the international agency of peace and security. We were here to pull him out."

"He's been pulled out. Forget about him."

"You mean you have him put away somewhere."

"Go through the house. Go through the garden. I'm telling you the bird has flown."

"Look, Simeon . . ." Messenger was trying hard to keep his temper. "I didn't come all this way to play guessing games with you."

"No guesses. Just accept the fact that he is beyond your efforts now."

"And that makes it sound like suicide," said Buthelezi. "Is that the truth of it?"

Simeon laughed. "Truth . . . It's a strange word to hear in these hanging gardens of all places and from you of all people. Your main concern, as I understand it, was to have him out of the grasp of those mercenaries and then clear of the Zimbabwe group. Well, that has been achieved. Be thankful."

Díaz and Da Gama were returning up the drive, piloting John Icarus before them and not too gently. Joachim walked a little way behind, mopping his brow and drawing sweat and white dust in equal quantities.

John Icarus extended his right hand, palm upward. Something glinted in the afternoon sun. "I found my ignition key, Simeon. Hell's teeth, I'm glad about that. I thought we were stuck here."

The sky rattled.

A spider shadow surged across the lawn and Jack Peterson brought the *Guadeloupe* down gently and easily. He jumped to the grass. "Any excitement?"

Buthelezi studied Simeon's features, found them inscrutable, and made his decision. "Nothing," he said. "Things took their natural course."

"And Prinz?"

"It is a far, far better thing than he has ever done . . ."

"He blew himself up!"

"Not quite, Jack, but he won't trouble us again. We're ready to go."

Buthelezi and Messenger started for the helicopter. "Now wait a minute," said Joachim. "You may be prepared to leave it at that but I have to present something tangible to my government."

"You have your two rescued nationals," said Simeon. Nelson and Sami had been hanging back on the fringe of the group. They winced visibly and Simeon was not slow to notice it. He winked at them.

"They are little use to us," said Joachim.

"But they are your subjects."

"They would be the last to admit that. They call themselves God's subjects."

"And that disturbs your composure?"

"That makes them small return for Arthur Prinz."

Joachim was pensive, Da Gama not likely to offer anything on his own initiative. Díaz found the rifle in his hand and let it fall to the grass.

"How tangible," asked Harold Messenger, "would you consider UN membership?"

He patted Andrew Buthelezi's shoulder. "That was your thought, wasn't it, Mr. Secretary-General?"

"Absolutely," said Buthelezi. It was good to have Messenger back. The man could even create happy endings.

"Then you don't want to take Messrs. Ojukwe with you," pressed Simeon.

"Actually," said Buthelezi, "if my aide comes with us, there won't be room."

"I have a hired car near the gate if it is any use to you," said Messenger. "Take it as far as you need it. Charge it to the UN . . ."

Messenger, statesman to the end, made his farewells to the brothers as Peterson swung the bird into action.

"Well, I guess the UN found its own place in your vision," Messenger told Nelson. "It's been good to meet you. I look forward to seeing you in New York some time."

"I don't think so," said Nelson Ojukwe.

"Nonsense. We are all workers in the same vineyard."

Nelson laid his finger on Messenger's jacket pocket. "Don't forget what you have in there," he said.

Messenger dug deep, found the crumpled piece of paper: "I Thessalonians, Chapter Five, verses one to three—as soon as I get hold of a Bible."

"Harold . . ." Buthelezi calling. Messenger made for the helicopter, swung aboard, and was gone in the slate-blue sky.

Later, when he and Buthelezi were still celebrating their happy ending, he would remember the promise, search out the Scriptures, and read: "Now as for the times and the seasons, brothers, you need nothing to be written to you. For you yourselves know quite well that Jehovah's day is coming exactly as a thief in the night.

"Whenever it is that they are saying: 'Peace and security,' then sudden destruction is to be instantly upon them just as the pang of distress upon a pregnant woman. And they will by no means escape."

It would turn Messenger's wine to vinegar.

The bone-dry locomotions of the *Guadeloupe* had barely passed beyond the threshold of the human ear when Famous Gogan came forth from the cascade at the elbow of Arthur Prinz.

A serenity had taken the man which rested him between bouts of feverish and futile activity.

As Randall and Withers moved forward to take possession of their chief. Rico Scarlatti whistled through his teeth. *"Finita la commedia,"* he said.

"What's that?" queried Simeon.

"The comedy ends. I would never have thought events could be so —symmetrical."

Prinz went his way among the laurels, beneath the bougainvillaeas, busy one minute, placid the next.

"In what way?" prompted Simeon.

"Last time I was here, I thought I knew what the phrase meant—it meant Shem dead and the whole world in mourning. It was irony honed to a fine point. But that was only half of it. Then Prinz had control of the minds in this place. Selective amnesia, he called it. Now who's the zombie? And can HE ever leave this place? No. Because everywhere else, somebody wants to kill him. *Finita la commedia!"*

Hither and thither went Arthur Prinz, from loggia to lake shore, from fountain to yew hedge and herb garden.

Walking a while. And washing his hands.

Touching a flower. And washing his hands.

As though there was some stain he just could not lose. The comedy ends.

Across the garden the Ojukwe brothers walked and talked, putting hands to box hedges and noses to fragrances, marvelling at the Creation.

In the middle afternoon, Simeon occupied the bench upon the lawn but with no thoughts of possession. He had Scarlatti on one side and Gogan on the other. Icarus and Zed stood nearby, swaying occasionally to blot out the southbound sun.

"Is that it?" asked Zed.

"That's it," said Simeon.

"Right. And we never did ask those two"—Icarus gestured at distant Sami and Nelson—"which way they aligned themselves."

"Don't worry about it." Simeon stretched out his legs. With the pressure gone, he was discovering his weariness. "They have their alignments. They don't want you any more than they want Eugenio's brand of worship."

"But that's ridiculous. They must come down one side or the other or they're not Christian at all. It's that simple."

"I'll tell you something." Simeon hitched in his legs and leaned forward intently. "Alongside their faith, your religions are as straight as a ball of wool the cat's been at. You can offer them nothing."

"And the things," said Scarlatti, "that they could offer you . . ."

Famous Gogan was ransacking his pockets, "I can offer you things," he said. "Both of you. Man, I nearly forgot."

He rummaged on, found what he sought, and closed Simeon's hand around it.

Simeon knew what it was without unclenching his fingers. As if through the flesh, he read: "FOR TOMORROW, JULIE."

His stomach kicked. His eyelids burned. Gogan was at his other hand, piling in four small screws.

"So this IS—" Simeon could not trust himself to say more.

But Scarlatti could. Simeon's speechlessness scored his senses like Shem's shed blood. "You pieces of filth," he said. "If that's the Protestant pay-off, I'd sooner have Arthur Prinz. At least he had the decency to lose his mind."

"Simeon was the only hope we had." The way Gogan said it, he didn't even sound sorry. Even so, the excuse was lost and lame after the other grandiose statements of conviction. "We couldn't have him letting go. Things would have swung all the other way."

"And now he's done his part, you can come clean. You b--"

"It's all right." Simeon had won his struggle for articulation with an ease that amazed and gratified him. He stood up. "It turned out for the best. I'm convinced."

"Convinced of what?" Even Scarlatti was not sure.

"Convinced that I won't ever find Julie while I dally with these people." Simeon offered the screws to Gogan. When there was no response, he let them drop and they were lost among the grasses.

"What about your—bench?" asked Zed.

"You want to burn something, burn that." Then he remembered what Scarlatti might have forgotten. "You said BOTH of us."

The lawman came to his feet. "Maybe you can improve on your last trick. But I doubt it."

"Shem's grave," said Gogan. "It's here. I can show you. I buried him myself."

"Well, thanks for that. But I'll find it."

Simeon and Scarlatti left tracks in the dewfall lawn. Simeon walked with both hands in front of him and the name plate between them for warmth.

They found the Ojukwe brothers squatting before a stone near the gate. It said: "SHEM FELL HERE AND MANY WERE RAISED."

"Eloquent," said Scarlatti. "A pity the mood didn't last."

Simeon scanned the circle he had joined by multiple elimination. So it had come to this. He addressed himself to Nelson Ojukwe.

"Tell me one thing—the people I thought were my friends . . . they seemed to be expecting something different."

Nelson straightened up. "People look for sky signs and miracles to bolster their faith when there is ample evidence in the way things are," he said. "God will act in His due time and you don't have to tour battlefields to be sure of being on the spot. I'll give you a scripture, Simeon—and it's not the same one I gave the UN. Second Book of Chronicles, Chapter Twenty, verses fifteen and seventeen. God says, 'Do not you be afraid or be terrified because of this large crowd; for the battle is not yours but God's . . . You will not need to fight in this instance. Take your position, stand still, and see the salvation of Jehovah in your behalf . . .' In other words, just get to know Him like Julie knew Him. And Shem, too, I fancy."

"Shem, too," affirmed Scarlatti. "If anybody said anything—fitting —when he was buried, the world has lost sight and sound of it. Do you think you could—?"

Nelson Ojukwe waited for them to bow their heads and longer

still. He saw how far he had come from a poor but faithful village to a misused Eden. He found himself again the spokesman of a flock.

Simeon closed his eyes and found Tomorrow Julie waiting to show him a healthy morning face. When Nelson began to put the new message into words, he fancied her head was lowered and her lips moved in accord. Lesson Number One: Julie was an object of love and not an object of worship. Lesson Number Two: There were no signs here to say "Megiddo." But that didn't prevent him from being sure enough for both of them.

Sc. Fic. a
Fate, Peter
Faces In the Flame

18121

Galien Township Library
Galien, Michigan

1. Books may be kept two weeks and may be renewed once for the same period, except 7 day books and magazines.

2. A fine is charged for each day a book is not returned according to the above rule. No book will be issued to any person incurring such a fine until it has been paid.

3. All injuries to books beyond reasonable wear and all losses shall be made good to the satisfaction of the Librarian.

4. Each borrower is held responsible for all books charged on his card and for all fines accruing on the same.

PRINTED IN U.S.A.   23-512-002